GRACE BENEATH THE FROST

CHRISTINE DILLON

LINKS IN THE CHAIN PRESS

www.storytellerchristine.com

Grace Beneath the Frost

Cover Design: Lankshear Design

ISBN: 978-0-6485890-9-9

This book is for the men in my family:

** **Dad** - thank you for your staunch support and for all you've taught me about life and ministry. Thank you also for pushing me to be more adventurous.*

** My brother, **Jeff** - watching you as a husband and father is so much fun. You inspire me with the generosity of your life and how you strive to make disciples.*

** My brother-in-law, **Remo**, thank you for your hard-work and steadiness. It is so great to see you and Jenny together.*

** **My nephews** - it is exciting to watch you grow and change. May you become men of whom it is said they were 'men after God's own heart' (1 Samuel 13:14).*

NOTES TO READERS

* All books are written from a worldview, be it secular, communist or New Age. This book is unashamedly Christian. If you're not a Christian, the views expressed by the characters might appear strange BUT it's a great opportunity. Why? Because this story allows you, if you're not yet a follower of Jesus, to see things from a perspective totally different to your own. Are the characters' views consistent and does their worldview make sense of the challenges in their lives?

* This is an Australian story and thus uses Australian spelling, grammar, punctuation, and word usage which may be a little different from what you're used to.

* This series highlights different parts of Australia. Most of this book is set in Sydney but there are scenes in Smiths Lake (New South Wales), Canberra, the Snowy Mountains, and Cairns (Queensland).

PROLOGUE

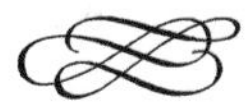

Sydney, Australia, 1992

"This can't continue."

Paul raised his head out of the depths of the newspaper and peered at his wife. "What can't continue?"

"This." His wife gestured between them both.

He stifled a sigh and put down the newspaper. "I'm not sure what you're referring to."

"That's just it. You're oblivious."

"To what?"

Wendy rolled her eyes. "To the state of things between us."

The state of things between them was fine. Wasn't it?

Wendy bit her lip, and he stifled another sigh. It was obviously not going to be a quiet morning of reading the paper. He leaned back in his chair and folded his arms. "What's bothering you?"

"See, even the way you ask that question implies I'm the problem and you're the consultant waiting to sort me out."

What did she expect? For most of the week, consulting was his job. How was he supposed to switch off when he walked into the house?

He unfolded his arms and tried to look more approachable.

Wendy was silent, her face turned slightly away from him. Was he supposed to say something? Perhaps not. With Wendy like this, whatever he said would be the wrong thing.

The uncomfortable silence stretched on, broken only by the muffled hum of traffic in the distance and the squeal of the train braking as it approached the station across the park.

Paul cleared his throat, the sound loud in the room. "I think things are more than good—we have this house, and the children are in excellent schools." Much more security than he'd had as a child. "Do you need a holiday?"

She turned towards him. "Do you really think it's just a matter of providing me with things? I'm your wife, not your housekeeper." She stared down at the Persian carpet. "I need you."

Good grief. She'd known he wanted to be a medical specialist when she married him. Did she think that happened within a nine-to-five working life?

"We barely see you," Wendy said. "And when you are home, you're buried in your study and only come out for meals."

Huh, yes. Meals where all conversation was dominated by the children. Those Victorian-era parents knew a thing or two when they said, "Children should be seen not heard."

"Do you really need to go to medical conferences every second weekend a month and write quite so many articles?"

"I do, if I want to be a leader in the field, not just a cancer specialist."

"A normal cancer specialist would be more than enough for me," she muttered.

But it wasn't enough for him.

"Why don't we talk about this next weekend, when I have more time, and—"

"And what?" she said, voice sharp.

He'd been about to say "when you've calmed down" but that would really get her riled.

"And when I can think straight," he said.

But she hadn't given him the chance.

Four days later, he'd come home to an empty house and a note.

We need to take a break. I've taken the kids to Mum and Dad's. I don't know if we'll be back. I'll contact you when I'm ready.

He'd waited and hoped, but she'd never been ready ...

CHAPTER 1

Easter, 1997
Sydney, Australia

"Never get emotionally involved with a patient." How many times had Paul heard that as a medical student? And he'd always followed the unwritten rule—an absolute must for a cancer specialist who heard more than his fair share of heart-breaking stories and saw too many poor outcomes.

He buttressed his heart. He controlled his emotions. His patients' pain slid off him. Warmth and empathy? That was for the nurses.

Meeting Esther for the first time, he'd had no clue he was in danger.

The door from Sister O'Reilly's office opened, startling him.

"Dr Webster—" A faint flush stained her cheeks. "Mary Brown just tapped on my door and asked if you'd forgotten her."

Now it was Paul's turn to be embarrassed. He had indeed forgotten Mary, and he'd never done that before.

"Yes, please send her in."

Sister O'Reilly looked at him. "Are you sure you're alright? You've seemed distracted all day."

He reached for Mary's file on his desk. "I'll be okay. Nothing a good sleep won't fix."

But that was precisely the problem. He hadn't been sleeping since Esther had died. Why, oh why had he failed to keep the normal emotional distance? Yesterday, he'd attended Esther's funeral. Broken another personal rule.

Mary entered his office.

"Sorry to keep you waiting," Paul said as Mary sat down. No point in telling the poor woman he'd forgotten all about her.

Thankfully it was Mary's final check-up, and the news was all good. He could do these kinds of appointments on automatic—which was useful today. By keeping the file open in front of him, he managed not to call her by the wrong name and must have made the correct comments.

"Still all clear. Hopefully I won't be back," he heard her say to Sister O'Reilly as she left.

These were the cases he longed for—breast cancer caught early and responsive to treatment.

Some of the doctors he'd graduated with couldn't understand how anyone could handle being a cancer specialist. Couldn't understand the challenge of fighting something so insidious, life changing, and sometimes life destroying.

But Paul loved the fight. Loved being on the frontline of such a worthwhile war. Loved seeing the success rates improve as new treatments became available.

He wasn't the sort to enjoy doing cosmetic surgery for people dissatisfied with their appearance. Dealing with disfiguring conditions like cleft palates made sense, but not doing surgery for people like his mother, people desperately trying to stop the ravages of time. Ridiculous.

Sister O'Reilly poked her head through the connecting door. "Is it okay if I head home now?"

He nodded. "Sorry I kept you late."

She turned to leave, then hesitated and looked back at him. "You will let me know if there is anything I can do?"

He'd always suspected a warm heart beat under her formal, old-fashioned exterior.

"Thank you for your concern."

Paul waited until she'd gone before scribbling the final notes for Mary and putting the folder aside to be filed.

He looked at the chair Mary had vacated. He hadn't registered anything unusual about Esther when she first sat in that chair. She was one more strained, pale face in a line of similar cases stretching back twenty years.

He hadn't even paid attention when rumours drifted back to him that Esther had caused a minor sensation prior to her surgery. Apparently, her father had organised a meeting in the ward to pray for healing. Then Esther had insisted her breast examination be redone just before surgery in case she was healed and didn't need a radical mastectomy.

Paul laughed grimly. He'd never seen such a miracle. He'd been prepared to write Esther off as some sort of religious nut after hearing about that incident, but things hadn't turned out as he'd expected. In fact, over the next months, Esther had changed in ways he couldn't ignore. A growing peace and calm and eventually a twinkling sense of humour had replaced her fear.

Before long, he had found himself looking forward to her visits. And no, he hadn't fallen in love with her.

Esther had been plucky and courageous, with a winsome sense of fun. She'd never seemed overawed by the fact he was a cancer specialist. People often treated him as a demigod, and it had been refreshing to be treated like a normal person. Not that she'd been rude. Not at all. But when they'd finally ventured beyond medical matters, she'd dared to call him out on some of his beliefs. He chuckled at the memory of her expression when he'd laughed at her belief in heaven. He'd said she was a gambler, trusting in blind faith. Not exactly a tactful thing to say to someone with her diagnosis. Esther hadn't backed down. Instead, she'd called him the superstitious one and given him two books—books he'd put off reading until the consistency of her beliefs had been too confronting to ignore.

He stared at the clock on the wall. He must get home. Not that home was any more than a place to sleep. These last five years had been the loneliest time of his life. He lived for his monthly visit from his kids. Lauren, almost eighteen, and Ben, nearly sixteen, who was just beginning to step out from under his sister's shadow.

If only Paul hadn't been so selfishly preoccupied with his climb to the top of his profession. He'd been stunned when Wendy had walked out, but he'd been too proud to fight for her and the kids and now he had no one but himself to blame for the barrenness of his life.

Maybe that was why Esther had managed to get under his skin.

Right. *Get up, Paul.*

He got up, went over to the locked cupboard and took out the grey leather briefcase Wendy had bought him for their final anniversary before she'd left. He'd grab a bite to eat on the way home. He'd barely slept last night. Too much on his mind. Too many whirling thoughts.

He flipped off the last of the lights, locked his office door, and strode towards the main doors of the building. The security guard said goodnight, and he was out into the cool darkness. Somewhere, the scent of a flower perfumed the air, the same kind of flowers that had been part of the floral arrangements at the funeral.

A wave of sadness coursed through him. Such a waste. Twenty-nine was too young to be gone. Yet Esther hadn't railed against God. He snorted as he opened his Land Rover door. When they'd stood around her hospital bed on her last night, all long faces and gloom, she'd chastised the lot of them for not understanding she was going to a better place.

Paul turned the car key and backed out of his reserved car spot. He didn't understand Esther. But then he still didn't know if Jesus had ever existed, and if he had, whether he was anything more than an impressive teacher. Esther had laughed at him when he'd expressed these kinds of thoughts. She believed Jesus was God and her confidence was unshakeable. Why?

CHAPTER 2

"Dad, that's the third time you've yawned in the last few minutes." Lauren frowned as she drove. They were past halfway on the four-hour trip to Smiths Lake, where he'd hired a place for a week of the Easter holidays. The long drive gave Lauren plenty of time to practise her driving before she took her test next month.

He sighed. She was growing up so fast, and he'd missed too much of the process.

"Dad. You didn't answer. Why are you yawning?" Lauren repeated.

"Sorry, I haven't been sleeping well."

"Have you been staying up too late?"

He laughed. "You're more like your mother every day."

Lauren raised an eyebrow at him. "And is that a bad thing?"

"No, not at all." And it wasn't. Wendy was caring but discreet with her friends' troubles; responsible, trustworthy, and fiercely loyal. Saying Lauren was her mother's daughter was a compliment. He hadn't known how good life had been until the separation.

Wendy being on holiday with them would have made the whole

thing perfect. She brought fun and a sense of meaning that had been missing from his life for too long. But she wasn't coming. That part of his life was over.

At least he still had time with the kids, although they hadn't wanted to visit him at all in the first year of their separation. It was Wendy who had eased them into it. He didn't know what she'd said to them, but it had worked. He'd soon learned that when Ben and Lauren were with him, he needed to give them all his time, even if he spent most of the weekend chauffeuring them to sport and other events. He'd resented it at first, but now he appreciated a weekend to switch off from work. Keeping busy and having active holidays made things easier. He wasn't great at deep and meaningful conversation, but the children did open up when they were on a boat or hike together.

He might not be anywhere near perfect, but even if he turned up once a year, he'd be a million times better than his own father. His father ducked out so early that Paul only had vague memories of him, a tall dark-haired man who smelled of tobacco. Paul thought he smoked a pipe rather than cigarettes, but he couldn't verify the memory because Paul's mother refused to talk about her ex-husband. There had been the occasional rant while he was in primary school about how his father was a wastrel and she should never have married him, but apart from that, no other information passed her lips. Nope, he had no intention of ever being like his father. He wanted his kids to look at him with affection and be proud of him.

Lauren indicated, checked her blind spot, changed lanes and overtook a caravan crawling up a hill in the left lane.

"Are you ready for a break?" Paul asked.

She nodded.

"Why don't you take the next exit?" He glanced at the petrol gauge. "Pull in at the petrol station, and I'll take over."

"Wish I could start learning to drive," Ben said from the back seat.

"The summer holidays will be here soon enough," Paul said. It only seemed like yesterday that Ben had his little-boy voice. Now he was pushing to fly the nest. How many holidays would they have together before his kids went their separate ways?

* * *

ON THE LAST morning of their holiday, Paul called up the stairs to the children. "Last chance for a sail. Is anyone coming?"

There was a loud groan from Ben's room. He preferred to exercise in the afternoons, when he was fully awake.

Paul carried his coffee out to the front deck with the view over the lake. Several small islands dotted the water, too small for living on but just right for sailing or kayaking around. A cool breeze ruffled the surface of the water and rustled the leaves of the gum trees.

He heard footsteps on the floorboards and Lauren came out to join him.

"Morning, Dad. Did you sleep better?"

He nodded. This break had been just what he needed, sailing every morning, then swimming or kayaking in the afternoons.

"If you give me a chance to grab some breakfast, I'll come with you."

He smiled across at her, delighted to have her seek out his company.

"Meet me down there. I'll get everything ready to go." Not that it would be hard, as the place they were staying had its own jetty.

He'd just finished his preparation when Lauren stepped onto the jetty, hair pulled back in a ponytail. He handed her the life jacket and she put it on with a little shiver. "You can feel the change in the season."

It wasn't a strong breeze but with the sail up, the boat began to move forward. There'd be more wind once they were out of the shelter of the nearest island.

On days like this, he was thankful to his mother for letting him go to the school near Melbourne where he'd learned to sail. He still didn't know how a kid from Canberra had received a scholarship to one of the best schools in Australia. Surely there must have been more deserving kids who lived closer to the school. Maybe his mother knew, but if so, she'd kept her usual silence on the matter. Even with the scholarship, she'd had to sacrifice to buy his uniform and all the extras.

"A little more to port," he said to Lauren. She adjusted the rudder and the boat responded with a tiny surge, as though glad to be free. The sail flapped, Lauren made another small adjustment, and the sound stopped as the sail filled more evenly.

They spent the next hour tacking to and fro, discussing Lauren's options for university.

"You're good with people. Do you think you'd like teaching?"

"I'm not sure. Maybe I can do a general degree first, and decide later."

Paul adjusted the sail to maximise the wind available and the boat tilted slightly.

"What do you want to do for your eighteenth? It's only a few weeks away and I expected you to mention it before this."

"I've talked it over with Mum."

A stab of jealousy slid under his rib like a knife. *Get a grip, Paul.* Of course she'd talk about things with Wendy first. Wendy wouldn't leave something significant like this birthday to chance.

"Jill and I are thinking of doing a joint celebration after the trials and before the final exams."

That made sense. Lauren's next few months would be dominated by her trial exams, which contributed a good percentage towards her final marks.

"Head down, coming about," Paul said. "Were you thinking of something for family too?" he asked once the boat was sailing on its new tack.

Lauren was silent, a flush spreading up her neck. He hadn't meant to put her on the spot.

"I don't really know what to do. It's difficult." She swallowed.

"You mean you're not sure if your mother and I can sit at the same table together."

She looked back towards their jetty. "Well, you never do, do you? You wait in the car to pick us up and only occasionally make arrangements on the phone."

He'd done things that way because he didn't know how he'd react to seeing Wendy. It was easier to keep away, but he hadn't considered how it was affecting his children.

"And Miranda, well, you know." Lauren's voice trailed off.

He did know. His mother refusing to be called anything other than her name was only one symptom of a broader problem. Wendy's parents happily answered to Nana and Pops and thought his mother was foolish for believing being called "Grandma" made her seem old and stodgy. He secretly agreed. Even after his marriage his mother had never said anything as friendly as "Call me Mum" to Wendy. He was the only one who could get away with not calling her Miranda, and even he called her "Mother", not "Mum". His mother hadn't made any comment when he'd told her he and Wendy were separated, although she complained he still didn't head home to Canberra often enough.

Much as he hated to admit it, he didn't enjoy visiting his mother. She was a cranky old woman.

Paul mentally shook himself. He was supposed to be talking about Lauren's birthday.

"Would you like me to talk to your mother and see what she suggests?" he asked.

Lauren turned to him. Her eyes looked a little wet. "I'd like that.

I do want to do something special with family, but I'm not sure it's possible."

"I'll call next week."

Lauren gave a small stiff nod. "Thanks, Dad. I'd appreciate it."

He kept thinking Lauren appeared tough, but her desire for family harmony revealed a touching vulnerability. That desire resonated deep within him.

* * *

THE HOLIDAY HELPED, but back at home, Paul still wasn't sleeping. He tossed and turned, pummelling his pillow to try to make it more comfortable. As always, a picture of that young woman filled his mind.

Esther.

Again. All this angst proved that he needed to keep his patients at a distance. He couldn't afford sleepless nights for each and every death of those under his care.

He blew out a long breath. Funerals were supposed to bring closure, so why did he still feel so unsettled? He pictured Esther sitting in the chair opposite his desk, her face alternating between gentle teasing and utter earnestness as she challenged him to properly examine Jesus' claims. What had she said? Something about how investigating Christianity would only take a tiny percentage of his time and it might be the best investment he'd ever make.

He'd never believed in haunting, but perhaps peace would come if he treated her challenge seriously. Esther believed Jesus was God. Paul had spent more time cutting his toenails than he'd ever spent on Jesus.

He laughed grimly in the darkness. Esther was convinced Jesus would come again to judge the world. If that were the case, then it made sense to be on Jesus' good side, although he doubted that being a friend of Esther's would gain him any points.

Paul turned over. He might not be a sensitive, self-aware sort of guy but he knew himself well enough that though he might decide to do a thorough investigation of Jesus' claims, there was no way he'd complete it. Not on his own, anyway. Too many things would get in the way.

Just like general busyness had prevented him from reading more than one of the books Esther had given him. Even then, he'd only casually skimmed its contents to make Esther happy.

Okay, so he needed someone to keep him on track. But what kind of someone? He didn't want a Christian. He wanted a sceptic. A man he could respect and who could be trusted to take the task seriously. Someone who could hear a raw and honest question and give a raw and honest answer.

The next morning, he woke with one name on his mind. It felt risky to ask, and he didn't even know how to find the guy.

He got out of bed and went to shower. While shaving he came up with a way to find out the information he needed. The question was, did he dare?

CHAPTER 3

Paul went into work half an hour early. The centre receptionist's eyes widened when Paul said good morning to her. Michelle greeted him every morning, but he'd never initiated the morning pleasantries.

He glanced around to check the place was still deserted. It was. Good. He took a deep breath. "I saw you at Esther Macdonald's funeral. Do you often go to client funerals?"

Michelle shook her head. "It was only the second time." She straightened a pen on her desk. "Esther and I had sort of become friends, you know."

"She was great at making friends."

Michelle smiled.

Paul felt his neck heat. "Last week was the first time I've attended a patient's funeral."

"Oh." She nodded politely.

She wasn't saying it, but she was probably shocked to have seen him there. If his colleagues had run a competition, he'd have been voted the least likely to attend such a funeral.

Paul cleared his throat. "There was another one of our patients at the funeral. Rob someone. He stood up and said he used to chat to Esther here."

Michelle smiled. "Yes, he and Esther used to joke a lot together. They arranged their appointments on the same afternoons."

"I'd like to get in touch with him." Paul checked over his shoulder. "I know you can't get his file for me, but could you give me a clue as to how I could find him?"

Michelle paused and fixed a steely gaze on him. "This isn't for any nefarious purpose is it?"

He blinked. "Nefarious. That's quite a word for a Monday morning. Yes, I can promise it isn't for any nefarious purpose."

"Ever since I heard that word on a quiz show last month, I've been dying to use it." Michelle tightened her lips to hide a smile. "I can't give you information off his file, but I think it would be okay to tell you what I overheard." She glanced around the room. "He's a science teacher at the local high school. That should be enough for you to find him."

PAUL SHIFTED down a gear as his car approached his street. He'd been debating with himself all day about whether or not he would contact Rob. What was less odd—trying to find his address in the phone book, or sending a letter to the school marked *Rob, Science Department*?

He switched on his indicator, pointed the remote gate opener, and drove under the apartment block to park the car. He'd write to the school. He didn't really expect Rob to answer. If Esther truly was in heaven—whatever that meant—she would surely know he'd tried his best. Anyway, he wasn't sure he believed in heaven. Esther had laughed at images of puffy clouds, long white gowns, and harps, and told him to expect a world more beautiful than the current one.

After he'd eaten, he got out some paper and wrote—

Dear Rob,

My name might be familiar to you, even if we haven't met. I was Esther Macdonald's cancer specialist. Like you, I attended her funeral last week.

I don't make a habit of going to patients' funerals, but I made an exception for Esther's. I was interested in what you said about her. You were right. She was real and winsome. I haven't heard that second word in years, but it described her well. You also said that you were one of her failures and that once you were cancer-free you tried to forget all you'd discussed together.

Paul nibbled the end of his pen and stared at the wall. How could he say this next part without appearing too vulnerable?

The reason I'm writing is that I'm also one of Esther's failures. She did talk to me about her faith, and I ignored most of it. Actually, I was quite dismissive of the things she believed. Because I was a scientist, I've always thought Christianity is a silly superstition, but Esther didn't see any contradictions between science and believing in Jesus. At her urging I read some of the Bible but I treated it fairly casually.

He wasn't going to tell Rob how much Esther's death had shaken him. It was too personal. All too often, he would remember Esther's glowing face as she talked about Jesus. It had seemed Jesus was more real to her than anyone else around her.

This week, I found the funeral programme on my kitchen bench with my scrawled notes. I, too, feel the way to honour Esther is to take up her challenge to investigate her beliefs.

I know I'll never get around to it if I try to do this on my own. I don't want to meet up with a Christian because they'll try to convert me. I want to be free to ask questions without censoring myself. I want to bounce ideas off another sceptic. The only person I can think of is you.

We don't know each other, but we both knew Esther and we're both scientists. Would you be willing to meet with me to discuss Luke? It only has 24 chapters, so it shouldn't take long. We could come each time with a list of questions and comments.

I know this sounds crazy but what do you think? Are you willing to be part of a two-man sceptics' club for six weeks?

Paul reread the letter, signed it, and added his home phone number. It would do. Now the ball was in Rob's court—and Paul wouldn't be unduly upset if he never heard from him. It would give him an excuse to avoid the task. The question was whether his conscience—or whatever it was that was bothering him—would let him off so easily.

CHAPTER 4

Lauren did most of the cooking when she and Ben came over. Paul had protested at first, but she'd said that once she learned a new recipe, she wanted to use it. So he'd relented. Truth be told, he hadn't wanted to win that argument. He recognised Wendy's recipe of fettuccine carbonara.

When Paul had driven over to collect Ben and Lauren, he'd intended to ask Wendy if she'd talk to him about Lauren's eighteenth birthday celebrations, but somehow it seemed easier to come home and phone later. Wendy had never shown the slightest interest in seeing him. He hadn't even caught a glimpse of her for over a year.

"Great dinner, Lauren," he said after the meal. "C'mon Ben. Your sister cooked, so you and I are on dishes."

"Do I have to?"

"I'd prefer to have self-washing dishes too, but that's not how it works." Paul gathered the plates as Lauren plopped onto the couch.

"Why doesn't he get a dishwasher that works?" Ben muttered behind Paul.

After the dishwasher broke down, Paul had never bothered to replace it. In the kitchen, Paul turned on the hot water tap. A minute later, Ben dragged himself in and reluctantly armed himself with a tea towel. Phew. Looked like he'd won this round, but what was eating at Ben?

"Shall I make some popcorn to go with the movie?" Lauren said, coming into the kitchen.

"I'm full from your delicious meal, honey. Why don't we make popcorn later? You sit down."

"Sure. I'll get the movie ready," Lauren said.

Ben snorted. "Crawler," he said under his breath.

Should Paul say something or not? Being an only child, he never knew what was considered a normal amount of bickering. Attending a British-style boarding school hadn't helped.

"Your sister isn't a crawler."

Ben glowered and turned away.

What did a parent do in situations like this? Paul kept washing the plates. *Help.* He didn't know who he was asking for help and didn't expect to receive any. Was that why people became Christians? Because they needed help? If people didn't have the answers, a divine answerer made sense. But it only made sense if God, or whatever divine power, knew about parenting and was wise, good, and willing to share. Paul wasn't sure God existed, and if he did, was he good? The state of the world suggested he was a hands-off kind of being, perhaps even some sort of sadist.

"How was your week?" Paul asked.

"Okay, I guess." Ben attacked the plate with a tea towel.

Paul wanted to tell him to be careful, but it wasn't worth it. Ben was obviously looking for a fight, and Paul didn't plan to give him a reason to start one.

Talking to Lauren used to be hard work until he'd begged Wendy for some hints about asking good questions. He tried again.

"What was the best thing about your week?"

Ben sighed as though he was faced with a major world crisis. "PE, I guess."

Did Ben have any idea how lucky he was to have a father around at all? Back when Paul was at high school, he would have given anything to wash dishes and chat with his father.

Every birthday, Christmas, sports match, graduation, and especially his wedding, had made the hole grow deeper. To this day, Paul didn't know how tall his father had been, his eye colour, or even his name.

Even when he'd heard his father was dead, the questions hadn't been stilled. Since they'd never meet, the most precious gift in the world would have been a photo. One photo. Surely his mother had a single photo somewhere. Or could she have destroyed every bit of physical evidence that her husband had ever existed?

Even if conversation was hard work at the moment, Paul wasn't giving up. "Is there any subject beside PE that you enjoy?"

"Not at the moment." Ben grabbed the cutlery, drying it before shooting it into the drawer with a loud clatter.

Paul was tempted to add his own world-shattering sigh to the situation. He didn't remember being this moody as a teen. He'd worked hard, and enjoyed most subjects. "What experiments have you been doing in science?"

Ben mentioned dissecting a frog and playing with dry ice. For the first time in ages, there was some animation in his voice.

Perhaps his usual indifference was just pretence, but how did a father go deeper with a soon-to-be sixteen-year-old son?

* * *

As Paul came through his front door, the red light on the phone in the entrance area flashed to let him know there was a message. He pushed the button and listened. It was from Rob, not only agreeing to meet but suggesting a time and a café near both of their workplaces.

Paul let out a gusty sigh. He hadn't expected Rob to agree so readily. Now there were no excuses. He found a piece of paper and wrote down the details, then took another deep breath as he picked up the phone to call Wendy.

This call would be more than simply business, which was the only type of interaction they'd had for a good long time.

Once he'd identified himself, she greeted him in return. Even hearing her voice say his name made his heart race.

"Wendy, how's work?"

"Fine, thank you."

He hated the blandness of their conversation.

"You didn't call me to talk about work," she said.

"N-no." *Pull yourself together, Paul.* "Did Lauren mention that we talked about her eighteenth?"

"She did."

"I'd like to do something special, but she's worried about things being awkward."

"Yes, I can understand that." Her voice was flat, emotionless.

He longed to elicit any measure of emotional reaction. "Have you got any suggestions?"

"An extended family dinner won't be much fun."

Paul appreciated that she didn't come right out and say his mother was the main problem. One of his many regrets about their separation was no longer having a reason to see Wendy's parents. They'd always treated him as an extra son.

"What if I took you and the kids out for something more classy?" he asked.

"Let me think about it, okay? Lauren might enjoy going somewhere special with you on your own."

That would solve all Wendy's problems. She could avoid Paul

and avoid offending his mother, who oscillated between ignoring them and being highly offended if no one had been in touch.

"I'll choose a restaurant that suits two or four," Paul said.

"Can I let you know in a week?"

"That'll be fine."

After Wendy hung up, Paul cradled the phone in his hand. If he could rewind the last decade, he would. He'd been blind not to see how his desire to be the best cancer specialist possible had stolen too much time from his family. Since when had he needed to be the best instead of merely excellent? He sighed. Probably since kindergarten, when his mother had insisted he keep away from the other children because their parents weren't what she considered suitable.

CHAPTER 5

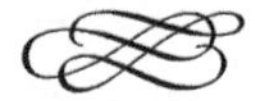

The morning of the first sceptics' club meeting came around all too quickly. Paul's stomach clenched with nerves as he entered the café and saw Rob's raised hand calling him over to the back corner.

"Have you ordered?" Paul asked when he reached the table.

Rob nodded.

Paul approached the counter and ordered a mushroom omelette with English muffins and his first coffee of the day.

Rob's order was just arriving as Paul pulled out his chair and sat down.

"Thanks so much for coming," Paul said. "I was never going to get around to doing this on my own."

"Me either. I'm a procrastinator from way back." Rob took the first bite of his breakfast.

Paul sat there, not sure how to start. It seemed abrupt and almost rude to get straight into business, but time was tight. He reached into his briefcase and pulled out a notebook. "I read up to chapter four and wrote a list of questions. I presume you have some, too. Shall we just go through them?"

Rob glanced at his watch. "I have to be out of here in an hour, so we'll have to get a move on."

The waitress arrived with Paul's coffee and he took a sip. He licked the foam off his lip. "Did you tell anyone what you were doing?"

"No, I didn't say a word." Rob flicked his gaze around the room. "Especially not my wife. She'd have nothing good to say about me reading the Bible. Luckily I didn't have to say anything to her because she's used to me going in early on Fridays for a meeting. She doesn't know the meetings are finished for the term."

So their time was limited. That suited Paul as well. "So what do you reckon about Luke? What were your first impressions?"

"I found the names fairly overwhelming," Rob said. "Weird names."

"Maybe our names would be unfamiliar to them," Paul said.

"But it was the angels that got to me," Rob said. "Luke said the whole thing was history, but angels seem to contradict that."

"Isn't that the point?" Paul said. "Angels weren't normal then, either."

"And the angels were nothing like I expected. People are scared of them!"

"Yes," Paul said. "Definitely not cute cherubs like in the paintings." He rubbed his eyebrow. "I wonder where artists got that idea from?"

"Definitely not from the book of Luke."

The waitress brought Paul's food and after a few mouthfuls, Paul looked back at his notes.

"The big issue for me is the virgin birth," Rob said.

Paul grinned and raised his eyebrows. "Whoever the father was, it wasn't Joseph. I checked up the Christmas story in Matthew and he thought Mary had slept around until—"

"Until the angel told him otherwise?" Rob grinned. "I looked up

Matthew too, and see--" Rob stabbed his index finger on the table. "Another angel conveniently turning up."

Paul considered this. "Why else would Joseph have married Mary when he knew the baby wasn't his? There has to be an explanation. If nothing else, the addition of the angel makes the story logical."

Paul jotted down a reminder to think about this later and added a question. *Why was the virgin birth so important?* If the whole virgin birth thing was a myth or scam, why did the author insist it had happened?

Rob chuckled. "Zechariah could have been a member of our sceptics' club. He didn't believe a barren woman could have a baby."

"And look where his scepticism got him. Unable to speak for nine months."

"You're the doctor," Rob said. "Could there be a medical explanation for that?"

Paul raised an eyebrow and sighed. "It's easy enough to explain one miracle, but even with what we've read so far, Luke is full of miracles—and angels."

Rob rolled his eyes. "Can't we remove the angels from the equation?"

"I'm not sure if removing the angels makes it any easier." Paul finished off his omelette. "It's not just one angel. The shepherds see a whole crowd of them. If it was one shepherd claiming they'd seen angels, then we could dismiss the report by saying the guy had been alone too much or had some sort of mental disease, but it's harder to explain when a whole group says they'd seen angels."

Rob snorted. "Maybe they ate some sort of hallucinogenic mushroom."

"Explaining away a miracle with something even less likely doesn't make sense. I'll have to think about it." Paul underlined the word angels in his notebook. "We're assuming there aren't angels, but isn't that as bad as assuming there must be angels?"

Rob harrumphed and looked at his watch. "I'll have to head off soon."

"Me too," Paul said.

"But before we go, what did you think of John?" Rob asked. "Such a blunt, Aussie kind of guy. Definitely not trying to make friends and influence people."

Paul chuckled. "Calling the religious leaders a bunch of snakes wouldn't have made him popular."

It would have been helpful to bring his Bible, but Paul hadn't wanted anyone to spot him with it. He was fairly well known around here, and being seen reading a Bible would get his colleagues talking. He'd look back at the story tonight. John might have been blunt, but Paul seemed to remember he also gave people hope.

They finished their coffee in silence. Rob put down his mug. "Thanks for this. I felt bad that I never bothered doing anything Esther suggested. She was obviously disappointed, even if she tried to hide it."

"Hope this whole experience wasn't too weird," Paul said.

"Not as bad as I expected. Like you, I prefer doing it with someone who isn't trying to convert me."

Paul stood up and took his suit jacket off the back of the chair. "I suppose we're both actually hoping we can disprove all this."

The words sank into his heart like a stone into oozing mud. Why was that his hope? What was so scary about these stories being true?

CHAPTER 6

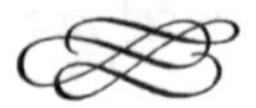

"Isn't Lauren's birthday coming up? Why haven't I received an invitation?"

Paul's mother's peevish tones tunnelled into his ear. He gripped the phone and took a deep breath to collect his thoughts. "Lauren hasn't confirmed what she wants."

"Well, she'd better hurry. Some of us have lives that cannot easily be rearranged to suit her."

Paul gnawed his lip. His mother had never liked Lauren. She was too much like Wendy. Anyway, what would his mother possibly have to rearrange? Hair and skin appointments? Playing bridge?

"Lauren is thinking of having a joint party with another friend after their August exams."

"But we're her family."

He was not going to let his mother rile him.

"At this stage, I don't know if there will be a family get-together," Paul said. "Wendy said Lauren might prefer to go out to dinner with different family members one at a time."

"So you still speak to that woman?"

Paul clamped his jaw tight. His mother seldom referred to Wendy by name. Her rudeness didn't usually take the form of overt insults. Instead, she was scrupulously proper—which Wendy had correctly interpreted as dislike.

"I seldom speak to Wendy."

As he said the words, a longing surged through him. What he'd give to sit and talk with Wendy like they used to before they were married. He hadn't been afraid to share his hopes and dreams, and she'd treated them with respect. She had never made him feel small or ashamed.

"I want to be kept in the loop," Miranda said. "You haven't been doing that much lately."

He used to take the children to visit their grandmother regularly, but they no longer stayed more than a few hours. Any longer, and the children were ready to riot. Miranda always greeted them effusively and gave them expensive presents, but it didn't take long for her to start harping on something or other.

"Sit up straight!"

"Don't they teach children manners nowadays?"

"Paul, I don't think you're getting your money's worth at those expensive private schools."

It wasn't long before they were all ready to bolt out the door. Had she always been like this, or was she getting worse? Maybe repeated patterns had worn a groove so deep she could no longer change.

"Mother, we're planning to go down to the Snowy Mountains for the long weekend. Would it be convenient for us to drop in for morning tea on the way?"

They'd leave after work on the Friday and stay somewhere close to Canberra, but it wasn't necessary to let his mother know they could have stayed the night with her.

"Just let me get my appointment diary, dear."

He heard her put the phone down and hurry across the kitchen.

He gave her the same appointment diary every year, a big black faux leather book with gold embossing.

She came back to the phone and made a big deal of flipping the pages and muttering. "So you're talking about Saturday the sixth?"

"Yes, that's right. We'll come earlyish, about nine-thirty, and need to leave by eleven. Does that suit you?"

"I'll be delighted to see you."

She was always delighted to see him, and she pretended to be excited to see the children, but the reality was they bored her.

His mother was talking about her recent fundraising events, which he found deadly dull, but punctuating her stream of words with occasional comments of "Yes" or "Uh-huh" was all that was required.

"And what have you been doing?"

She wouldn't be interested in their holiday. What she wanted to know was whether he was doing well at work, had he received any recent accolades, or written for any publications. Sometimes he found himself agreeing to write an extra article for some magazine simply so he'd have something to tell her. She basked in his reflected glory, and there was a shelf in his mother's living room filled with scientific magazines or books he'd contributed to. Pity clenched his heart.

They talked for a few more minutes before he hung up.

He rang his mother once a month, but the call always left him sad and empty. When he was small, he hadn't known his relationship with his mother was abnormal. Perhaps she'd been different before his father's abandonment, but when he'd tried as a teenager to wheedle information from her about his father, his mother's mouth had clamped tight. There were no photos on display or in any drawers. He'd looked. Nothing to suggest he'd ever had a father.

He'd been excited the day he went to get his driver's licence because it was his opportunity to see his birth certificate for the first time. Somehow, she'd managed to block the details on the certificate as she handed it over and then snatched it back before he could see them.

Soon after, in a fit of annoyance, he'd told her he was going to order a copy of his birth certificate, and his mother had slapped him. Both of them were so shocked she'd laid a hand on him that he'd backed down.

Shortly before his wedding, when she finally handed over his birth certificate, he found she'd outsmarted him as it was obviously much newer than the one he had glimpsed and there was nothing listed in the place where his father's name had been. What had his father done that she'd go to the trouble of expunging his name from the certificate? However difficult his mother was, his father must have been more so. After that, Paul had decided the man who had fathered him would have no place in his life.

CHAPTER 7

It was a chilly Friday morning and Paul rubbed his hands together before getting into the car to drive to the second meeting of the sceptics' club.

This morning he met Rob at the front door, and they ordered their food and coffee before sitting at the same table as last time. Paul was eager to discuss what he'd been reading but didn't want to scare Rob away with his enthusiasm. Better to ease in.

"Do you like teaching?"

Rob nodded. "Love it. Well, most of the time. Every so often I have a student who doesn't want to be there, but I win most of them over in time."

"Do chemistry teachers still teach the first twenty elements in the periodic table with, 'Harry he lives behind Belfast Castle, near our friend. Never nab magnesium alloys since police seek clues, are kittens cats'?"

"Yep. No point in reinventing something that works."

The waiter arrived with their eggs and toast.

"So, what did you think of the next section?" Paul asked after a few mouthfuls.

"It was different from the first chapters, wasn't it? More stories. People doing stuff. Easier to read," Rob said.

"Yep. It hasn't been anything like I expected. I'm not sure where I got the idea that the Bible was a list of rules. Maybe from my school chaplain. He droned on and put lots of us to sleep. Didn't seem to believe anything he was saying." But now reading Luke was keeping Paul up past his usual bedtime.

"I'm still getting stuck on the miracles," Rob said.

They were a problem for Paul as well, and he was becoming aware of how strong his preconception was that miracles simply couldn't happen. "I'm trying to treat miracles as a hypothesis which needs testing."

Rob pursed his lips and then said, "Okay, I can work with that."

Paul looked across at Rob. "Since by definition, miracles are something abnormal, I'm asking myself if there is any evidence that Jesus performed miracles."

"Even asking the question assumes Luke wrote a historically accurate eyewitness testimony."

"Mmm. Let's leave that discussion for another time and just treat the Bible like any other book, looking for themes and asking questions."

Reading one of the books Esther had given him was beginning to convince him he could rely on Luke's history, but he wasn't going to admit it. Instead, he reached into his briefcase, took out the book concealed in a paper bag, and laid it on the table. Hilarious—he wasn't even willing to be seen with such a book in public. "This is the book Esther gave me." He tapped the paper bag. "I've found it helpful. It's written by an ex-history professor who looks at whether Jesus ever existed and whether we can trust documents that have been transmitted for nearly two thousand years."

Rob chuckled. "The paper bag makes it look like offensive material. I'll take it to school and read it."

"Won't take you more than a few hours."

"It's obvious Luke had an agenda with what he wrote."

"Doesn't every writer?" Paul leaned back in his chair. "Newspapers do, advertisers do. Even when I write a supposedly unbiased medical article, I'm still trying to persuade people to accept my views."

Rob grunted.

If they didn't get on with discussing the chapters, they were going to run out of time. Paul took a deep breath. "I'm struck by the way Jesus speaks. His absolute assurance. It would sound arrogant coming from most people, but I can't find any evidence that Jesus was arrogant." He clicked the end of his pen. "In fact, I'm amazed by the lack of sensationalism in the writing."

Rob scratched his chin. "I noticed that too."

Paul's eggs were getting cold on his plate. "Somewhere Jesus tells people not to tell anyone about the miracles."

Rob looked at the paper next to his plate. "Yes, he said that to the leper. Almost like Jesus doesn't want to be noticed." Rob took a slow sip of coffee. "And Jesus was more confrontational than I expected. If he wanted to stay out of trouble, then he should have kept away from the religious leaders."

"Didn't it strike you that Jesus wasn't interested in being politically correct?" Paul said. "He was more interested in exposing hypocrisy."

Rob chuckled. "Aussies would have loved him. He'd have hammered the hypocrites and kept the politicians honest." He looked at his watch. "Sorry, I'll have to run. Chapters nine to twelve next time?"

Paul nodded as Rob got up. "See you next Friday." Paul still had fifteen minutes before he needed to move.

They were just skimming the surface with their study and could easily spend an hour discussing each chapter. Esther had once told him how she'd read the Bible over and over, as well as doing in-depth studies of each book. It sounded peculiar, but she said she enjoyed it. He'd always thought Christians were boring, but the more he read Luke, the less boring it all sounded. Jesus said and did unusual things, and his disciples went from being astounded to being afraid. Would he have been afraid if he'd been there among them? Perhaps. If the stories were true, he would have been in the presence of someone with real power. Power to control the waves. Power to cure sicknesses with a word.

What a boon it would be to be able to cure cancer with a simple command. He'd be rich with power like that. But Jesus didn't use his power to gain money or influence. Yet another issue to ponder.

Paul glanced at his notes. He'd copied out a few sentences, including one when Jesus said, "It is not the healthy who need a doctor, but the sick. I have not come to call the righteous, but sinners to repentance."

He'd always figured Christians thought they were better than other people, but Jesus was nothing like that. In fact, Jesus was nothing like he'd expected. Luke's Jesus was confrontational yet gentle. Confident yet humble. Goal-focused and yet he still managed to care for those that others ignored.

If Jesus was around today, would Paul have liked him? He put down his coffee mug, empty except for tepid dregs. Yes, he would have liked Jesus. Just as he'd liked Esther.

Yet Paul had always preferred to maintain a respectful distance. He'd always thought his scepticism didn't matter. Now he was beginning to suspect it mattered rather a lot.

CHAPTER 8

Paul pulled into the carpark at the restaurant he'd booked two weeks before.

"Lauren, I've got something for you before we go in." He'd debated about where to give her the present. The light wasn't as good in the carpark as in the restaurant, but he had wanted some privacy in case he'd got things wrong.

He reached into the back seat, dragged the wrapped box forward, and gave it to Lauren. "Happy birthday, sweetheart."

She held the box up to her ear.

He laid a hand on her arm. "I don't think I'd rattle this one."

Her eyes shone in the dark and she carefully removed the tape and paper from the professionally wrapped box. Inside was a flat-tish white box.

"Ooh," she said, eyes wide. "This looks exciting."

She opened the box and touched the beautiful sapphire pendant on the end of a gold chain and the matching stud earrings. "Oh, Dad, they're gorgeous." She held up her hand. "They match the ring Mum gave me."

He smiled at her pleasure. "Your Mum sent me a picture of the ring she was giving you."

The ring had been in her family since the 1920s, a Ceylon sapphire set in gold.

"Put them on. They should be perfect with that dress."

"So that's why Mum told me not to wear jewellery tonight."

He grinned at her as she put on the earrings.

"I hope this restaurant has a decent mirror because I'm going to have to go and check myself out." She fumbled with the clasp of the necklace and then ran her finger over the pendant. "Thanks so much, Dad."

They got out of the car and he offered Lauren his arm. He'd taken Wendy here once or twice when the restaurant first opened. Fortunately, the decor had changed significantly enough not to pierce him with memories.

Paul went around to the far side of the table covered with a starched white tablecloth and pulled out the chair. Lauren blushed prettily and sat down.

He'd gone to a good deal of thought about what to do for Lauren's eighteenth, wanting a father-daughter date that would fittingly mark her transition to legal adulthood. His little girl could now vote.

He took his own seat opposite her.

"Your mother told me how much fun you had looking for your dress."

He'd been thrilled that Wendy had actually talked about something beyond essential information.

Lauren opened her mouth and then closed it again. One day she was going to ask him about what went wrong between him and Wendy. He'd better be ready.

The waiter approached and handed them the menu. Lauren's eyebrows shot up.

"You only turn eighteen once," he said. "Choose what you want."

She was silent reading the choices. "Good thing they explain what each item is, or I wouldn't dare order." She tapped the menu. "Is it okay just to have a main and a dessert?"

"I thought you might do that. I'll do the same."

The waiter returned. "Are you ready to order?"

Lauren nodded.

The waiter turned to Lauren. "What would you like, madam?"

Lauren giggled, then flushed when the waiter winked at her. "This one." She tapped the menu.

"Ravioli di melanzane e scamorza, for the lady." The syllables rolled off his tongue with practised ease. "Anything else?"

She shook her head.

"And you, sir," the waiter said, turning to Paul.

"I'll have the rigatoni alla Genovese."

"And any wine with that?" The waiter looked at them both.

"No, thank you," Lauren said. Instead, she chose mineral water with lemon and he ordered the same.

After the waiter left Lauren said, "You sounded almost Italian."

"I always choose the easiest things to pronounce."

She laughed. "Now I'm going to powder my nose or whatever sophisticated women of your era said."

Ouch. It always stung when one's children talked about previous eras as though they were several centuries earlier.

Lauren touched her earrings. "Of course, all I want to do is look at my gift properly. I won't be long."

After things had fallen apart with Wendy, Lauren had barely talked to him for a year. He couldn't blame her. Thirteen wasn't a great age to have to deal with divorce. He'd rung Wendy about it.

"Well, what do you expect?" she'd said. "You were never there for her. You ought to understand, since your father was the same."

He'd been silent. The one man he hadn't wanted to imitate, and he'd repeated his father's sin. He wanted to say that it wasn't the same, that Wendy had left him, but he couldn't. She'd left because she was tired of trying to get his attention.

Lauren came back out and sat down. "They are perfect, Dad. I don't know how you got such a good match with the ring."

"Luck, I guess. And several weekends of ringing around and looking."

She smiled, a lopsided dimple flashing. "Thanks for making the effort."

Seeing her reaction, he'd gladly do it again.

"Are you any closer to making your final choices for next year?"

"It's not easy. They give us this book with all the possible choices for each university. I know what I don't want to do."

"And what's left?"

"I hope you're not disappointed, but I don't want to do medicine or anything to do with science."

"Medicine is something you should only do if you're really keen. It's so many years of training." And harder for women who wanted to get married and have a family. He loved his job, but Wendy had only been half joking when she called medicine his mistress. He didn't want Lauren under the same pressure.

"All my choices are related to history, English, and geography."

"Are you thinking of teaching like your mother?"

She shrugged. "I'm not sure yet. I think I'll just start and see where it leads."

The food arrived.

"Now to avoid getting anything on this dress."

Paul shook out his linen serviette. "That's why these are so big. I'll tuck it in my collar if it makes you feel better."

Lauren leaned forward. "We'll look ridiculous."

"One of the things you'll have to learn in life is that it's always easier to do ridiculous things with someone else." Like he'd done with Wendy the day her sandal strap had broken on a trip into the city before they were married. He'd taken off his shoes to make her feel less self-conscious. Together they'd endured the disapproving stares of some of Sydney's more respectable citizens.

"What happened, Dad?" Lauren asked.

"Sorry, I missed your question."

"I asked what happened between you and Mum." Lauren looked at her plate. "Of course, you don't have to tell me."

Paul took a deep breath. "It's a fair enough question, and you're old enough to hear. I prefer you asking rather than speculating."

Lauren's throat flushed pink. "Did you have an affair or something?"

"No, neither of us did that."

Her shoulders relaxed. "I'm glad. That would have made me mad."

He'd expected her to ask that sort of question as soon as she became more aware of romantic relationships. He was surprised she hadn't already had a boyfriend, but perhaps he and Wendy were to blame for that. Maybe she didn't trust herself to get it right.

"And neither of you have married again."

"Would you have found that hard?"

She avoided his gaze. "Uh-huh."

It was only recently that he'd begun to do some mental digging into his past with Wendy. It might be a midlife kind of thing, to look back, reflect, and evaluate.

"You asked if either of us had an affair. We didn't, but your mother called my work my mistress, and she was right in terms of the time and energy it took up."

"I don't get it. Mum is proud of what you do."

A warmth filled his chest. Was she indeed?

"Maybe—but when you were younger, I spent long days at work, especially with all the extra training. It was hard for her. She was working full-time and looking after everything at home as well."

Lauren was halfway through her meal, and he'd barely started.

"But she didn't have to work, did she?" Lauren asked.

"Not for financial reasons, but she'd trained hard and she enjoyed teaching."

They'd had one doozy of a fight about it when Wendy had insisted she needed help with the children. He'd suggested she quit work, that he was perfectly able to support the family. Wendy had blown a fuse and called him a chauvinist. He'd walked out and spent the night at a hotel.

"Some of my friends' mothers work and some don't." Lauren fiddled with her fork. "I think the ones who don't work or work part-time seem more relaxed."

Paul wasn't going to comment. Call him a coward, but this was a conversation a man could seldom win. Perhaps things had been easier in his grandparents' generation.

Lauren asked a few more questions as he finished his main meal, then the waiter cleared their plates and offered the dessert menu. They each ordered two flavours of gelato.

"Looking back, most of the fault was mine," Paul said once the waiter was gone. "I did take on things at work that weren't necessary. Your mother felt she was alone and carrying all the family responsibilities."

He'd been happy and assumed she was too. All he needed was to know she was at home waiting for him, but she'd needed more. Not only more support, but she'd needed to feel appreciated and special. He'd neglected that in a major way.

They chatted a little longer and sampled each other's gelato choices.

"Anything else? Coffee?"

She shook her head. "I need all the sleep I can get."

He raised an eyebrow. "When did you get so wise?"

She winked at him and sat back in her seat with a contented sigh.

He was so proud of his daughter and how she was maturing.

And talking about being proud, it was music to his ears that Wendy was proud of his work. Had she had a change of heart? He'd tried to move on from Wendy several times, but he'd never asked any woman for a third date. He always found himself comparing them with Wendy, which wasn't fair to the women. He preferred being alone rather than settling for a poor substitute.

But Wendy. What did she think of him now? She was willing to say a few words on the phone, but the subject was always the children. If he attempted to enquire about her, she cut him off and said she had something to do. Was she busy, or was busyness a convenient excuse, the ploy someone uses when they are avoiding something? If so, what was she avoiding?

CHAPTER 9

Paul whacked the squash ball against the wall. It bounced back, and he hit it again. He'd do another twenty minutes on his own, as his colleague had to leave early. Not that it mattered. He came for the workout, and they always reserved the court for a double session.

John had asked him to play soon after Paul's separation from Wendy. It hadn't taken him long to get the hang of the game. Without John, he could work on his weak points and figure out how hard he needed to hit the ball to get it to bounce off the back wall of the court and still hit the front wall. He swung and the ball fell short. Again. By the tenth time he was getting a fifty percent success rate. Not enough if he was to use the technique on John.

He and Rob had missed several weeks of their club but this week they'd managed to complete the third session. It had been a hard one. The chapters had pounded on about what it would mean to follow Jesus, with lots of talk about denying themselves and taking up a cross.

He'd been shocked by the two predictions Jesus had made about his own death. Who had that kind of knowledge? Was this evidence proving Jesus really was God? Or had Jesus deliberately provoked the Pharisees to fulfil his own prophecy? But what would be the point of that? Only a madman would want to die.

Thwack.

Paul struck the ball again, and it ricocheted back so fast that he missed it. He put one foot back in the serving box and served to start another solitary volley.

There were other things in Luke supporting Jesus' claim to be God. The number and spectrum of miracles was the most obvious. Everyone recognised that Jesus had an unusual authority, not just in the way he taught and claimed the Old Testament prophecies were fulfilled in him, but in his authority over demons, sickness, and death.

The ball came back at an unexpected angle, and Paul launched himself forward to stop it bouncing on the floor a second time. He skidded on a droplet of sweat that slicked the floor and missed the ball. Blast. He walked to the back of the court and collected the cloth to wipe the floor.

At medical school, they'd been shown gruesome photos of leprosy patients with missing extremities because they didn't feel pain and so didn't pull away from danger. The healings Jesus did weren't ordinary at all. Atrophied muscles and nerve cells had been instantaneously restored.

Paul started another volley, deliberately moving around to areas that made returning the ball harder. The first few months he'd played against John, he'd lost every game. Now he won about thirty percent. He grimaced to himself. Playing John each week kept him humble.

One of the verses that hit him hard was the one about what good is it to gain the whole world but lose your soul. Surely no one could read the story of the rich fool and not ask if they were a fool. Looking back, he'd certainly been given more than his fair share of gifts. Even things like being an only child ensured all his mother's money and effort was directed his way. He'd sometimes resented her preoccupation with him, but maybe he'd have resented it more if he'd had to share her with siblings. And without the scholarship, he'd never have received the privilege of one of the best educations in Australia.

He hit the ball again and settled in for a few more strokes with his racquet. Looks and well-directed charm helped in life too. He had the world, yet he'd squandered what mattered most. Not that he'd realised how precious his family were to him until Wendy had taken the children and gone to her parents. He hadn't seen them for more than a month, and he'd learned day after day how much his family meant to him.

Yet, if he understood what Jesus was saying, there was something worse than losing his family. Jesus called it losing your soul. Paul didn't know what a soul was, but at the very least it would be the essence of what made him human. Was it some part of him that lasted beyond the grave? He'd always assumed people died and that was the end, but Esther had been certain she was going to see Jesus. If she was right, presumably the other place was real as well.

He reached for and missed the ball, and it rolled into the back corner. More than time to stop anyway. He exited the court and picked up his water bottle. He drank half the bottle in thirsty gulps, then picked up a small towel and wiped his face and head. He was drenched with sweat, which was why he played squash. It was a fast, hard workout.

Paul headed for the showers, greeting a few regulars on the way. He and John always came straight after work and played while most people were having dinner. It ensured they didn't need to wait for a shower.

Hell. Not something he'd ever taken seriously, along with an imaginary Satan in shiny black lycra with red horns and a pitchfork. Paul was more inclined to accept angels, although he didn't know if he believed in them either.

He'd always believed Satan was a myth the church used to manipulate people. Yet Jesus took Satan seriously. Jesus not only talked with Satan but cast demons out of people. Esther had said people couldn't pick and choose the bits of the Bible they wanted to believe. It was all or nothing, and he wasn't anywhere near accepting it all. Wasn't sure he wanted to.

Once in the shower he scrubbed his scalp vigorously. Rob had been quiet during their last discussion, so Paul hadn't dared to raise the most confronting verses. The verses where Jesus said he'd come to bring division, not peace. That families would split down the middle over their response to Jesus. Rob said his wife was vehemently against Christians. What was her story? That kind of anger usually had a reason behind it. Whatever the reason, Rob was tiptoeing around to avoid her discovering that he was studying the Bible.

Perhaps there was less pressure for Paul, but there would still be consequences if he ever made a decision to follow Jesus. What would Wendy think? She had attended church regularly as a child, but her family had only attended at Christmas and Easter by the time he met them. He and Wendy had been married at the beach rather than in a church.

He had no idea what Wendy, Ben or Lauren thought about Jesus. He suspected they didn't think about him at all. He could predict his mother's response. She wouldn't be happy to share him with anything or anyone else. Beneath her frantic busyness, her life was empty. She'd once called him the sun in her universe, an expectation that had made him happy he lived in Sydney. What was the sun in his universe? Early in his marriage he would have said it was Wendy, but he'd proved that a lie. She'd accused him of blind selfishness, and she'd been right.

He towelled himself dry, dressed, and headed out to his car. He'd grab something for a late dinner, Chinese maybe, and be home in less than twenty minutes.

He pulled out into the post peak-hour traffic.

He'd like to think his family and colleagues would be tolerant of any decision he made, but Australian society was contemptuous towards Christians. Not that much had changed since Jesus' day. Taking up a cross daily didn't sound like fun.

Look at what had happened to Esther's family. She'd grown up in the church, but her father had gone ballistic and thrown her out of home when she questioned some of his teachings. It sounded like something that happened centuries ago or in less tolerant cultures, not in 1990s Australia.

There'd been something about Esther's funeral that had puzzled him, but he couldn't work out what at the time. It was only recently that he'd remembered that her father wasn't there. The front pew had only held Esther's mother, sister, and grandmother. Definitely no male relative. Had their conflict endured even beyond death? Paul shuddered and gripped the steering wheel. What was it about Jesus that divided people like that?

Paul had been thinking of this process as a personal journey to honour the memory of a friend, but he'd been naive to think a decision could be made in isolation. He could say no to Jesus, continue with the status quo, and no one would be any the wiser. But, if he decided to follow Jesus, there would be major upheaval.

He blew out a gusty breath. His natural inclination was to forget the whole thing. Change wasn't something he embraced at the best of times.

HANDS OF STEEL were squeezing the air out of his throat. Paul's chest heaved with the effort to breathe. He reached up to pull the hands off but gripped nothing. A mist swirled around him, but not like any mist he'd encountered. The mist had form and weight. Cloying weight. It was fear itself. The fear enveloped him, filled his nostrils, and oozed into every nook and cranny. He struggled, but he seemed to be tied down by cords. He was powerless before the terror. His blood pulsed in his head.

The hands around his neck squeezed tighter and his heels drummed on the bed. Lights exploded in his mind and the fear thrummed.

Paul gurgled through his constricted throat and woke to find himself lying on his queen-size bed. He wasn't even panting. What had happened? Whatever it was, it was unlike any nightmare he'd ever experienced.

He turned his head. The bedside clock glowed 02:10 and convinced him he was awake. The nightmare had been so real, he hadn't been sure of his state of consciousness.

Was the nightmare somehow linked to yesterday's pondering or merely what he ate for dinner? He shivered and patted the bed. All the blankets were on the floor. In the cold of the night, the whole thing seemed improbable, but enough of the fear lingered to ensure he wasn't going back to sleep any time soon. Not if a repeat of the experience, whatever it was, awaited him.

CHAPTER 10

Paul approached the reception desk at the medical centre and greeted Michelle as he now did each morning.

"Oh, Dr Webster, there's a letter here for you." She opened one of the desk drawers. "The mail room found this letter caught at the bottom of the mailbag. It wasn't discovered until yesterday and they're afraid it has been there quite a while. They sent their apologies."

She handed it to him. Blazoned across one corner were the words *Strictly Personal*. Strange. He couldn't think of anyone who would write to him at work rather than at home.

"Thanks, Michelle. Better late than never."

She looked at him oddly. Had she expected him to chew her out? The letter's late arrival wasn't her fault.

He went into his office, put away his things in the locked cupboard, and then slit open the envelope with a letter opener and unfolded the three pages. The words looked like they were written by an elderly person. He flipped to the last page. Esther! Her name was scrawled, with an untidy line in brackets underneath.

(My grandmother wrote this for me).

He put the letter down. There was no way he was reading this here. Not with a whole day of non-stop appointments ahead of him. A letter from someone buried weeks ago would unsettle anyone. And he was unsettled enough already on the issue of Esther.

* * *

It wasn't one of his nights for squash, so Paul hurried home, warmed up a frozen meal in the microwave, and sat at his kitchen table. He would read while he ate. He laid the letter flat on the table next to his plate using the salt and pepper shakers to weigh down the edges.

Sweat prickled along his hairline.

Dear Dr Webster,

This is one of many letters I've written to people in the last few weeks. If you're reading this, it means I've gone to be with Jesus. Most of the letters will have been distributed after my funeral but as I'm sure you wouldn't have been at the funeral, I made sure the address was on the envelope so my mother could post it.

Pity she'd never known he had been at the funeral. He'd even stood up and said something about her impact on him, but he'd slipped out immediately afterwards because he'd been terrified he was about to cry. He did recall hearing something about personal letters while he was still in the foyer but he'd assumed they would be for close friends and family, not someone like himself. He turned back to the letter.

First of all, thank you for all the hard work you put into making sure I knew what was going on and answering my numerous questions. I thought we wouldn't connect at first, but you became more approachable over the months.

She was being gracious. He'd prided himself on his professionalism, but Esther had shown him he needed to be more human in what was often the most stressful experience of a person's life.

I wanted to write and encourage you again to take the time to thoroughly investigate who Jesus is. I know the all-too-human tendency to put things off, but if Jesus is who he claims to be, then it matters.

Fear flooded into his heart. He took a shaky breath and fumbled his fork, dropping it with a clatter on his plate. As he'd thought more about last night's nightmare, he'd become convinced it was linked to his investigation into Jesus. He planned to ask Rob if he wanted to continue or quit. They'd agreed to do the study because of Esther, but both still hoped they'd find proof that the whole thing was ridiculous.

You're going to think me crazy. You've probably often thought this but have usually been too polite to say.

Paul's face warmed. He hadn't always been polite. Several times he'd called her crazy or at least implied it. Esther had never snapped back, although at times he'd sensed she was hurt—maybe not personally, but sad on his behalf.

I wouldn't be surprised if you experience some trouble if you start reading the Bible and asking serious questions.

Paul blinked. Trouble? What was she talking about?

By trouble I mean that things might happen that make you want to quit doing a thorough investigation.

Was that what had happened last night?

If you want a better explanation, I suggest you find Joy Wong (the centre cleaner) and ask her about spiritual opposition. She has had lots more experience than me.

He put the first page of the letter behind the others and continued reading.

Sorry for this waffly letter, but at least I can blame you for it since you've made sure I'm pumped full of drugs.

He laughed. There was the sense of humour he'd enjoyed so much.

As I've said to you before, dying can be a good thing. It has shown me what really matters. Aside from my family, you and several others are on my heart. I want you to have the best possible opportunity to meet Jesus, yet I find myself afraid to speak the truth to you. Have you ever noticed how much of human interaction is dictated by fear?

Was Esther right? Certainly most people's daily interactions kept within the strictures of those behaviours that were considered polite and professional. That wasn't necessarily a bad thing, was it?

He gripped his fork. Was fear part of his complicated relationship with his mother? With her, he walked a tightrope between giving her enough time, so she didn't feel neglected, yet avoiding too much time in the negativity of her presence. He had never dared to confront her on issues.

And Ben and Lauren? He always aimed to give them a good time when they visited, but was some of the reason because he feared the silence if the three of them had just each other for company? He didn't want to risk rejection.

Wendy? He'd left things as they were rather than chase after her in case she rejected him more fully and he lost access to the children. Esther might be right. Fear of rocking the boat and ending up with less time with Ben and Lauren kept him quiet when perhaps he should speak. He sighed. Another thing to think about.

He turned to the final page.

So here goes. I want to state upfront that being a Christian is so wonderful that I want all my friends and family to know Jesus too.

Wonderful? Paul shook his head. What kind of God allowed one of his loyal followers to get cancer?

I don't believe that our meeting was accidental. The God who made the universe orchestrates events to allow people to come to know him. Amazing thought, isn't it? That he would allow me to have cancer so you could meet him through knowing me.

Whoa. Paul's eyes widened. Did Esther truly think her God allowed her cancer for Paul's sake? Not that it was just for his sake. Esther's cancer had allowed her to meet others as well. There'd been a man at the funeral who said his wife met Esther in chemo and as a result had become a Christian before she died. It seemed horrible for God to allow his followers to go through suffering and death for other people, yet Esther didn't resent it. He'd have resented it if he were in her place.

Many years ago, a man called C.S. Lewis (a professor at Oxford and Cambridge) wrote that Jesus was either a liar (who said he was God but wasn't), or a lunatic (like those people in asylums who claim to be God) or Lord of all. I find those categories helpful.

Of course, I know some people would prefer to think Jesus was simply a teacher or a good man whose model we can follow. But those categories don't fit, because Jesus repeatedly claimed that he was God.

He'd hoped that there would have been no evidence that Jesus had claimed to be God. But that wasn't the case.

None of my teachers ever did that. I suspect people prefer to confine Jesus to these gentle categories because then we're in control and don't have to submit to him. Ignoring him is easier than letting him take charge.

Paul nodded. Yes, this described him perfectly. Jesus' claims were disruptive, and he was used to jogging along in comfort. Yet, if he himself had cancer, what he had now couldn't begin to help him navigate through it.

So is Jesus a liar, a lunatic, or Lord? You know what I think, and I've staked my eternity on the decision. Please investigate thoroughly. Eternity is too important not to make the effort.

He licked his suddenly dry lips. It wasn't hard to imagine Esther pleading with him.

I've prayed a lot for you these last eighteen months. Prayed that you would have the courage to not only read the Bible but to do it with intellectual integrity. Prayed that you won't look for loopholes that give you excuses to ignore Jesus but will read with an honesty that allows for the possibility that Jesus might be who he claims to be.

Esther had known him too well.

May you one day have what I have and discover that what you feared is what you've been searching for your whole life—even when you weren't aware of it.

Sincerely, your friend,

Esther

Paul put his head in his hand. Esther seemed to read his mind. She'd have claimed that any insight came from God, but it was still disconcerting. It was as though she was looking straight through him, sifting his motivations. Just when he'd been willing to give up the hard work of thinking through things he'd rather avoid, this letter had arrived.

A month ago, he'd have said the letter getting lost on the way to him was a coincidence, but was it? Esther would have teased him by calling it a miracle. Yet he'd still prefer to label it a coincidence, because the thought of a God arranging such things scared him.

There. He'd admitted it.

This God scared him. He didn't want his comfortable life turned on its head. He didn't want to have to lay down his own ambitions and dreams. Most of all, he didn't want to submit to a God who might demand anything of him. What if this God asked too much?

No! He was not thinking any more tonight. He washed up, wandered back into the living room, plopped down on the sofa, and switched on the TV. He'd been entirely too serious lately. He needed to lighten up.

That night, the nightmare resumed.

CHAPTER 11

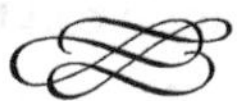

Winter seemed to be arriving early with three blustery days of wind and rain. Paul's nightmares continued and were taking a toll.

Mid-morning, the sun came out and flooded through the side window of Paul's office. He couldn't wait for lunchtime to escape into the park next door. He seldom ate there, but today he'd make an exception.

For once, he accepted Sister O'Reilly's offer to order his lunch when she ordered her own. When his Cornish pasty and fruit arrived he headed outside. Glorious. Now if only there was no one seated in the sunny spot.

He strolled across the park and clicked his tongue in annoyance. Someone was there. He changed direction and stopped. Wasn't that Joy Wong? If so, it was another coincidence. The coincidences in his life were multiplying. He hovered, undecided whether to move on or to approach Joy.

"Jerk," he muttered to himself. Why shouldn't he talk to whomever he wanted? He was letting his insecurities about what people might think get in the way. He mentally shook himself and walked towards Joy.

She had her eyes closed, and he cleared his throat. Her eyes flew open, but she didn't seem shocked to see him.

He gave a tentative smile. "Ms Wong, would it be okay if I joined you?"

"Of course, Dr Webster, but do call me Joy."

He nodded and took a seat across from her but not directly opposite. "Paul."

Joy looked like she'd already finished her lunch. "I hope you don't mind if I eat," Paul said.

"Not at all." Joy gestured around. "I've never seen you out here."

"I normally eat in my office and take a short break or catch up on paperwork, but today I wanted some sunshine."

Esther had told him to talk with Joy, but how could he start? Jumping right into discussion about his nightmares with an almost complete stranger was awkward. Although he talked about difficult subjects every day with his patients, he'd always avoided personal conversations. They made him feel too exposed.

"Did you receive a letter from Esther after the funeral?" Joy asked. "I noticed your name on the list. At least I presume it was yours—it only said Paul W."

"That's the odd thing. My letter got lost and only arrived a few days ago."

"Glad it finally reached you. Those letters meant a lot to Esther." Joy gave Paul a warm smile as though they'd known each other for years. "Esther said she'd told various people to come and talk to me if they had questions."

Paul swallowed some crumbs from his pasty down the wrong way. Here was his opening, but fear swirled through him once again. The nightmares were so real, to the point where he almost doubted his sanity. He'd not prepared himself to see Joy, yet here she was. He swallowed and laid down the rest of his pasty.

"Esther's letter strongly challenged me to investigate Jesus' claims for myself."

Joy raised an eyebrow. "And are you going to do that?"

He nodded. "I've already started. I'm reading through Luke with another of Esther's friends from the clinic."

Joy didn't say anything. There was something about her that made her easy to talk to.

"We decided to read four chapters a week on our own, then talk about them when we get together on Friday mornings."

"I've been praying for you," Joy said quietly.

Paul blinked. When Esther had told him she was praying for him, he hadn't known what to think. Being prayed for seemed sort of invasive, but it also touched his heart that someone he didn't know took the time to pray for him.

"I've been praying you'd read God's word, understand it, and become more and more curious about it."

He squirmed in his seat. "The first few weeks that was what happened, but then something weird happened—"

"Yes?" Joy said.

Would she think him crazy?

"If you're reading the Bible and asking serious questions, you're almost certain to run into trouble."

Trouble. There was that word again. "Esther's letter mentioned spiritual opposition, but I don't understand what she means."

"There are two great powers in this world, although one is far greater than the other," Joy said. "Do you know who I mean?"

"I presume one is God."

"Yes, he's the far greater power. And the other?"

Paul glanced around the park. No one was nearby but he still lowered his voice. "Do you mean Satan?"

Joy nodded. "Someone you westerners persist in disbelieving." She chuckled. "That suits him, because it's much easier to work behind the scenes when no one thinks you're real."

"This is so far outside my experience that I don't even know what questions to ask."

Joy smiled. "Would you like me to tell you a little about Satan before we talk about your experience?"

Paul nodded and picked up his pasty again. Eating gave him something to do as he listened to a topic he'd never expected to ever talk about. Esther certainly had a lot to answer for.

"The Bible only gives veiled hints about Satan's origins. He seems to have been an angel who became proud and rebelled against God. Other angels joined him in his rebellion, but they were all defeated and banished from heaven."

It all sounded like something from a speculative novel, but Joy talked about Satan and angels like they were a perfectly normal topic for a sunny winter's day.

"Ever since his banishment, Satan has worked against God's plans and purposes. He tries to destroy humans and prevent them from deciding to follow Jesus." She fixed her gaze on him. "He uses many different methods. Distraction is the most common, but sometimes he uses nightmares so vivid they seem real, where you are terrified and may feel like you're being strangled—"

Paul's head snapped up. "How did you know that was what happened to me?"

"I didn't, but it happened to me before I became a Christian and a few times since."

"I've had them the last four nights in a row. I don't usually remember my dreams, but these can't be forgotten."

"Do the dreams leave any lingering fears?"

"Yes." Paul shuddered. "And the fear comes back whenever I pick up the Bible or think about what I've been reading."

Joy reached into her bag and pulled out a piece of paper and a pen. "And have you been thinking of giving up your Bible reading?"

"Uh-huh."

"That's the whole purpose of the nightmares. To stop you from getting any closer to the truth. Whatever you do, don't stop."

"But I can't handle more nightmares. I've already nearly lost my temper twice this morning from lack of sleep."

"Let me tell you what I do when I experience these things. As I said, Jesus is infinitely more powerful than Satan, so we have to claim his protection."

"But I'm not a Christian. I respect Jesus, but I'm not sure he's God. And I'm definitely not ready to follow him." Joy was still smiling her gentle smile at him. "Why would he help me?"

"Helping is part of his nature. Why don't you say something like, 'In the name of Jesus, leave me alone'."

Paul looked hard at Joy. Was she joking? Was that it? He wasn't even sure what she suggested was possible. "I can't move in the dream. How would I be able to talk?"

Joy laughed. "Just try it."

Paul rubbed his temple. How on earth had he got himself mixed up in all this stuff?

"As a Christian, I can claim my position as an adopted child of God. I say something like, 'I am a daughter of the King of the universe. In the name of Jesus, leave me alone'."

"And does it work?" Paul couldn't quite conceal the scepticism in his tone.

Joy nodded. "Satan flees whenever a person stands under Jesus' protection." She chuckled. "The Chinese have a proverb that's based on a story. There was a fox who boasted that all the other animals were afraid of it. The other animals said, 'We're not afraid of you, but we are afraid of the tiger walking behind you'."

"And you're saying it's the same with a Christian? They can't stand against Satan, but if Jesus is behind them then Satan is afraid?"

Joy flashed a smile at him. "Exactly." She picked up her pen. "I'm going to write down a few Bible references that tell us more about

Satan and his purposes. Not many, because the Bible doesn't say much."

She wrote down some references. Genesis 3 was on the top, along with something from a book called Corinthians and another from Peter. He'd have to check the table of contents in his Bible to find them.

"There, that's more than enough. Would you feel uncomfortable if I prayed for you now?"

He leaned back slightly. "A bit."

"I won't close my eyes or do anything other than say a few sentences."

Paul did a quick check around the park. He couldn't see anyone he knew. He stared ahead while Joy prayed.

"Dear heavenly Father. Thank you that you love Paul and want him to know and trust you. Help him to keep reading Luke and help him to understand what he reads. Help him not to fear but to learn to trust you. In Jesus' name, Amen."

"Thank you," Paul said, a catch in his throat. "First time I've heard someone pray for me."

"I'll keep praying." Joy stood up. "Please don't be afraid to come and ask me any questions."

Afraid. Interesting she should choose that word. He had been afraid—afraid enough to never approach Joy. Seeing her right in front of him had given him the courage to at least say hello, and Joy had made it easy. She'd given him a lot to think about. Now he'd see if her suggestion cured the nightmares.

CHAPTER 12

The hands were around his throat again, and his chest was being crushed.

"Help," he croaked. "Help." Nothing happened except his breath wheezed through his constricted airways.

Joy. The name leapt into his mind. She'd told him what to say. He remembered, but he no longer had air for a full sentence. "Jesus," he gasped. "Jesus!"

The pressure on his neck and chest disappeared as though snatched away. He took a deep breath of cold air. Beautiful cold air. Thankfulness filled him. "Thank you. Thank you, Jesus."

* * *

THE ALARM STARTLED HIM. Paul turned over, hit the button with his hand, and stared blearily at the clock. 5:45. He needed to rush to get to his fourth meeting with Rob. He swung his legs out of bed and shivered. Brrr. If it was cold now, what was the weekend going to be like in the mountains? He'd spent the last two nights packing for three days of hiking with Ben and Lauren.

He was in the shower before he remembered the events of the night before. His flesh tingled. All he'd said was "Jesus" and the fear had disappeared in a flash, replaced with such peace that he'd slept soundly all night. A new kind of fear settled in his belly. Was this how the disciples had felt when they'd seen some of Jesus' miracles? The terrible awe of meeting someone way outside anything they'd ever known? The whole thing would take some getting used to.

When he arrived at the café, Rob was already seated. He suspected Rob got there early to ensure they had the most private table.

This week's reading had several hard-hitting chapters, but last night's had been the most confronting. There'd been no warning that he'd find it difficult—an ordinary story about a father and two sons. It wasn't as if it was the first time he'd read or heard the story, but last night it hit him in the heart like a punch from a heavy-weight boxer. Bam!

Oh, how he longed for a father like that. Someone who always had his best interests at heart. Someone who was waiting for him no matter what he'd done. Someone who loved generously, eternally, unconditionally.

He'd sat in his armchair with tears in his eyes. How could a man in his fifties be crying for a father? His mother had been wrong to deny him the right to meet the man. Even if his father had been the wastrel and weakling she claimed, he would have liked to have met him and make the judgement for himself.

Paul ordered his breakfast and walked towards what he now thought of as their corner. He wasn't going to mention chapter fifteen in their discussion, and he hoped Rob wouldn't notice. The Parable of the Prodigal Son might undo him in front of Rob and everyone in the café.

They caught up a little as they ate.

"I nearly backed out of meeting this morning," Rob said as he finished a mouthful of eggs.

"Me too," Paul said. "But I made a promise to Esther's memory that I'd finish Luke, and I intend to do it."

Rob nodded. "I feel the same. She used to say if I did this, then if I was ever bothered by another Christian, I could tell them I'd already thoroughly investigated the Bible."

Paul laughed. "She used the same line with me." Esther had been confident Luke would impact him, and she'd been right. Whether or not he ever chose to follow Jesus, his view of Jesus was now completely different from the impressions gleaned through school chapels, books, and the media. He'd had to read *Pride and Prejudice* for senior English, and who'd ever want to be like the ridiculous clergyman Mr Collins? And as for the media, they almost never had anything positive to say about Jesus or Christians.

"Ready to start?" Rob asked.

"Yeah, sorry. Was thinking my own thoughts." Paul glanced at his notebook. "One issue that keeps jumping out at me is something related to my job."

Rob raised an eyebrow.

"When people get cancer they often ask, 'Why me?' It's as if they think a good person or a nice person shouldn't get sick."

"Yeah," Rob said. "People asked me that when I got cancer. As though it was my fault for not living right or that it was some sort of divine punishment." He chuckled. "My wife went ballistic with one person for suggesting that. Told her off for believing in a god at all, let alone one that randomly hands out punishments to someone like me."

Wendy used to defend him from his mother's criticism. He'd loved her for it. No one else, including himself, ever stood up to his mother.

"Yet Jesus is clear that the people who died when that tower collapsed weren't worse than anyone else," Rob said. "Although I'm not quite sure what he means by his statement about worse things happening to people if they don't repent."

Paul had puzzled over the same lines while he drove into work yesterday. "Do you think he means hell? If people don't repent and get right with God, then one day they'll die and go to hell?"

Rob shifted in his seat. "I'm not at all sure I believe in hell."

"Me either, but Jesus talked about it in chapter sixteen. If he really was who he claimed to be, then presumably he knew what he was talking about."

Rob used his toast to mop up the last of the egg on his plate. "That's just it. I'm still not sure who Jesus was. I haven't noticed him making any claims to be God."

The fear from Paul's nightmares pressed in against him. He sent up a tentative, "Help, Jesus". The fear disappeared, but the temptation to say nothing lingered. He mentally squared his shoulders.

"That's what I thought too, because I was expecting Jesus to come right out and say, 'I am God'. But when I went back and looked at the stories, he's more subtle than that." Paul flicked back a page in his notebook. "If you look at the religious leaders and their reactions to Jesus, it's clear it wasn't just jealousy and dislike. It was because they knew Jesus was claiming God's authority. That's what all the fuss was about when Jesus healed people on the Sabbath. Jesus was claiming to be above all their rules, and the only one higher was God himself."

"I hadn't noticed that," Rob said.

"And the demons tell others that he is."

Rob held up his hands in mock surrender. "Okay, okay. You're beginning to sound like a Christian."

Paul's eyes widened. He'd never been accused of that before.

He looked at the underlined part of his notebook. "I found the story about the rich man and Lazarus at the end of chapter sixteen fascinating."

Rob raised his eyebrows at him.

"Jesus' values are topsy-turvy compared to what most of us believe. Most of us respect money and power and success, but

Jesus doesn't. He implies those things get in the way of us knowing God."

"They certainly make us comfortable and self-sufficient," Rob said, taking a swig of his coffee. "One of the best things about having cancer was that I've learned to value small things again, and realised how much we need other people."

Paul had never thought of himself as a wealthy man, but he had plenty compared to most of the world—even compared to the average Aussie. He never had to budget, and if something broke, the funds were always there to replace it. "This story emphasises the loneliness, discomfort, and desolation of hell."

"Not a place to spend a vacation." Rob laughed.

Rob might be able to joke about it, but Paul didn't want to even visit hell, let alone spend an eternity there. He'd always assumed if there was a heaven, then he'd go there. Of course he would. But it was becoming clear that if Jesus was in charge of who went where, then Paul was headed to hell. He folded his hands around the comforting warmth of his coffee mug.

"That banquet story. I wonder what modern excuses we would offer to avoid going." Paul hadn't meant to voice the question aloud.

"Instead of getting married, buying land, and all those other reasons?"

Paul nodded. "The original invitations were given to those we'd expect, the good, hardworking members of society."

If this parable was about Jesus' invitation, which seemed likely based on the clues about the wedding being a feast in the Kingdom of God, then a last-minute decision was a huge gamble. Cancer usually gave people a chance to say their goodbyes, but so many people died with no warning. He wasn't willing to assume he'd get a last-minute chance to accept Jesus before he took his final breath.

"Most of the reasons people gave in the story are still the same today," Rob said. "They're busy with work, busy with family, busy planning the next vacation."

Just like Paul had been. He'd never considered Jesus might have any claim on his life. "I guess most of us simply don't want to go. We assume being at Jesus' banquet would be rather dull."

Rob grunted and caught the eye of the waiter, pointing to their empty plates.

While the plates were being cleared, Paul breathed a silent sigh of relief. He'd avoided talking about the father parable. Less than six hours of work, then he and the children could head to the Snowy Mountains.

* * *

PAUL SKIPPED lunch so he could get his paperwork cleared and be ready for the Queen's Birthday holiday. It was becoming an annual tradition. Snow seldom fell in the Snowy Mountains before the peak of the ski season in July and August. It would be cold, but they could hike rather than ski. The cusp of winter was better for hiking than summer, with its clouds of mosquitoes and massive biting flies.

He pressed the buzzer to request the last patient for the day.

"Good afternoon, Elizabeth. More good news for you today."

Elizabeth sat down with a shaky smile as the tension eased out of her shoulders. He ran through the routine questions checking whether she'd had any unusual pains, tiredness, or shortness of breath. She hadn't. Then he checked how she was coping with the lingering effects of chemotherapy. He even chatted about her work and family for a few minutes.

"Okay, one more appointment in six months, then a full year before the final check-up."

Elizabeth said her goodbyes. He wrote up the relevant medical notes before poking his head into the side office where Sister O'Reilly reigned. She not only prepared people for the practical side of treatments but soothed their fears and mopped their tears. All the things he was no good at.

"I'm about to finish and head off. See you Tuesday morning." He took a step back and then stepped forward again. "Are you doing anything special this weekend?"

Her eyebrows rose towards her hairline, but she recovered in milliseconds like the consummate professional that she was. "My husband and I are going for a quiet weekend in the Blue Mountains."

"Have a good time. You deserve the break."

She gave a tight smile but looked pleased.

Paul shut the door, closed the blinds, and changed into clothes more suitable for driving. Time to get a move on. Wendy would make sure that the children were ready on time.

Just after he arrived home, Wendy pulled into the car space next to his. It had been months since he'd seen her. Did she have any grey in her hair, or did she dye it? All things he couldn't see for himself as Ben and Lauren exited the car and got their packs and boots out of the back.

Jesus said that if anyone followed him then he had to hate his family. Surely this was hyperbole. Elsewhere, Jesus told people to love others and he demonstrated it every day. It seemed his point was more that he was claiming he must be first in people's hearts. First? Paul had reached the point where he respected Jesus and even thought he might be God, but first love? Impossible!

He opened the back of his vehicle and Ben and Lauren transferred their gear across. No, Wendy was his first love, with these two close behind. Wendy, who wouldn't even get out of the car to talk to him. A yearning filled him. What would he have to do for Wendy to let her guard down? To see that he was willing to change?

CHAPTER 13

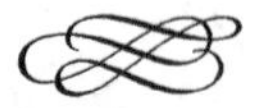

"Dad, why do you make us visit Miranda?" Ben clambered into the back of the four-wheel drive parked outside the bed and breakfast where they'd spent the night. "She doesn't want to see us."

"Don't ask Dad questions like that." Lauren jumped into the driver's seat.

"You always defend him," Ben said. "None of us like her."

"Ben, please don't talk like that." Paul looked over his shoulder into the back seat. "I know she's hard to like, but as your grandmother she deserves respect."

Ben looked away, hiding his sullen face. He'd been cranky since he woke up and having to see his grandmother wasn't improving his mood. Paul watched as Lauren carefully backed the car out of the parking space. Her driving test was next week, and he couldn't see any reason she wouldn't pass first time. How had the tiny premature baby he'd held in his arms become this gorgeous woman?

* * *

THEY PARKED at his mother's place, and Paul and Lauren got out of the car. Ben emerged with all the attitude of a bear forced out of the warmth of hibernation. Paul sent a brief look his way that he hoped conveyed both empathy and a clear message to buck up and meet the challenge.

Ben hung his head but shuffled towards the front door. Lauren rang the bell, and waited.

The door opened. His mother looked like she was expecting the Prime Minister, yet somehow managed to appear stiff rather than welcoming. "Come in out of the cold. Let's not waste time since this is such a short visit."

Paul saw Ben wince at the words. Miranda was definitely getting more critical as she aged.

The central heating hit them with a blast of too-hot air, and they all peeled off their outer layers.

"Please take your shoes off."

They always did—as if they'd dare to walk on the pristine cream carpet with shoes on.

They settled themselves in the elegant lounge, with Ben looking like he had a broomstick strapped to his back. On the last visit, he'd been constantly reprimanded for his casual seating posture.

Miranda went into the kitchen to get the morning tea, and Paul followed to help. It was really too early for morning tea, but they had a long way to drive before they would leave the car and set off and anyway, teenagers were always hungry. He wanted them to hike ten kilometres before nightfall.

His mother switched on the kettle. The table was covered in an array of cookies and slices. His mouth watered. She was a terrific cook and would pack up the leftovers for them to take with them.

"How have you been going, Mother?"

She shrugged. "Oh, you know, always plenty to do."

Her skills at cooking and organisation were appreciated, but did she have any friends?

She took the covers off the various plates. "Why don't you get your children to put those out on the coffee table?"

Your children. He gritted his teeth and took the first plate off the table, his favourite chocolate slice, picked up the pile of Royal Doulton plates, and went through into the lounge. "Can you help your grandmother bring the morning tea through?"

Lauren sprang to her feet, but Ben looked like he'd been asked to paint the whole house before lunch.

"Snap out of it," Paul whispered as he passed Ben. "It's only for a short while. You'll survive."

While Ben and Lauren walked back and forth between the kitchen and the lounge room, his mother asked what he'd been up to. He gave her the kinds of answers she expected—work, squash, the house—but he didn't mention the sceptics' club. One part of him wanted to tell her, if only to see if he'd get the reaction he'd expect—utter horror and a question about why he was wasting his time, or if she'd be shocked into revealing some of her past. He knew nothing about her religious upbringing, if any. In fact, she never mentioned much at all from her past. Her parents had died before he was born.

The kettle whistled, and she poured water into an elaborate teapot that matched the rest of her set. She'd expressed an interest in fine china, so he'd bought her the full tea set in separate gifts over the first five years of his working life. Back then, they'd been an expensive gift. Now he could have bought the whole set without much thought.

He carried the tray with the teapot, sugar lumps, and milk out to join the children, and set everything ready for her to pour. He'd have preferred coffee, but his mother considered tea the appropriate drink for someone of her perceived station. Never mind, he only had to drink it when he was here. It was useless trying to change her. She would just stab him with her piercing stare, and he would back down.

The tea was soon poured.

"Concentrate, boy," she said as she handed Ben a teacup and saucer. "I don't want my china broken."

Ben muttered something and put the tea cup on the side table. He'd wait until it was cool then drink it quickly to minimise the possibility of dropping it. By the time Ben had been cautioned about dropping crumbs four times, as though he were three years old, he'd stopped eating altogether. That was a hardship, as all the family favourites were in front of him. Wendy made similar biscuits and slices, but they were missing that mysterious something to bring them up to his mother's standard. Miranda had always refused to reveal what she referred to as the family's secret recipes.

"Now tell me what you're up to, Lauren."

Lauren put down her tea, which she handled like the queen herself. "Not much, I'm just getting ready for my next lot of exams."

"And did you do well in your last lot?"

Lauren nodded. She hated talking about marks. His mother almost purred, as though she'd gained the marks herself.

"And were you driving today?"

Lauren nodded.

"I suppose Ben will be wanting to get his L-plates soon." Miranda looked across at him. "Hope you take more care with your driving than with your eating."

Ben blushed scarlet and picked up two crumbs that had landed on his shirt. Paul turned to his mother. "Mother, Ben will do very well."

Miranda tightened her lips.

Lauren gave her brother a tight smile. "Since we're camping, I couldn't bring the beautiful jewellery Dad bought me for my birthday. I'll bring it next time."

Good on Lauren, for deflecting attention away from Ben.

"Paul always had exquisite taste." Miranda eyed her tea set with a smug smile.

"Well, I did send Wendy my shortlist before making the final decision."

"Humph," his mother muttered, like he'd had the audacity to burp loudly in public.

He should have known better than to mention Wendy. Mentioning Wendy always made Miranda mad and, if she was mad, he wouldn't be the one to suffer.

"And what about you, Ben. What are you up to?"

Ben shot Paul a mute cry for help. As most of his life was study, which Ben considered boring, and sport, which didn't interest his grandmother, Ben didn't have much he could say to compete with Lauren, whose world was broadening month by month.

"I love watching him play volleyball," Paul said. "He's very skilled, and getting better all the time."

"Volleyball won't get you far in life."

Suddenly he'd had enough. "Well, Mother, sport was the making of me. It taught me to work with others and to lose gracefully. Two things that have a broad application to life."

And the year living in the Snowy Mountains before his senior years of school had taught him confidence and fostered ingenuity and leadership. "This hike we're going on isn't just for enjoyment. We'll all learn things along the way."

His mother frowned but kept her mouth shut.

Ben's tea was finally cool enough, and he drank it quietly, doing his best to avoid any more negative comments.

"Thank you, Mother, that was delicious as usual."

She smiled, all graciousness again. "I've packed up the leftovers for you. Before you go, I've got a present for Lauren." She reached into a drawer, drew out a card and handed it to Lauren. "It's to go towards a car. I'm sure you're planning to buy one."

Lauren flushed with pleasure. "Maybe not right away, but soon."

"Well, that should help." She stood up and went over to kiss Lauren's forehead. "Happy birthday."

As they left the house with a box full of leftovers, Paul made a mental note to speak to her about how she treated Ben. It wasn't fair that she fawned over Lauren and only criticised her grandson.

CHAPTER 14

Paul pulled into the carpark at Round Mountain. Lauren was already lacing her boots.

"We're setting off as soon as we can," Paul said.

"I thought this track had huts. Why can't we stay in those and save the hassle of setting up tents?" Lauren said.

"Wait until you see them. Then you can decide." Paul grinned. Once Lauren saw the corrugated shack with the smoke of ten thousand fires ingrained into the walls, she'd have her tent up in a jiffy. The huts were only for emergency use and although the weekend promised to be cold overnight, no snow was predicted.

Paul checked the ground for anything they might have dropped and locked the car. Then he picked up his pack and followed the others. The pack was heavy on Paul's shoulders. Everyone was carrying a portion of their tents, the food, and had snowshoes tucked into the various straps on the outside of their packs, just in case. They'd been coming to the Snowy Mountains for the past three years and never had to use them but leaving them behind wouldn't be wise.

The path was relatively flat, but there were higher ridges along the horizon. Tomorrow they'd climb Mount Jagungal. If the weather report was correct, they'd see a view worth the effort.

Their boots brushed through the ankle-high snow grass with a steady swish, swish, swish. It wouldn't be as much fun in the morning when the grass would be laden with melting frost. Paul took a deep breath, savouring the sharp cold of the air. He'd spent the happiest year of high school up in these mountains. Despite having to do normal classes, they'd been supplemented by long hours of hiking and camping. He'd learned to kayak and cross-country ski—things he'd never have done if he hadn't received that scholarship. He whistled through his teeth and laughed when he realised it was the theme song of *The Man from Snowy River.*

"What's so funny, Dad?" Lauren asked.

"Just happy to be back."

She laughed. "What is it you say? A few days up here and all comes right with the world?"

Well, it was true. Just the thing to settle him after those nightmares.

"Tell me what makes you happy, Lauren."

She tucked her thumbs under the shoulder straps of the pack. "I like the mountains too. Actually, I look forward to all our holidays."

She'd been a pain the first two as she'd struggled to relate to him. Wendy had managed to reassure her that she wasn't being disloyal enjoying time with her father.

"And I like being with friends and doing things with Mum."

"Like what?"

"Anything, really. Cooking. Craft. She's been teaching me to use the sewing machine."

Wendy loved to create, whether it was cakes, cards, or cross-stitch. He used to resent that she was always doing something, but he'd come to love the whirr of the machine and the glossy swing of Wendy's hair as she peered at her craft. How he'd give up all his holidays to be able to sit and watch her sew, to see the slow smile that spread from the corner of her mouth and set her whole face alight.

Lauren chatted on for a while. She'd grown in confidence over the last year. He looked ahead to where Ben was walking like a machine. What was going on in that mind of his? There had to be some things they could talk about.

Ben stopped, pulled out his camera, and squatted down to take a close-up of something. Paul strolled forward. A beetle was climbing a stalk of grass.

"Good spotting."

Ben grunted before straightening and sliding the camera back into its case. They set off together. One disadvantage of being a trio was that they couldn't walk together. There was always someone left on their own. As Lauren was easier to talk to, it was tempting to walk with her. Ben was hard work, although Paul had seen Ben talking easily with his volleyball friends.

"What do you most like photographing?"

"Lots of things," Ben muttered.

Paul resisted an exasperated sigh. "Such as?"

"Oh, insects, waterfalls, stuff like that."

"But what made you pull out your camera for that beetle?"

Ben kicked a stone in front of him, and it skittered off the track. "The way it gleamed in the sun."

So there were opinions and preferences behind the grunts. Now Paul just had to master the right kind of questions. They lapsed into silence as a crow cawed its lonely call somewhere in the distance. Out here, it was okay to be silent.

* * *

"HERE'S THE HUT." Paul turned to Lauren, who after looking around inside, declared she preferred the tent. Paul chuckled.

"Thought you'd say that. These huts are famous for their extra guests."

She gave a horrified squeak and bounded out the door.

Already the warmth was leaching out of the day. It would be dark in a little over an hour.

"I asked a friend where to camp, and he suggested we walk a little further—there's a tiny creek and better shelter. Let's have a drink of water and keep going. It could get crowded around here later."

The sheltered spot was just as his friend had said. A few scrubby trees and the remains of an old wooden fence forming a windbreak.

They were able to find two relatively flat areas to set up and were now so familiar with the tents that they were up with a minimum of fuss.

"Lauren, you can decide later whether you want to be in your own tent or with us. If it's really cold, we can pile in together and use your tent for our packs." He looked around. "Ben, can you please gather some sticks to add to the ones left by previous campers?"

Paul dug in the lower section of his pack for the cooking gear and various food items. Tonight they'd eat the heavier ones—potatoes, already wrapped in foil for the coals of the fire, and he'd fry bacon to add to grated cheese and chives. They had a tin of peaches and custard to warm for dessert.

Ben's wanderings startled a group of kangaroos who took off with long leaps towards the nearest gully. He came back and dropped a pile of dead branches in a heap.

"Let's see if we can break some of the longer branches into more manageable pieces," Paul said. Once they were done, he let Ben demonstrate his recently learned skill of lighting a fire.

"Good job, son."

Ben grunted and went to get a few more meal-related things out of his pack. They'd do a repack tonight to redistribute the weight.

"I'm going to sort out my stuff before it gets dark." Lauren scrambled to her feet. Paul had already laid out his mat and sleeping bag, so he went to fill the billy with water from the creek while there was still some light.

By the time the potatoes could go on the coals and they had all found a comfortable spot by the fire, the sky was pearly pink. The evening star glowed low in the sky.

They'd spread out rain jackets to sit on. The fire radiated heat and emitted an occasional sputter and pop and they stared at the flickering branches, mesmerised.

"Why is grandma like she is?" Ben asked.

Paul would have loved to know the answer to that question. He leaned against the log a previous camper had placed as a convenient back rest. "I don't know what she was like before my father left, but I imagine that's a large part of it."

"But you've never become bitter and cranky," Ben said. "And neither has Mum."

Maybe that was because their split wasn't because of endless arguments, adultery, or general angst.

"Your Mum isn't the cranky kind. I don't know what went wrong in my parents' marriage, but it must have been major because Mother won't speak about it."

Had his father beaten her or played the field? He couldn't remember alcohol or violence, but he'd been young. Perhaps he'd blocked it out.

"Do you hate your father?"

Paul stared into the fire. "Not hate, but I wasn't ever sure whether I wanted to meet him."

"I can't imagine you not being around," Lauren said. "In fact, I think we see more of you than before."

Paul grimaced. "And for that I'm sorry. I should have spent more time with you when you were younger." Instead of wasting his time building sandcastles of ambition for the tide to wash away.

"We don't have to stop at Grandma's on the way home, do we?"

"No, we won't have time."

Ben's shoulders relaxed.

Pain filled Paul's heart. He should have tried years ago to pull his mother up for her sharp criticisms. He'd talk to her on his next visit, although he doubted she'd listen.

He stretched his legs and shifted to sit on a log. It didn't matter whether she listened or not. It was his job to protect his children from her bitterness. How would Jesus have handled his mother? Would he have forgiven or confronted her?

CHAPTER 15

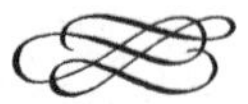

Early in the second week after their hike, Paul heard the phone ring through to Sister O'Reilly. She always fielded his calls, so he kept scribbling in his notes. It had been a busy morning.

"Dr Webster," Sister O'Reilly's voice came through the intercom. "This one's important."

He pushed the glowing light for line one on the phone. "Dr Webster speaking."

"Son of Miranda Webster?" the voice on the other end said.

His mouth went dry as dust and his heart thumped in his chest.

"I'm calling from Canberra Hospital ICU."

"Yes." Paul gripped the telephone receiver.

"Your mother had a heart attack sometime during the night. Her neighbour called for help when she didn't see your mother as usual in the morning."

His mother's long-running feud with her neighbour might have saved her life.

He forced words past the constriction in his throat. "How serious is the situation?"

"We think you should come as soon as possible. As you'd know, the long delay before she was found makes things difficult. She really should have surgery, but at her age that's quite a risk ..."

Paul ran a hand through his hair, his gut in a tight knot.

"I'll get there as soon as possible." His mind whirled with all the things that would have to be arranged. "It won't be much before seven or eight this evening."

They talked for another minute, and Paul took down the details for his mother's room. Then he put down the phone and went to knock on the door to Sister O'Reilly's side office.

"My mother's in hospital. I need to get to Canberra."

Together they went through his appointments for the next few days, sorting them into 'delay and make another appointment' or 'normal chemo', which Sister O'Reilly would deal with.

"I'll let you know what's happening," Paul said.

"You do what you need to do. Mothers are important," Sister O'Reilly said.

Her mother had died the previous year and she'd taken two weeks off, weeks that had proved how much he relied on her.

"Don't worry, Dr Webster. You leave things with me." Her fingers flew over the keyboard as she noted all his instructions.

She looked up from her keyboard. "I'm popping out to get some lunch. Can I get you something?"

He handed over the correct amount of money and went back into his office to make a phone call. It was lunchtime, so he should be able to catch Wendy.

"Paul, is something wrong?" she asked. He'd never disturbed her at work before.

He explained what had happened. "I'm going to drive down to Canberra this afternoon."

"Of course."

"Would it be better for you or me to tell Ben and Lauren?"

She was silent for a moment. "I'll tell them at dinner."

He didn't think they'd be too crushed, and that was sad. He would want people to care if his life was in danger, and for his death to be more than an unremembered blip in human history.

He thanked Wendy and put down the phone. If things had been normal between them, then it would have been wonderful to have had her beside him. Her grandmother's death in the early years of their marriage had brought them closer as they'd cried and mourned and remembered her together.

Joy Wong had said she'd been praying for him. He could write her a note and ask her to pray for his mother. It wouldn't hurt, and if Jesus was who he claimed to be, a reality Paul was slowly coming to accept, prayer might help. Right now, he could use all the help he could get.

* * *

HE WAS on the road by two. He had three hundred kilometres to drive. Once out of Sydney, it was mostly highway with no lights or delays.

He'd never expected his mother to have a heart attack. She kept herself trim and looked fit, but she had never discussed her health with him. He had no idea if she had high blood pressure or cholesterol or some other issue. In fact, his mother had seldom discussed anything personal with him. He only knew about the feud with the neighbour because he'd seen it in action. Maybe anger and bitterness had put a strain on her heart.

He and Rob had noted something similar as they discussed Luke 17–20 last Friday. Jesus' words had shocked them both. If someone sinned against them, they must keep forgiving, not seven times, but seventy times seven. He didn't think of himself as a man who held grudges, but he'd never felt badly wronged by anyone, at least not as an adult.

Jesus said a lot about forgiveness. Tonight Paul could look at the

Bible he'd slipped into his bag and check why Jesus kept saying his work was to bring about the forgiveness of sin. Why was that so important?

The light ahead changed to orange and Paul geared down. Soon he'd be on the highway with no more traffic lights.

During their last discussion, Rob had reminded him of the story about the paralysed man. He'd wanted healing, yet Jesus' first words to him had been, "Son, your sins are forgiven."

Rob had reckoned the man might have felt ripped off.

Paul changed lanes to overtake yet another car pulling a large caravan.

He and Rob had discussed why Jesus thought this man needed his sins forgiven before anything else. They'd ended up agreeing it was unlikely that the man was paralysed as a punishment for sin. Not after what Jesus said, about how people weren't crushed under a tower because they were more sinful than others.

The questions about the story had been swirling around in his head. There was something he was missing. Why did Jesus think forgiving sin was so important?

The road stretched out in front of him, blasted straight through hills of solid sandstone. Did Jesus see sin as the biggest problem in people's lives? Bigger than paralysis? Bigger than messed up relationships? Bigger than poverty? It must have been important, because Jesus was willing to offend the religious authorities rather than let the paralytic go home unforgiven.

Paul pushed the small of his back into his seat and stretched his neck and legs. This was the most boring section of the route. He much preferred driving along the edge of Lake George.

Jesus kept saying he came so people could be forgiven. Paul still didn't get it. At Esther's funeral, Joy Wong had told a story about the criminals crucified next to Jesus. Compared to those men, Paul was one of the good guys, but how much would his life impress Jesus? Jesus had never been impressed by those regarded as the good guys of his own era. It wasn't their deeds that Jesus criticised them for, but their motivations.

Paul liked to think he did his job out of the goodness of his heart, but did he? Or was it because he wanted his mother's approval, to prove that he was nothing like the man who'd fathered him?

Ten percent of his high school classmates had studied medicine or law. Most of them, including himself, had mixed motives. His mother had pushed him to do medicine for the money and prestige.

He stared at the road in front of him, shifting in his seat. Jesus hated self-righteousness and loved the humble. The way he could look right into people's hearts would have made him an uncomfortable friend.

A sign flashed by letting him know there was a rest stop ahead with toilets and drinking water. More than time for a break.

Paul drove the kilometre then took the side road before pulling up. He got out stiffly and did some stretches to limber up. No. Jesus would not be impressed with Paul Webster. Not one little bit.

CHAPTER 16

Paul's mother lay on a bed, surrounded by a range of paraphernalia reading her vital signs. Her skin was pallid without makeup. She had never been the kind of mother to stroll around in curlers and her dressing gown, and even at six in the morning she wouldn't have been caught without makeup. Now she was almost a stranger.

He ran his eye over the various digital read-outs. His mother's oxygen levels weren't great, and it wasn't a good sign that her bed was closest to the nurse's desk where they could most easily keep an eye on her.

A nurse walked over to him and said, "Dr Brandon has just arrived and would like to talk to you."

Paul stood, gave his mother's hand a squeeze. "Mother, I'm going to find out what's happening."

The nurse directed him to a small room outside the entrance to intensive care. He waited five minutes before a young doctor came in and shook his hand. "I'm Nelson Brandon, one of the team looking after your mother. I believe you're also a doctor?"

Paul nodded. "Oncologist."

"I admire you guys."

Paul laughed. "But you wouldn't want to be one?"

Nelson grimaced as he sat down across the table from Paul.

"The paramedics found your mother on the floor at eight-thirty this morning," Nelson said. "She might have got up to get her angina medication."

"I didn't even know she had angina."

Nelson checked his notes. "Apparently she's been on medication for the last twelve months, but she didn't get any further tests."

"Probably putting it off." As she did with anything that indicated her age.

"Pity, because she might have been able to avoid the attack. Her neighbour, Penny, was on the ball, and the paramedics arrived fifteen minutes after her call."

"How did Penny work out that my mother needed help?"

"It says in the history that when she didn't see your mother at eight, she was concerned enough to go and look in the windows. She spotted your mother's foot in the kitchen doorway."

Every morning for the past ten years, his mother had stood at her front gate, glaring at Penny and the dog who liked to mark the base of his mother's postbox. Paul would have to drop in and thank Penny.

"The paramedics had to resuscitate her, but they didn't know how long she'd been there."

Paul's gut knotted. "Cardiology was a long time ago for me. How long is she likely to be in a coma?"

"It's fairly normal for up to seventy-two hours after resuscitation, but any longer than that could be problematic."

"So the next few days are critical."

Nelson nodded, reached into a desk file, and removed two forms. "Your mother is currently on anti-clotting medication, but we'd like to do further tests once she's more stable. Do you know if you're her next of kin?"

"I presume so. She doesn't have any other close living family that I'm aware of."

"This is the consent form for surgery." Nelson handed over the first form. "And this one doesn't need to be filled in immediately—" He handed over the second form. "We'd like you to think through about whether to resuscitate or not if your mother has another heart attack."

A heaviness dragged at Paul's limbs. Despite dealing with medical things day in and day out, he'd never dealt with them for close family before.

"I'm sure she wouldn't want it."

They discussed the medical situation for a few more minutes. Once he was alone, Paul filled in the forms.

The nurses must have turned his mother while he'd been away, for she was now partially on her side. He pulled up a seat to be close to her.

"Mother, you have gotten yourself into the wars." Despite how she would have protested, she finally looked like what she was, an old woman. Shrunken and faded.

"Mother, I don't know if you can hear me, but I'm going to talk anyway." His throat tightened. Just in case he didn't get another chance. "I wanted to thank you for all your sacrifices in raising me. You did your best to give me opportunities."

When an extra class for academically gifted kids had opened up in upper primary school, she'd changed her timetable to suit his. She'd urged him to sit the entrance exams for the selective high school, and he'd been accepted. Even though they didn't have to use the place because he won the scholarship to his private school, she'd been ready to do anything extra that going to the selective school would have entailed.

"And thanks for allowing me to go away to boarding school." In the late fifties and early sixties, that had meant they'd only seen each other twice a year. He'd gone off happily enough, but it must have been a major sacrifice for her. In his last year, she'd travelled all the way to Melbourne by bus and train a couple of times to attend his final sports match and speech night.

When he came home for holidays, she always cooked roast chicken for his first night home, just the way he liked it.

Paul yawned and he closed his eyes for a few moments.

He woke with a start as a nurse came over to their area, and as he did so, he wiped the dribble of sleep away from the side of his mouth. The nurse bustled around, then left.

"Mother, I'm going to stay the night at your place and come back in the morning. I've taken a few days off work." Three days, and he'd almost used one. Hopefully by tomorrow he'd know whether he'd need to take Friday off as well. That would give him the weekend if needed.

PAUL RETURNED to the hospital early, after a poor night's sleep and a quick breakfast. Today he'd buy flowers as a thank you gift for Penny. The doctor had been clear that his mother would have been dead without Penny's actions.

His mother had been moved into a more private corner but looked much the same. It was still touch and go. He'd already checked out the café downstairs. It would be a long day.

He pulled out his Bible and notebook. He'd probably have to cancel this Friday's meeting with Rob, but he'd still do the preparation. He turned to Luke 21 and began to read. An hour later, he'd read the next chapters and taken notes. He stood and headed out for a short walk. Then he came back to the bed and sat down.

"Mother, do you know I'm here?" He glanced around to check no one could hear him. "I don't think you could possibly guess what I'm doing while I'm sitting here. No, it's not the daily crossword, and I'm not reading the paper. It's not even a medical journal."

His mother kept breathing at the same rate.

"Of all things, I'm reading the Bible." He glanced towards the nurses desk. "Not a book that I ever thought I'd read, but I was challenged to read it by one of my patients."

His mother lay completely still.

"Talking to you is harder than talking to Ben on a bad day. At least he grunts an occasional response." Paul had been doing a lot of thinking about Ben and how they could spend more time together. It had to include some sort of activity—anything that required communication wasn't going to work for either of them. He'd thought of kayaking, rock climbing, and abseiling, and discarded every idea. Maybe Wendy would have some suggestions.

His mother's chest rising and falling was the only indication she was alive. "I don't know if you have ever read the Bible, but I've found the book of Luke surprising. I always thought Jesus was a wimp with a gentle smile who got himself crucified. Instead, I've discovered a man who was always in control and knew where he was going, yet was full of compassion."

He sat and thought about what he'd said and then looked more closely at his mother.

"Mother, I'm going to tidy up your hair a bit." He carefully moved her head and tucked her hair back. Her hair was coarse below his fingers. He leaned down and kissed her forehead. She was a private, self-contained, rigid sort of woman. Fiercely proud of him but not affectionate.

He picked up his Bible off the chair so he could sit down again. It fell open to where he'd been reading. "And Mother, Luke is full of stories. Stories Jesus told and stories about Jesus."

This forcing himself to make conversation was too hard. Back in medical school, they'd had a lecture about how to help families visit family in ICU or what to do when someone was in a coma. He hadn't paid much attention at the time, as he'd just met Wendy and had been daydreaming about when he'd next see her, but he did remember the suggestion to read or sing. He wasn't going to croak a song, but he could read. Maybe his familiar voice could pull his mother back to the surface.

"I'm going to read from Luke 22." He turned to the correct page and began to read.

> ... the Passover was approaching, and the chief priests and the teachers of the law were looking for some way to get rid of Jesus, for they were afraid of the people.
>
> Then Satan entered Judas ...

Paul kept reading. Sometimes he paused to think about something but most of the time he just read, putting as much expression into the reading as he could. Jesus' last meal with his disciples. Jesus' predictions that Peter would deny him. That denial must have stung, given Peter was one of his best friends.

The more he read, the more obvious it was that Jesus had gone to Jerusalem deliberately. He'd gone there to die.

Midway through chapter twenty-three, the nurses came in to turn his mother. He stood up hastily and put the Bible out of sight. What a hypocrite. He'd just mentally criticised Peter for being a weakling under more dangerous conditions, and he didn't dare to be seen reading a Bible. What did he fear? Someone joking about it? Pathetic.

The nurses left, and he finished reading about Jesus' death and burial, then took his mother's hand. "Mother, I'm going to go and get some fresh air. Be back in an hour."

* * *

OUTSIDE, the cold seared his throat. He pulled his scarf up to cover his mouth. The old Royal Canberra Hospital had been close to Lake Burley Griffin and much better for walking. This area was mostly bike paths, but he'd asked if there was a quieter place to walk and was directed off to one side where there was some green space.

He strode along swinging his arms. It might be cold, but there was always something invigorating about Canberra's winters. There were things he loved about the place—like the central lake and all the bike paths—but it was also a little sterile. A little too over-planned. He preferred cities that had grown and spread more naturally.

When he set up the sceptics' club, he'd deliberately excluded Christians, but now it would be great to have someone to answer his questions. He'd sensed during the last two meetings that Rob was pulling back week by week, probably more scared of his wife's reactions than he dared to admit. Joy was the only Christian he knew. She was a nice enough woman, but meeting with a man would be better.

Back in senior school, he'd had an enthusiastic history teacher. They'd not only delved into Roman roads and military but also their criminal justice system. Paul had taken a ghoulish interest in all the gory details. Jesus would have been lashed with the standard forty lashes minus one. Based on what he'd already read about Jesus' powers, he could have escaped crucifixion, but he still wasn't sure why Jesus didn't use his power. He'd have to ask Joy, or better yet, write and ask her some of the many questions he had.

His mother hadn't been a churchgoer, and he'd never heard her mention Jesus. The chapters he was reading might be the only chance she'd ever have. He'd walk a little further and then go back and finish Luke. Maybe even read her some of the earlier chapters. If Jesus was God, then Jesus could presumably help her understand. Couldn't he?

CHAPTER 17

The third day after his mother's heart attack, Paul was dragged out of a deep sleep by the ringing of the phone. He got to his feet and stumbled out into the hallway.

"Hello?"

"Is that Paul Webster?"

"Yes ..."

"Your mother's situation has deteriorated ..."

Paul barely heard anything more, but managed to ask a few questions. He rushed to dress, before driving faster than normal to the hospital.

He walked into his mother's room to find the nurse tidying the bedding. She avoided looking at him, murmured some generic condolence, and left him alone.

He hadn't made it in time.

He stared at his mother, hands clenched. Her skin hung loosely, revealing her as she truly was, a woman well into her seventies. He barely recognised her without that bitter expression which no amount of cosmetics or plastic surgery could disguise.

A wave of fury swept through him. How dare she die now? Last night, he'd finally decided he was going to insist on knowing about his father if his mother woke up from her coma. Now the door had slammed shut in his face.

He dropped into the chair next to the bed, leaned his head on his hands, and took some deep calming breaths. How awful that she had died alone and without hope. So different to Esther who'd been surrounded by loved ones and had died confidently, asserting her hope that she was going straight to be with Jesus. Even if she'd been deluded, her beliefs had made a difference. His mother had no such hope. Depressing.

NEARLY TWO WEEKS LATER, Paul unlocked his mother's front door again. The house was silent except for the ticking of the clock on the mantel. He might not have looked forward to his visits home, but right now he'd welcome even one caustic comment from his mother.

He'd been surprised that Wendy had come to the funeral yesterday. She'd come to support Ben and Lauren, but she'd been the friendliest he'd seen her in years. He'd had to restrain himself from hugging her. Instead he'd given her cheek a quick peck and clamped down on the wave of emotion that swept through him at the familiar citrus scent of her perfume.

Without Wendy, the crematorium chapel would have been even emptier. Only their family of four, and one of the chapel officials. With Esther's funeral in mind, Paul had requested they simply do a few Bible readings. He offered the eulogy, and Wendy and the kids seemed to appreciate what he'd said.

At Esther's funeral, there had been real grief from people who loved her. Esther's death had left a hole. Yesterday, Lauren had been the only one to shed any tears. He'd felt empty and sad. Sad because his mother's life had had so little positive impact on anyone apart from himself. His mother had been like one of those mud bubbles he and Wendy had seen on a holiday in New Zealand. It rose to the surface and popped, leaving very little evidence that it had ever existed.

Paul propped open the front door and went back to his Land Rover to pull out several empty cardboard boxes. The first thing on his list was to empty the fridge and kitchen cupboards.

He planned to do some sorting and packing up, then spend the rest of the afternoon on his search. If there was anything here about his father, he'd find it.

Wendy and the kids were staying at a bed and breakfast. She was taking them to the National Art Gallery this afternoon. Tomorrow morning, Ben and Lauren would come over to help and choose any items they wanted.

The weight of everything that needed to be done settled heavily on his shoulders. Anything that needed proper sorting, he'd pile into boxes to take back to Sydney. This wasn't his childhood home, and he had no sentimental attachment to it. He'd get it ready for market as soon as possible. His mother's solicitor had told him he was the sole beneficiary.

He opened the fridge, and the sour smell of the milk left forgotten in the jug his mother always insisted upon, assaulted his nose. He pinched his nose as he picked up the jug, turned the tap on full, and watched the curdled contents swirl down the sink.

He then worked methodically through the kitchen and laundry, ticking off each completed task on the list he'd taped to the kitchen bench.

The first night after his mother's heart attack, he'd been itching to look for any important papers or photographs that might give him clues about his father, but he hadn't dared. His mother was neatness personified. If she'd come back to her house, she'd have known immediately that it had been searched.

There was no attic or garden shed, and there was nothing under any of the guest beds. The most likely places were her desk and her bedroom—a room he'd never entered.

He had a quick drink and took an empty box with him to the desk in the third bedroom.

The desk drawer was locked. His palms turned clammy as he searched for the key, which he eventually found at the bottom of a vase on the mantelpiece. He hurried back to the desk and inserted the key, which jammed. He let it go, taking some deep breaths to calm down. On the next attempt it turned easily, obviously well-used. He reached in and rifled through the papers. Bank books, cheque book, insurance records, a few share certificates. Important, but not what he was looking for. He piled the contents of the desk in the box. He'd take it home to look through later.

After emptying each drawer, he pulled each one out to look behind it but found nothing. He finished checking the room, ate something to keep up his energy, and then moved on to his mother's bedroom. The door was closed, as it always had been. His pulse sped up and he couldn't help glancing over his shoulder as though he was doing something wrong. Would this be where he found what he was searching for? He turned the handle and opened the door. Inside, a bed with a flowered double quilt and matching pillows dominated the room. The green of the walls perfectly matched the soft furnishings. Built-in mirrored wardrobes covered one wall.

There was a mirrored dressing table covered with glass bottles, makeup and other things he didn't know the uses for.

He opened his mother's wardrobe, expecting a hand on his shoulder at any moment demanding to know what he was doing prying into her things. He rifled through everything. There was nothing but clothes. He carried a chair in from the kitchen and peered into the top of the wardrobes. Nothing at all. Could his mother have burnt all the early photos? He'd seen some baby photos with him on his own or with his mother. They'd been in a brown album with gilt edges and old-fashioned adhesive photo corners. Where would that be? He frowned, trying to remember. Maybe in the cupboard of the room he always used. He'd finish here first.

Apart from several photos of him on the dresser, there was nothing personal here. This was strictly a bedroom, with clothes, personal items, and a radio.

He finally found the photo album in the second bedroom, the one his mother had always called his room. When he opened it, the baby photos he remembered were at the front, but then there were two or three pages where the photos had been removed. Removed and put somewhere, or thrown away? It depended on whether his mother had intended to obliterate her past or merely hide it. Sadly, he didn't know her well enough to guess which.

He placed the album in a box of things he'd definitely keep.

Most of the wardrobe was filled with empty hangers, but he could see what looked like a cardboard box tucked in the top corner nearest the roof. Hands shaking, he went to get the chair, placed it on the floor, and climbed up to retrieve the box. It was heavy in his hands. He clambered down to place the box on the floor. Opening it, his breath whooshed out in disappointment. Only old assignments his mother was proud of and an array of sports trophies and academic certificates. All things to sort later. He pulled everything out, but there were no photos. No evidence that he hadn't been the product of a virgin birth.

* * *

THE NEXT MORNING, he was washing the few breakfast dishes when Wendy's car pulled up. Ben and Lauren got out first, followed by Wendy. His eyes stung. He hadn't expected her to come and help.

The doorbell rang and he went to open the front door. "Come in, come in," he said too loudly and too cheerfully.

Ben squinted at him, removed his shoes, and then slouched into the living room and sat down in his usual seat.

"I thought we'd get things done more quickly if I helped," Wendy said. "Is that okay?"

He nodded, not trusting himself to speak, and led the way into the kitchen where yesterday's list was still taped to the counter. "There are still a few things that need doing."

Wendy read down the list. "Ben, can you come in here and choose which jobs you'd prefer?" she called over her shoulder.

He didn't look like he wanted to be here, but Paul was pleased to see he immediately obeyed Wendy and the sullenness was absent. Perhaps the bad attitude was only directed towards him.

Ben agreed to pack up the books in the two bookcases. The two women would tackle his mother's room and the bathroom. He'd finish the study and spare bedroom, then they'd work together on anything else.

"Paul, what do you want done with your mother's clothes and personal things?" Wendy asked.

"Why don't you and Lauren take anything you want? Call me when that's done, and I'll see what's left." He pointed out the heap of boxes in the living room. "Please label anything with the contents and whoever it is going to."

"I brought garbage bags. I thought they'd be easier," Wendy said.

"Thank you for coming to help."

She avoided his gaze. "Of course I'd come."

He hadn't been at all confident that she would.

They all set to work. Every now and then he'd hear Lauren and Wendy laughing together. Several times he passed Wendy carrying bags or boxes towards the main door, where there were now two piles—boxes and items to take home, and bags designated for the local charity shop.

"If you push things towards the door of the bedroom, I can do the carrying for you."

Wendy looked at him as though puzzled. "That would be kind. Thank you."

After lunch, they all went from room to room. Paul photographed each piece of furniture and Lauren labelled everything while Wendy wrote a master list. He had a nearly empty storage area at his house and Lauren was going to take some of the furniture in case she flatted with friends during university.

"Ben, is there anything you want?"

He shook his head. "No furniture, but I'd like the clock on the mantelpiece." He'd stared at it for hours as a toddler, waiting for the quarter-hour chime. On the hour he'd bounce up and down on chubby legs, clapping in time with the strikes.

They all liked the clock, but it was fair that Ben had something.

"Why don't you go and put it with the stuff to go home today." Paul tossed two clean towels towards Ben. "Wrap it in those."

A few minutes later, Ben came back. "Dad, I checked inside the clock for the key and I found a second key." He held it out. "It looks nothing like the clock key."

Paul took it, heart racing. The key had a number on it. He'd seen a key like this before for a safe deposit box, where people stored jewellery, other valuables, or family papers. All those things were fine, but he was hoping for something worth even more to him.

One photo. Just one. Was that too much to ask?

CHAPTER 18

The next morning at nine o'clock on the dot, Paul rang his mother's solicitor. He'd tossed back and forth last night, barely sleeping. He'd even murmured a prayer that he'd find the right bank, that there'd be a safe deposit box, and that he'd be able to look inside.

The previous evening, once he'd loaded Wendy, the children, and some of the things they'd chosen in their car, he'd hurried back into the house to look at the things in the box he'd cleared out of his mother's desk. It was most likely the safe deposit box would be at his mother's bank.

The bank hadn't admitted his mother had rented a box, but they'd told him what proof of identity to bring with him. When he said he didn't live in Canberra, they'd squeezed him in for a two o'clock appointment.

The solicitor promised him everything he needed, confirming Paul had inherited everything his mother owned. That would include anything in a safe deposit box.

Hanging up the phone, Paul drank another cup of coffee. He'd just have time to visit the two real estate agents he'd selected as the best possible ones in the area. He'd grab some lunch on the way to the solicitor and the bank.

He was thankful his mother's will and estate were so simple. As sole executor and beneficiary, and with a will properly lodged with her solicitor, there'd been no need for months of waiting. Working out what to do with any financial assets would give him another excuse to talk to Wendy. Maybe he could convince her their talk needed to be over dinner.

* * *

AT THE BANK, Paul introduced himself at the enquiries desk, mentioned his appointment, and was directed to a seat to wait. Despite the cold of the day, he sweated. So much rode on whether his mother destroyed everything or had merely kept her secrets hidden away. Had she ever intended him to know anything about his father? Surely it didn't matter if he was dead. Once Paul had a name, he could hunt for the death certificate. And as long as he'd died in Australia, Paul would find him.

He rolled his shoulders and mentally reviewed the documents he'd brought: death certificate, solicitor's covering letter, will, crematorium bills, other related information. Driver's licence to show he was the person he claimed to be. Payslip to prove where he worked.

"Dr Webster."

Paul jumped at the quiet voice behind him.

"Sorry to startle you. Please follow me."

He was led through to an office where a second man was waiting.

"Let's look at the documents you've brought," the first man said.

Paul pulled out the envelope and handed everything over.

"I'll need to take copies of these." The second man left the room with the envelope, and Paul attempted to engage the other man in conversation. It proved almost impossible.

Eventually the other man returned with the envelope. "This is all in order. Where is the key?"

Paul pulled out his keyring and detached the key they'd found in the clock. It matched the one the banker had. The second man placed some forms on the table. "If you'd fill these in, we'll all sign them."

Paul resisted the urge to bite his thumbnail. What, if anything, would be in the box?

At last one of the men went and brought back the box. "Please check that your key works."

Paul inserted his key into the keyhole. It opened with a click.

"If you could take the contents out of the box, we'll record the number of items and leave you alone with the box," the taller man said.

There were four envelopes in the box, with only one labelled. Paul waited impatiently until both men had signed another document.

"When you're finished please ring the buzzer and one of us will return," the first man finally said. "You can let us know then whether you'll be taking things with you or continuing to use our service."

It was all Paul could do not to push them out the door, but he thanked them and waited until they were gone. He leaned his head in his hands and took three steadying breaths, filling his lungs and letting the air out slowly.

He opened the labelled envelope first. It claimed to contain insurance documents. Sure enough, there was a notebook listing all the contents of his mother's house with photos of the major pieces of furniture.

The smallest envelope contained what must have been his mother's wedding and engagement ring. The diamond was a mere chip, suggesting his father may not have had much money. The wedding band was engraved inside.

Russ & Miranda, 17 Nov. 1945

Russ. His father had a name. His stomach cramped. What had once been a shadowy outline suddenly had form.

"Russ, Russell," he said out loud. At least it wasn't a common name like John.

He reached for the third envelope and peered inside. It was full of documents. His original birth certificate was on top, and his father's name was listed. Russell James Webster. His hand shook as he scanned the document.

Occupation: Engineer/returned serviceman

Born: Melbourne

Age: 26

His mother had been born in Newcastle and was two years younger.

He sat staring at the words on the certificate, each fact as precious as black opals. Each fact full of possibilities that he could follow up. His pulse pounded in his ears.

He pulled out another document. His parents' marriage certificate, with the name of his grandfather. He knew nothing about his father's side of the family, and not much more about his maternal grandparents.

He stared at the marriage certificate and ran his finger over his father's signature. It was steady, with copperplate clarity. If he hadn't known his father had abandoned them, he'd have guessed he was a strong, steady kind of man. The kind of person he'd always wanted for a father. First impressions could obviously be deceiving.

There was only one more envelope to open. It was thick and had the right feel for the photographs he hoped for. Nausea swirled in his stomach as he tipped the contents on to the table. A man in military uniform stared at him, eyes and chin like his own. Ben had his nose, and Lauren had received his wavy dark hair.

Paul's stomach churned. What an amazing, confusing, exhilarating thing to have a father. Of course, he'd always had one, but he'd been nothing more than a vague concept. Now Paul had a name for his father, a photograph, a history. Russell James Webster had lived.

With trembling hands and blurry vision, Paul spread the photos out on the table. Wedding photos—not many, but covering the key events. His mother walking down the aisle. The two of them coming out of the church arm in arm, his father's smile shy but proud, and his mother looking like she'd won the lottery. Cutting the cake—not a big cake, as it was 1945, but someone must have been saving their sugar rations. A few formal photos. Photos of two older folk who he presumed were his father's parents. More family that his father's desertion had deprived him of knowing. Bile rose in his throat. There was never going to be a happy ending to this story.

He looked past the wedding photos to the final half of the collection. A lump clogged his throat. His father cradling Paul as a baby, a look of fierce pride and protectiveness on his face. Paul squeezed his eyes closed. What had happened to change his father's attitude? What made a man abandon his wife and infant son? Another woman?

Paul opened his eyes and shifted his gaze to the next photo. He gasped. His father stood clasping Paul's hands as Paul stood on his father's shoes, both facing the camera. His father's face was turned towards Paul's, which laughed up at him. Paul clenched his fist as a wave of pain coursed through him. It made no sense. That man didn't look anything like someone who would abandon his family. If it wasn't another woman, had he committed a crime or got himself entangled in gambling debts? Neither of those things seemed to explain his mother's bitterness.

Paul looked at his watch. It was nearly three o'clock, and he still had to drive back to Sydney. He gathered the photos together and pressed the buzzer. The shorter banker entered the room a few minutes later, holding a folder.

"Are you wanting to leave anything here?"

Paul shook his head. "There's nothing valuable, just family stuff. I'll take it all."

The man opened his folder and laid another form on the table. "If you'd read and sign here, here, and here." He indicated each blank signature spot with his finger.

Paul read everything and signed before putting all four envelopes into his briefcase. Within minutes, he was in his overloaded car and heading for home. He'd have to return to Canberra at least once more, but the major things were done or well on the way.

Somehow, in the next few days, he was going to find the time to search for his father's death certificate. Would it be in Melbourne, Canberra, or somewhere else entirely?

CHAPTER 19

The sceptics' club hadn't met since Paul's mother's death. Today was the last Friday morning Rob had free, and he'd rung Paul to ask if they could finish Luke this morning.

Paul hadn't had time to read the final chapters again, but he'd read them out loud to his mother while he was at the hospital. It would have to do.

"Sorry to hear about your mother," Rob said as Paul sat down in his usual spot.

Paul gave a tight nod. "Thanks."

"I remember how much sorting there was to do after my mother's death," Rob said, stirring his coffee.

"The sorting wasn't too bad, but the whole thing was rather a shock. I had no idea my mother had any heart problems. It made me realise there was so much I didn't know about her."

And it was a reminder, if he needed such a thing in his job, that life was fleeting. There were no guarantees that he'd get any warning when his time was up.

"I felt the same after Dad died," Rob said.

At least Rob had known his father's name.

"If this is our last time to officially meet, I guess we'd better get started," Paul said. Knowing time was short, he'd prioritised his questions. "My first question is a biggie." He cleared his throat. "I used to think Jesus got crucified because he angered the wrong people or got caught up in politics, but Luke makes it obvious that Jesus acted deliberately, that death was something he chose."

"I agree, but I'm not sure why," Rob said. "I don't get why he had to die."

"I had the same question. Do you remember the Chinese woman who spoke at Esther's funeral?"

Rob nodded. "Joy something or other?"

"Yes, Joy Wong. She works in our centre. I wrote her a note and asked her this exact question." Paul pulled a letter out of the back of his notebook. "She left this answer for me. Is it okay if I read it?"

"It'll give me a chance to finish my breakfast."

Paul laid down his fork before unfolding the letter. "I'll jump right into the place where she is answering our question." Paul cleared his throat again.

> YOUR QUESTION IS AN IMPORTANT ONE. WHY WAS JESUS' DEATH EVEN NECESSARY? IT ISN'T CLEAR TO MOST OF US AS WE READ LUKE, AND IT REQUIRES AN UNDERSTANDING OF THE WHOLE BIBLE AND THE WAY THAT GOD SET UP THE UNIVERSE.

Paul looked up to check Rob was listening. Rob gave him an awkward thumbs-up around his fork.

> BACK IN THE GARDEN OF EDEN, ADAM AND EVE REJECTED GOD AS THEIR CREATOR, KING, AND FATHER, AND THE RESULT WAS DEATH. THINK OF IT LIKE A TREE AND A BRANCH. GOD WAS THE MAIN TREE, AND PEOPLE WERE THE BRANCHES. THE BRANCHES RELIED ON GOD TO PROVIDE LIFE THROUGH THE ROOTS AND TRUNK. WHEN ADAM AND

Eve ate the fruit and went their own way, it was as if the branch chose to remove itself from the tree.

"Joy has drawn two diagrams to illustrate." Paul held them up for Rob to see before turning back to the letter.

Death is the natural result of rejecting God. Some die early and some die late, but there is no exception to the rule. Everyone dies.

Long before Jesus came to earth, God began to prepare people for what was to come. He used the temple and sacrifice system to teach them why Jesus had to die.

"I don't know much about the Jewish system but did hear something about sacrificing lambs." Rob said, wrinkling his nose. "Sounds rather bloodthirsty."

Paul thought so too, but reading Joy's letter a few times had made things clearer.

Once a year the Israelites celebrated the Day of Atonement.

"I haven't heard of that. Have you?" Paul asked.

Rob shook his head.

Before I tell you what happened on that day, I will explain how their temple worked and what it meant to them. For the entire nation there was only one place of worship, the temple in Jerusalem.

"I think the only part that's left is what they call the Wailing Wall," Rob said. "All those bearded religious Jews slipping prayers into the cracks between the stones and rocking back and forth."

Paul remembered seeing this in a documentary.

The main part of the temple had two parts. The most important part was the inner room, called the Holy of Holies. No one could enter because that room was like God's symbolic throne room. A thick curtain separated it from the rest of the temple. Every part of the temple, including all the furniture, had meaning. It was a vast object lesson—I think that's what you Australians would call it. If anyone wandered into the Holy of Holies, they died immediately.

"Whoa," Rob said. "That sounds a bit over the top."

"Joy answers your objection immediately." Paul looked back at the letter.

It does seem unreasonable that merely going through the curtain could result in death, but God wanted to teach the Israelites that he was holy. That is, God is completely separate because of his perfection and goodness. People's lack of holiness means we must be separated from God. The holy and the unholy cannot mix. There you have a major problem. God is holy and can't be friends with sinners because of who he is, yet he longs to relate to us.

Rob rubbed his head. "It's too early in the morning for this."

"I've made a photocopy of the letter so you can read it later." Paul slid the copy in its envelope across the table.

Once a year, on the Day of Atonement, the high priest functioned as a middleman or mediator between Israel and God. He had to bathe and put on clean ceremonial robes to represent purity. Then he took two perfect sheep or goats. One was killed as the sacrifice. Its death was on behalf of the people's sin. The second was called the scapegoat. It symbolically carried the sins of the people out into the

DESERT. THE PRIEST THEN CARRIED THE BLOOD FROM THE SACRIFICED GOAT INTO THE HOLY OF HOLIES. ON THAT DAY, GOD SAID HE HAD FORGIVEN THE SINS OF THE PEOPLE FOR THE PAST YEAR AND HE COULD CONTINUE TO LIVE WITH THEM AND BE THEIR GOD.

Rob belched. "Seems a complicated way to do things."

"All that was the background to help us understand why Jesus had to die."

"Don't let me stop you," Rob said.

Paul laughed awkwardly. "I'm just glad I didn't have to try and explain all this myself."

YEAR AFTER YEAR, THE ISRAELITES SAW THE SAME CEREMONIES REPEATED. OF COURSE, THE PROBLEM WAS THAT THE BLOOD OF SHEEP AND GOATS REALLY HAD NO POWER TO FORGIVE SIN. WHEN JESUS CAME, HE WAS CALLED THE LAMB OF GOD AND HE REPEATEDLY SAID HE'D COME TO DEAL WITH SIN.

Rob leaned back in his chair. "I think I see where Joy is going with this. Jesus is the sacrificial lamb."

"Uh huh," Paul said. "And if Jesus was God, then he is also the perfect mediator."

Rob shook his head. "That's where I get stuck. I'm not convinced Jesus is God."

"Put that aside for a minute. If Jesus is God, then he can represent God perfectly, in a way the priest, who was a normal man, couldn't."

"Oh," Rob said. "I think I just saw a reason for why the virgin birth was important."

Paul leaned forward.

"If Jesus had been born like us, he would have been born with our nature and could never be perfect."

Paul nodded several times. "I think you've nailed it. This also helps me understand why the resurrection was necessary. Without the resurrection, there is no final proof that Jesus was who he said he was or that sin had truly been dealt with."

"I'm still dubious about the resurrection," Rob said.

"I admit that's the hardest miracle of all to accept. I don't know if I believe it either, but Joy's letter helps me to see the logic of it."

"It seems to me there are a group of linked issues." Rob ticked them off on his fingers. "Is Luke itself a good history? Is what he wrote reliable? And was Jesus really God?"

Paul had already accepted Luke as historically accurate. If it wasn't, it was an outstanding fake. No con artist could have resisted hyping up the miracles.

"Then we have two huge miracles we have to either accept or explain." Rob held up his index finger. "One, that Mary had Jesus despite being a virgin, and two." He held up another finger. "That Jesus rose from the dead. Both of those are big obstacles to me and I'm still not sure how confident I am of Luke's history."

"I'm making some progress here." Paul tapped his head. "But not so much here." He indicated his heart. "When we started this investigation, we presumed the Bible wasn't true and therefore, all the miracles were made up. But if we make the opposite assumption—that there is a God—then the miracles are easy to accept because a God who can create an entire universe can easily manage healings, virgin births, and resurrections."

Rob grunted. "I guess I don't actually want these things to be true."

"I get that. I've always thought of Christians as foolish and superstitious. It was the fact that Esther wasn't, that made me willing to even consider there might be something worth looking at."

"When you think about it, it's pretty weird that we'd bother doing all this because of someone we knew for less than two years."

"It says a lot about the kind of person she was."

And was such a contrast to his mother, whose life and death had barely made a ripple in the universe.

Paul glanced at his watch. "We're just about out of time. No time to talk about the resurrection, although I believe that is the key to the whole thing. If Jesus rose from the dead, then all the other miracles are possible."

"I'd agree, but it's an awfully big if," Rob said. "If Jesus really rose from the dead, you and I are in trouble."

That's what Paul was afraid of. On the second day he'd sat with his mother at the hospital he'd not only read the final four chapters of Luke but several of the earlier chapters too. Following Jesus could prove to be tough. Ben and Lauren would give him freedom to believe what he liked as long as he didn't try and force his beliefs on them, but he wasn't sure about Wendy. *Wendy.* Thoughts of her had kept him awake at night.

Paul looked across at Rob. "I do appreciate you embarking on this quest with me. You could have written me off as a crackpot, and I wouldn't have blamed you."

"I would never have done this on my own," Rob said.

"I wonder if people in heaven know what we're doing on earth."

Rob laughed. "As someone who still doubts heaven exists, I am not going to speculate on what heaven might be like."

"Wise man." Paul finished his now cold coffee and grimaced. "What's the next step for you?"

Rob shifted in his seat and looked up at the ceiling. "Oh, I don't know." He shrugged. "Probably try and forget everything and hope Jesus leaves me alone."

Paul grinned. "I think I'm hoping for the same thing, but I'm not sure I can. Luke wasn't anything like I expected, and Jesus has impressed me."

Impressed him far more than he was going to let on to Rob. Paul's quest wasn't finished. He was going to keep reading, at least Matthew, Mark, and John. Then he'd have to see what was next. It would be great if Jesus could just be a useful model of how to live with some wise teachings he could apply in his life. But that wasn't an option, not based on what he'd read so far. Jesus demanded all or nothing. Paul didn't want to give all, yet was equally afraid to ignore what he'd learned.

Rob stood up and extended his hand. "Good luck."

Paul shook Rob's hand. "You too." He didn't know what else to say, but luck seemed to have little to do with what they'd been doing. Esther would have said God was orchestrating the whole thing. The arrival of her letter, this weekly get-together, and the timing of his mother's death.

They went out together to the carpark. As Rob got in his car, Paul leaned forward towards the open window. "Do you really think your wife would give you the cold shoulder if you became a Christian?"

Rob grimaced. "She's cut herself off from friends who have become Christians. I'm not willing to risk it." He clipped in his seat-belt. "I like my life the way it is."

Paul stood up straight and watched Rob pull out of the carpark. Rob tooted his horn and accelerated away.

What would he do in Rob's place? Paul liked to think he'd have the courage to do the right thing if necessary, but his past history suggested otherwise. He hadn't had the guts to sort things out with Wendy or to pursue her and show he cared. Instead, he'd sat waiting. Waiting for what? Waiting for her to make a move. Why should she have to take the risk? It had been his responsibility, and he hadn't bothered. He used work as an excuse, but it was really because he was too proud. Too proud to risk being rejected. He wasn't any better than Rob. Both of them lacked courage to take the first step.

CHAPTER 20

What was it about Paul's workplace lately? Yet another letter marked *Strictly Personal* had arrived. Yet another letter that gave no clue as to the sender. The last such letter had rocked him. He wasn't going to read this one until he got home, just in case.

He put the letter in his briefcase and locked it away, but it may as well have been in plain view. He'd forget it while he saw a patient, but the second they were gone, his gaze drifted towards the locked cupboard. As each new person entered his office, he had to drag his attention back to the job. It would serve him right if the letter turned out to be something mundane. This was worse than childhood Christmases, when his mother would place wrapped gifts under the tree a week before the twenty-fifth. Cruel.

It had been a stressful week. Every lunchtime he'd made a call to a different births, deaths and marriages registry. There was no death for a Russell James Webster in Victoria, the ACT, or New South Wales. He'd check the other states next week. Before he'd rung the first office, he'd strained his mind trying to narrow down the possible year of death. He'd definitely finished high school when his mother told him, and he thought he'd finished university as well. He had a vague memory he'd even finished the exhausting early years in different hospitals, moving through his internship, residency, and even beginning his specialty. Those years blurred together into a mess of sleeplessness, fear, and increasing exhilaration as his diagnoses and treatment made a real difference in someone's life. Yes, it may even have been after his marriage. He thought his father must have died in the early to mid-seventies, but he'd ask that the checks be made up to 1990 just to be safe. His father might have moved to Britain or Canada. How could his mother have gone to the grave without leaving more clues?

It was a relief when the last patient was gone for the day, and he could play a vigorous game of squash. He'd won for the first time in ages, and his colleague had asked, "Anything you want to talk about?"

Paul had muttered something non-committal and headed home as quickly as possible.

Back home, he opened his takeaway Chinese, leaned against the kitchen counter, and grabbed a fork. He didn't have patience for chopsticks tonight.

He opened the letter and scanned the first sentence.

THIS LETTER IS LIKELY TO BE A SHOCK TO YOU. I HAVE NO IDEA WHAT YOU KNOW ABOUT ME.

What mysterious person was writing to him? He flipped the page to search for the signature.

SINCERELY, RUSS WEBSTER

He choked and dropped both the letter and his fork. His father! But his father was dead. Had been for years, according to his mother. Who was this man, and what did he want? He clenched his fists to stop the shaking that spread up his arms. Was this man an imposter intent on some cruel joke? If it was his father, why had his mother said he was dead? Where had he been all these years, and why was he writing now?

Paul took a deep breath and picked up the letter from where it had fallen face down on the floor.

He reread the first line and kept reading.

I HAVE BEEN WAITING MANY, MANY YEARS TO WRITE TO YOU.

Bile rose in Paul's throat. Nearly fifty years? That wasn't normal. Paul scrunched up the letter and hurled it across the room. His heartbeat pounded in his chest. *God, what are you doing?*

He took a deep, quavering breath and sat down hard on the floor. Nausea almost overwhelmed him, and he had to draw up his knees and put his head between them.

Slowly his breathing evened out. He raised his head tentatively and shuffled across the floor to the scrunched-up letter. He smoothed it out carefully.

I PROMISED MYSELF I WOULD WRITE WHEN YOUR MOTHER WAS GONE.

Yet he'd been willing to let his son think he was dead. If this man who claimed to be Russ Webster had been standing here, Paul would have knocked him out. How dare he abandon his wife and child and not contact them at all? Did he expect to be welcomed back with open arms?

I'M GUESSING YOU EITHER KNOW NOTHING ABOUT ME OR WANT NOTHING TO DO WITH ME, BECAUSE YOU'VE NEVER COME SEARCHING AND MY NAME ISN'T THAT COMMON. SURELY YOU COULD HAVE FOUND ME IF YOU'D WANTED.

He had wanted, but without a name it had been difficult, if not impossible, to make a start. He'd sometimes wondered if his surname really was Webster, but that question was now answered. The surname he'd lived under was his by law.

Perhaps your mother never mentioned me. There is so much we don't know about each other, you and I. You must know your mother and I had a terrible marriage. I have forgiven her long ago.

He'd forgiven Paul's mother. Surely it should be the other way around? As far as Paul knew, his mother had never forgiven her husband for abandoning his family. Her bitterness had warped her and maybe even contributed to her death. Paul clenched his fist. He'd have preferred that his mother had come out of her coma so she could have gone to her death with past grievances dealt with, but sometimes you don't get what you wish for.

There has never been a week that has gone by that I have not longed to see you.

Paul snorted. His father had a strange way of showing his longing.

I've written you a letter almost every week, but I've never sent them. I was afraid Miranda would destroy them and you'd never get to see their contents. I have all the letters ready for you in numbered boxes.

Paul leaned back against the cupboard. Boxes? The picture was mind-boggling.

He stared at the letter. Thinking about his father felt almost disloyal. Even if he met this man, there were no guarantees. Once he heard his father's story, there would be no going back. He might discover that his father wasn't someone he wanted to know, and any good memories of his mother might be besmirched as well. Paul pulled on his earlobe. What did he want to do? Keep reading or ignore the letter?

Cursed curiosity! Curiosity was going to keep him reading, but it wasn't going to make him careless. This man still hadn't proved he was his father.

I HAVE FOLLOWED YOUR TRAINING AND CAREER WITH INTEREST. THIS MAKES ME SOUND LIKE A STALKER, AND IT OCCURS TO ME THAT YOU MIGHT HAVE NO REASON TO TRUST ME OR EVEN TO ACCEPT I ACTUALLY AM YOUR FATHER. ON THE NEXT TWO PAGES OF THIS LETTER I WILL PHOTOCOPY SOME PHOTOS AND ONE OF THE LETTERS I WROTE YOU. I HAVE THE ORIGINAL PHOTOS, BUT I'M NOT WILLING TO PART FROM THEM UNTIL I KNOW WHAT YOUR REACTION WILL BE.

Hands shaking, Paul flipped the page. There were three photocopied photos. Two matched photos he'd found in the safe deposit box. The third was the first family photo he'd seen—his parents sitting on a picnic blanket with him as a toddler, standing between them.

He gulped as his chest tightened. The man was being clever. The third photo guaranteed he'd have to meet the letter writer if there was even the slightest possibility he could get a copy of the original.

He turned the photo page and looked at his father's letter. It was dated January 27, 1959.

TODAY YOU STARTED HIGH SCHOOL. I FIND IT HARD TO BELIEVE IT HAS BEEN SO LONG SINCE I SAW YOU. YOU'VE CHANGED FROM A TODDLER WHO LIKED NOTHING BETTER THAN TO BE TOSSED INTO THE AIR, TO A FIRST FORMER WITH KNOBBLY KNEES PEEPING OUT BETWEEN THE TOP OF LONG SOCKS AND THE BOTTOM OF YOUR GREY SHORTS.

Paul closed his eyes. He'd forgotten about the games he'd played with his father, but the memories of his giggles and his father's hoots of laughter were now clear in his mind. He remembered the fear mixed with joy of flying up into the air. He'd never doubted his father would catch him.

He reread the previous paragraph. It sounded like his father had seen him at school. Perhaps he'd visited on a day when lots of parents were milling around and one more wouldn't be noticed. Paul didn't know if it spooked him or comforted him. It did suggest his father lived in Victoria. His mother had said they'd lived in Sydney until his dad left. She hadn't moved to Canberra until Paul was in high school. It was closer to his school, but she'd refused to answer when he'd asked why she didn't move all the way to Victoria. Had she guessed Russ would move back to the area he'd grown up in?

> It hurts to know you wouldn't recognise me even if I spoke to you. When you were born, I didn't even want to go to work because it meant leaving you.

Then how could this man have abandoned him?

His mother had never been particularly motherly. She did all the outward things that she considered proper, but hugs or kisses hadn't been her thing. If she did hug, it was a hug of possession that made him struggle for freedom. Even when he'd been little and skinned his knee, she'd never hugged him. Instead, she'd dust him off, wash the cut, and tell him not to cry. If it hurt enough to cry, he'd cry under his bed, out of her hearing.

Paul finished reading the old letter and then turned to the final paragraph before the signature.

I would love for us to meet but realise you might find that difficult. My address and phone number are below. I'm praying you will call.

Praying? Was that merely a figure of speech, or was his father someone who prayed like Esther or Joy? Yet another thing to find out.

Paul scrambled up from the floor and stretched his back. He wouldn't rush into a decision. This was too important for rushing. He wanted to consider the implications from every angle and decide if he'd write, call, or arrange to meet face to face.

CHAPTER 21

Yet again Paul was on the road to Canberra. The real estate agent had called earlier in the week and said they had a buyer.

Paul reached into the glovebox and pulled out his sunglasses. It was a spring-like day plonked into winter, and the whole weekend had a terrific weather forecast. He wasn't going to waste it.

The family and the agent had agreed to sign the papers at eight on Friday evening, allowing him to fit in a trip to the Snowy Mountains. He still hadn't decided what to do about his father. Maybe a long walk in the snow would clear his head.

* * *

By leaving Canberra at four-thirty in the morning, he'd avoided the traffic and managed to get the first Skitube and hotel transport of the day. He'd left some of his gear at his hotel and been on his way by ten. Ahead of him, a group of four moved purposefully, their clothing bright splodges of red, blue, and purple against the sparkling white snow.

Anticipation sparked in his stomach. The mountains felt like home. His time there during high school had given him a love for the wild, solitary spaces and he'd even considered a career up here before his mother's ambition had lit his own.

Even though he was only planning a day hike, his pack was fully loaded with a tent and sleeping bag in case there was a sudden weather change. Unlikely, but he preferred to be alive than freeze to death regretting his decisions.

In summer, the ground was covered in low-lying bushes and tiny flowers. Now, snow blanketed everything. Overhead, a wedge-tailed eagle floated, alert for any animal foolish enough to venture out from under the snow. Paul craned his neck and shaded his eyes to watch the bird soar upwards on the thermal air currents. The only sound was the drip, drip, drip of melting snow and an occasional burst of laughter from the people ahead of him.

His snowshoes crunched through the thin crust on the top layer of snow, and the bright orange markers stretched out along the path in front of him. The greatest danger today would be sunburn, so he wore snow goggles and had applied sunscreen to all of his exposed skin.

He continued walking, revelling in the beauty of the blue sky against the crest of the mountains. The path wound down to the main river crossing. He matched his steps to those in front of him marking the way, but he still checked every step in front of him with a ski pole. Somewhere under the snow there was water. Water that he had no intention of falling into.

As Paul admired a belt of snow gums with branches twisted like arthritic fingers, a clump of snow fell with a thump. A flash of dark feathers on two stilt-like legs burst out of the trees, shaking its snow-dusted feathers like an offended old woman. He laughed, and the emu swivelled his head to look his way, then dashed back into the shelter of the closest cluster of trees.

On the drive up this morning, Paul had been thinking about his father. Which did he prefer? The reality? Or a fantasy father he could create any way he liked? All his life, he had managed to simultaneously hold two contradicting ideas in his mind—the despicable man who'd abandoned them, and the almost-perfect father he'd daydreamed about. Yet at school, only a tiny number of the fathers he knew were ones he'd wanted for his own. Some boys wished they'd never had a father, and others wished their father was not so strict or rigid or distant.

A father who'd abandoned his family was hardly likely to be in the top echelon of fathers.

"Come on, Paul," he muttered to himself. What was the big deal? If his father turned out to be a disappointment, at least he lived far enough away to not be an annoyance. And if he did become a nuisance, Paul could easily get an unlisted number. Anyway, his father might turn out to be okay. An old man would be different from one who'd not yet been thirty when he left.

He'd call next week.

Decision made, Paul strode out.

He had lunch overlooking the Blue Lake, a circular lake in an indent surrounded by rocky hills. There were a few patches of clear water, but the lake was mostly iced over. He spotted the foursome walking on further ahead. Maybe they were camping out. Lucky them. He'd camp if he had company, but not on his own.

He lingered, watching the shadows across the surface of the lake. At two o'clock, he set off on the five-kilometre return walk. Plenty of time to get back.

He was two-thirds of the way back when his right snowshoe caught on a branch protruding from the snow. He stumbled and landed heavily. The weight of his pack unbalanced him, and it took a minute to get his feet untangled and get up. The snow had broken his fall, and he was fine, but the same couldn't be said for his snowshoes. One of the straps was broken.

No need to worry. He'd prepared for such glitches. He took off his backpack and found the spare strap he always carried.

The whole issue was quickly sorted out and he set off. Soon, the snow-covered river crossing was ahead of him. His stomach gave a nervous lurch. The sun had partially melted the top layer and the slush weighed down his snowshoes.

One cautious step at a time.

He plunged his ski pole into the snow, searching for rocks underneath. He only stepped forward when his pole was firm on rock. Two-thirds of the way across, his feet slid, and he took a few quick steps to prevent himself falling. His left snowshoe cracked against a rock.

When he pulled his foot out, the snowshoe dripped water and dangled off his foot. Unbelievable. Having never broken a strap before, he'd broken two in one day, and he didn't have another spare strap. He walked cautiously over to a protruding rock, dusted the snow off the top, and sat down to remove the broken snowshoe.

His heart pounded away in his chest and sweat prickled beneath his clothing. He shouldn't have stayed so long at his picnic spot. He checked his watch. It was nearly four, and sunset was just after five.

He couldn't guarantee anyone would check the hotel book, notice he wasn't back, and come galloping to the rescue. The silence closed in on him, and the serene sky mocked him. The eagle was soaring again. He could do with a pair of wings at this moment.

God, you say you care for the sparrows and notice them when they fall. Can you see me here? I know I have no right to ask, but I could do with some help.

He didn't suddenly hear the comfort of human voices or see his snowshoe miraculously mended, but he did think of something that might help. He swung his pack off his back, opened the top, and rummaged inside. Sleeping bags had cords. His cord might just be long enough and strong enough to get him the kilometre and a half back to the hotel.

He hadn't paid much attention to the sleeping bag when he packed last night. The bag had straps. They'd be even better than the drawcord. *God, let them be long enough.*

Hands shaking, he used the broken strap to measure the length. It might just work, but if and only if there was still a roll of duct tape in the bottom of his pack. The boys at school used to joke about his roll of tape, but it had proved useful for temporary repairs in the past. The question was whether it was there. If it was, would it still work in the low temperatures? His anxious fingers felt into the bottom of the pack and he laughed out loud as his fingers touched the roll.

His fingers grew increasingly cold and clumsy while he cobbled together a strap. Before he set off, he put on his headlamp, ready for when it got dark. The sun was already alarmingly close to the top of the mountain, and it was going to get dark earlier than he'd calculated. The strap held, but he'd have to place every foot carefully, while at the same time moving as fast as he could. Even though he'd packed the tent for emergencies, he wasn't sleeping out here if he could avoid it.

He put a handful of nuts in his pocket to munch on as he walked. *God, give me a clear mind and keep this strap together.* Did God care about snowshoe straps? Maybe not, but he couldn't fail to see God's care when reading the Bible. A father's care. Funny really. He'd been looking for a father all his life, and God was there for the asking. All he had to do was accept his offer of salvation and he could be part of God's family. Out here in the awe-inspiring mountains, that seemed a big deal.

He trudged on, carefully placing each foot and keeping his eyes on the orange poles. The light was definitely lessening now. His heartbeat was loud in his ears and he gripped the straps of his pack. He mustn't break into a panic-stricken run, as the temporary strap would never hold up to that sort of abuse. *Help me, God. Keep me calm.*

He began to whistle the tune of *Amazing Grace* he'd heard at Esther's funeral. He couldn't remember the words, but it was comforting all the same. God had always seemed irrelevant and kind of distant. But out here, in the icy silence and with the darkness increasing every minute, he hoped God was looking out for him. There was so much he still needed to put right. *God, help.*

Paul switched on his headlamp, fingers fumbling for the switch. He loved the clear skies during daylight hours, but at night, those clear skies meant deep, penetrating cold.

"God, don't let there be more snow or any wind. Get me home safe," Paul muttered, slapping his gloved hands against his body.

The next orange pole glowed in the light of his headlamp. *Concentrate, Paul, concentrate.* As he reached every pole, he made sure the next was visible before moving forward.

The pack was heavy on his shoulders, but he was thankful he'd been his usual over-the-top safety-conscious self as he put on an extra layer of thermals. Stripping down to put them on was agony, but the relief afterwards was worth the effort. With his scarf around his ears and mouth, and gloves, he was warm, as long as he kept moving. His eyes darted between the ground in front of him and the next pole, and his snowshoes crunched with every step. *Jesus, keep that strap holding.* He was under no illusions regarding the strength of his temporary repair. His left hip ached from placing his feet so carefully.

Again, he resisted the desire to run. *Jesus, keep me calm.*

He'd always thought Christians were pathetic to use Jesus as an emotional crutch, but today the prayers were pouring out of him. Embarrassing, really, to bother the King of the universe with such small requests.

He reached into his pocket and pulled out a small handful of nuts. The saltiness and crunch filled his mouth. *Keep me alive.* He still had things to do. Things to make right.

Above him, millions of tiny points of light glowed like shards of coloured glass. Breathtaking, but he couldn't afford to look up and risk an awkward step. *God, you've been patient with me. Thank you for sending Esther to my clinic and giving her the courage to talk to me about you.*

Esther could so easily have seen him as a hopeless case. She'd seen beneath the shiny facade to the shallow emptiness below. Before Esther had shown him her technicolour world, he'd lived a relatively grey existence. It had seemed safer. But Esther had a sense of purpose not even cancer could slow down. The worse her situation, the more connected, outgoing, and courageous she became.

Jesus, I want more out of life. I don't want to be afraid to meet my father, or of my family rejecting me.

The men he knew didn't admit fear, yet they were all afraid of something.

He blinked. Where was the next pole? He'd been looking at them so long that he hadn't noticed there wasn't one in front of him. Panic stuck its claws in and crushed his chest.

"Jesus, help." His voice emerged in a strangled gasp.

Paul leaned forward, hands on his knees, his breaths loud in his ears. He held his breath and let it out slowly. *Jesus, help me find the track.*

He stood up and turned slowly around. His tracks were crisp and clear behind him. He could just make out what might be the track. He slowly retraced his steps until a pole loomed up in front of him. Three more steps, and he wrapped his hands around it. *Thank you, Jesus. Thank you it's not snowing. Thank you I could see my tracks.*

He clutched the pole and turned until he could see the next pole ahead of him. He must keep moving.

Ten more poles, and he took a brief rest to drink some water. The coldness seared his throat and he coughed. The second mouthful he warmed in his mouth before swallowing. As he tilted his head back, he saw lights. Rows and columns of lights. He was nearly there.

He walked forward. Light. Nothing beat light on a dark night. He imagined the warmth of the fire waiting for him. Light was hope and warmth and life. Light added colour to a grey world. *Jesus, thank you.*

He was closer now. A door opened, and yellow light poured out. Someone came outside and looked up at the stars. Then there was a brief flash of flame and the red glow of the tip of a cigarette.

It was difficult to judge distance, but he must be nearly there. He took another step and heard the ripping sound he'd been dreading. His broken snowshoe flopped at the end of his boot. He bent down and detached both snowshoes. He took a step and then another. His boots sank into the snow. How deep was it? At knee level, his boots hit rock. Solid ground. Holding the snowshoes in his hand, he flailed forward. Fifteen steps in, already breathing heavily, he went up a small rise and saw a sign with a big P on it. He'd made it to the carpark.

"Are you okay, mate?" yelled the smoker.

"I am now," Paul said, voice shaky.

"The boss was just about to send a search party out for you."

"I'll let him know I'm okay," Paul said, stamping his feet. He opened the door into the boot room. A wave of warmth hit him, and he shivered. He staggered over to the pine bench and sat down. Something shone on the wall. His headlamp was still on. He pulled it off just as it gave a weak sputter and died. Another tremor hit him. He'd taken the spare batteries out of his pack last week and forgotten to add new ones to his emergency supplies.

In the past he'd have pooh-poohed anyone who claimed Jesus performed miracles, but there were too many 'coincidences' tonight to avoid the inference that God had saved him. *Thank you, Jesus.*

The outside door opened and the man came back, bringing a blast of cold air and the strong smell of cigarette smoke. He squinted at Paul. "You look all done in. Can I get you a drink?"

Alcohol or coffee wouldn't be wise.

"A strong, hot tea with some sugar would be great. Thank you. I'll sit here and defrost," Paul said through chattering teeth.

"Righty-o," the man said.

Paul unlaced his boots and peeled off his socks. They were soaked through but he'd be fine. Now he needed a hot shower, a hot meal, and a good night's sleep.

He got two of the three. The hot shower revived him. The hot meal powered him up the stairs. But he couldn't sleep.

What happened out there, God?

Whatever it was, God had his attention. What now? His mother's life had ended without warning. Out in the snow, things could easily have gone from bad to worse. People died every minute, and it wasn't always major events that carried them off. Sometimes it was as simple as a broken snowshoe strap, a dead battery, or losing sight of those life-saving orange poles. He wasn't any more ready to face eternity than his mother had been. The difference was he now knew enough about Jesus to make his decision. But following Jesus wasn't just a matter of information.

It was a matter of trust. Jesus was either God, or he wasn't.

Paul adjusted his pillow. Jesus had answered his prayers tonight, but Jesus wouldn't be content with such a rescue. Jesus wanted more. Jesus wanted to rescue Paul from his sin and his failures, and give him a new start.

Paul turned over in the super-comfortable bed, a bed that should be lulling him to sleep. He'd like to blame his sleeplessness on the tea, but even coffee didn't usually stop him from sleeping. God was still trying to gain his attention.

"Okay, God, you win." Paul sat up, pushed two pillows behind him, and switched on the bed lamp. His Bible was back home on his bedside table, but every hotel room he'd ever been in had a Bible somewhere. He opened the bedside drawer, but it wasn't there. He got up and padded over to the desk. Yes, there was a Bible, hidden in the bottom drawer, almost out of sight. He brought it back to his bed.

He had no idea how one became a Christian, but it couldn't be too complicated. God wouldn't go to all the trouble to die for people and make sealing the deal impossible. Years ago, in the privacy of a previous hotel room, he'd glanced at one of these free Bibles, wondering why his hotel rooms always had one of them. If he remembered correctly, there was some sort of explanation in the front or back. He opened the front. It wasn't there, but he found it at the back.

Know Jesus as your Saviour

There were four main points.

1. God loves you

He read the verses underneath the point. John 3:16 and Romans 5:8. They weren't too difficult to understand. While he was still a sinner in rebellion against God, God had reached down and saved him. Not just physically, but God was ready to rescue Paul spiritually as well.

2. You are a sinner

The bluntness of the words on the page was a punch to his pride. So hard to accept. He'd always thought of himself as a man sacrificing himself to a great cause, the fight against cancer, but would he still fight if the job came with no salary and no prestige? No, not him. Selfishness permeated everything he did. Selfishness had made him turn a blind eye to Wendy's discontent in their marriage. He'd assumed Wendy would stick with him no matter what. He snorted, the sound loud in the room. Wendy hadn't been fooled. She knew there wasn't much substance under his polished exterior.

His selfishness ran deep. Having a daughter like Lauren was great because she was easy and made him look good. He'd prefer not to have to put in the hard work with Ben. His attitude to his father was the same. He wanted a perfect father. If Russ wasn't perfect, then Paul wasn't sure he wanted to invest the time. *Selfish, selfish, selfish.*

And, of course, he hadn't given much thought to the sin of all sins. He'd lived as though God hadn't existed. As though he was irrelevant. He'd preferred to believe silly myths about God rather than check out the truth of them, because he didn't want God in his life. Didn't want someone who commanded his respect and obedience. All he'd wanted was a universe where everything was at his beck and call.

He glanced at the next point and the two verses.

3. God's remedy for sin

He knew that one. He still might not fully understand it, but who would ever fully understand God? One of the verses was one he'd read last week. John 1:12. "Yet to all who did receive him, to those who believed in his name, he gave the right to become children of God—"

What an amazing thing that the God who'd made the stars out there tonight was willing—no, it seemed he also wanted—to adopt Paul as a son. What kind of God did such a thing after the way Paul had ignored and mocked him?

Paul skimmed the final point and read the sample prayer.

God, I confess that I am a sinner and need salvation. I believe Jesus died on the cross for my sins and rose again to bring me new life. I ask to receive your forgiveness and grace, and choose to follow you as my Lord and Saviour. Amen.

That was simple enough. Should he get out of the bed and kneel down? It seemed unnecessary, as Jesus had never been impressed with outward show, but maybe he should. It was a humble posture, and humility was something he needed to practise.

He flung back the bedcovers, swung his legs round, and got into a kneeling position. With the Bible open in front of him, he used the suggested prayer to guide his own words.

"God," he whispered into the quietness of his room. "God, I've gone my own way an awfully long time. I've ignored you. I've treated you as unimportant. In fact, I haven't honoured you at all by my thoughts or words or actions. Please forgive me. Thank you that you died for me despite the way I've treated you. You've given me another chance. I can't guarantee that I'm going to be an easy-to-love kind of son, but I know you'll keep loving me anyway like that father in the story loved his two sons. Help me to follow you, and don't let me forget you." He paused and then finished with a rush. "I don't know what else to say. Thank you. Amen."

He got stiffly to his feet. He'd done it. There was a paragraph in the back of the Bible, point four, that promised Jesus had heard. He didn't feel too different. He wasn't sure what he expected. All he felt was a sense of peace because he had made the right decision. That would have to be enough for now.

He put the Bible in the bedside table drawer, ready for the next person who needed it.

CHAPTER 22

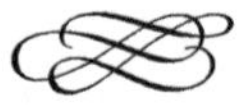

Paul held his phone, the handset slick with sweat. "Is Russell Webster there?"

"Speaking."

"This is Paul—" His voice shook and he gripped the phone harder. "You gave me your phone number to call."

Russ' sharp intake of breath could be clearly heard. "P-Paul, I hoped you'd call."

"I was too curious not to. I've spent the last weeks searching the death registers for your name."

"Death registers? Why would you do that?"

"Mother told me you died years ago."

There was another whistling breath. "I guessed she'd be angry but didn't think she'd go that far." Russ paused for a long moment. "If you thought I died so long ago, why did you only start looking now?"

A smothering numbness settled on Paul. Where should he even start? He took a deep breath. "Because I knew nothing about you, not even your name, until Mother died. She'd hidden all the information about you in a safe deposit box at the bank."

"What information was there?" Russ' voice was puzzled. The complexities of the birth certificate saga would have to wait.

"Things like your marriage certificate with your name and occupation." Slowly they were finding a way forward. "Did you keep working as an engineer?"

"No, I left that long ago. I worked as a gardener up until I was seventy. Now I do my own garden and volunteer at the nearby nursing home."

There was a story there, but it would have to wait until another time.

"And your family?" His father's voice trembled.

"I'm still officially married, but we've been separated for over five years. Lauren is eighteen and in Year 12. She's applying for university and got her driver's licence last month."

"Watch out, world." Russ laughed but he still sounded nervous. "And don't you have a son as well?"

"How do you know that?" Paul said, voice sharper than he'd intended.

"I saw the marriage announcement and later the announcements for two children in the papers. Might have missed others."

Paul took a breath. This man was either creepy or had a father's interest in him all along. But if he'd been interested, why wait all these years? Anger sizzled deep in his belly and he squeezed his eyes shut for a moment before answering. "Ben is about to turn sixteen."

They talked about the family for a few minutes and then Paul asked, "Look, what am I to call you?"

His father paused. "What about Russ for the moment? Maybe later you'll feel able to call me something else."

His father assumed there would be a later. Paul wasn't sure. "Okay, Russ." The name sounded abnormal on his tongue. "I'm not going to make any promises at this stage, but I do want to know more about you. All I know is your name, approximate birth year, and occupation."

"Fair enough. I know more about you, but before I get to that, I want to say that leaving you was the hardest choice I've ever made. If I could have taken you with me, I would have, but you never took a child from his mother in the fifties. I would have been accused of kidnapping if I had."

That was probably true. Courts back then would seldom have awarded custody to a single father.

"I was born and raised in Geelong."

Paul's eyes widened. "Geelong? But … I …" He forced himself to stop speaking. "Please, go on."

"Dad was an engineer, and he loved to work in his shed. I spent hours with him working on various projects." Envy curdled in Paul's stomach.

Russ mentioned his siblings, both dead, and a few other small facts before jumping to the year he finished high school. "As a 1920s baby, I was turning eighteen right on the eve of the war." He sighed. "They wanted engineers, and all I'd ever wanted to do was follow Dad."

Paul clenched his fist.

"The government was calling for aircraft engineers."

Russ' voice became flatter as he started to talk about the war, mentioning that he served in Syria, North Africa, and Sicily. There was silence at the end of the phone for a long while. "We were just stupid kids who thought it would be all fun and games, especially as we weren't on the front line."

"And it wasn't?"

Russ sighed. "No. We lost sixty-three of us—good men, the same age as me. Mostly pilots, but those of us in support roles weren't always safe either."

There were years of memories there, but Paul might never get to hear them. "How did you meet Miranda?"

"Ah, that was at a Saturday night dance in Williamtown, where we did our training. Those dances were the highlight of our week. Your mother was the best-looking girl there, and I was gobsmacked when she took notice of me. Made the other blokes envious."

"But you didn't get married then?"

"No. It didn't cross my mind, but I did ask her to write when I was posted to Syria."

"And presumably she wrote back?"

"The post wasn't regular, but she wrote just enough letters to keep the relationship alive. I wrote every week. There wasn't much else to do out there in the desert." He sighed. "I discovered later that she told everyone I was in the Air Force and let them assume I was a pilot." There was a long pause. "I discovered lots of things later, like how she played the field and used me as an excuse to end things if anyone got serious."

Paul had been prepared to be sceptical about anything Russ said, but so far, everything fitted in with what he knew of his mother.

"When I was demobbed, I found Miranda was determined to marry me. I'd barely seen a woman for five years and here was a beautiful one throwing herself at me. She offered me a chance to forget, and we were married a few months later." He sighed again, louder this time. "She saw me as an educated man who offered financial stability, and as her ticket out of a life of scrimping and saving."

Russ' sighs suggested a world of pain behind the mere words.

"I'm surprised we lasted five years," Russ said. "I nearly left earlier, but once I found out Miranda was pregnant, I couldn't leave. You were the light of my existence, and I held on as long as I could."

Anger surged in Paul's throat, but he tamped it down. Russ had begun to win him over, yet he'd still abandoned his family. What had happened that he considered a good excuse?

"After the war, I resigned as an engineer. Your mother couldn't forgive me for wanting to be a gardener."

There were so many questions that Paul wanted to ask, but he'd have to wait. This conversation was as tenuous as a single spider's thread.

"After I left, I moved back to Victoria. It was months until I was able to find work at the grammar school."

Paul stiffened. "The school I ended up in."

"Uh-huh. One of the senior teachers and I knew each other from the war."

Here was the beginning of the explanation as to why he'd received a scholarship to a school in another state. He'd always been puzzled, as he hadn't sat any scholarship exams.

"I once saved my friend's life, and he managed to convince the principal that neither you nor I would let the school down."

"But why would the school give an unknown kid a scholarship?"

Russ coughed. "The principal risked a twenty-five percent scholarship the first year and said it would be only for that year if you didn't do well. But you did well, and the scholarship increased until it reached sixty per cent in your final two years."

Paul sat up straight and the recliner clicked into its upright position. "No school would have risked that without a guarantee the fees would be paid."

"They were guaranteed."

Paul's gut tightened. "You guaranteed them?"

There was a long pause. "Your grandfather and I. It wasn't as if I had anything else to spend my money on."

His father must have lived like a hermit to pay those fees. Paul had assumed his mother was struggling to pay his way, yet she always seemed to have enough.

"Is there any chance I could come and see you?" Russ asked, voice quavering. "I could catch the train or fly up."

Paul was silent, his mind a whirl of alternating, yes, no, and maybe.

"Or we could w-wait. I don't want to put any pressure on you," Russ said.

There was no mistaking the anxiety in his father's voice. If their positions were reversed, Paul might be feeling the same instead of walking a tightrope between overwhelming curiosity, fear of disappointment, and flashes of anger.

"I think I need more time to digest all you've told me, but I'll call to let you know."

"Thank you, for calling … thank you. I'll wait for your call."

He sounded like a stray dog, hovering at a safe distance, eager for a pat but expecting nothing more than a kick.

"I'll be in touch."

Paul put down the phone and stared at the coffee table spread with brochures promising adventures for the next possible holiday. Seeing a piece of paper among the clutter, he reached for it and jotted down some of the details of Russ' war service and a few of the dates before he forgot them. Things to follow up. Little breadcrumbs that gave hints of the bigger story.

He still had so many questions, but the main question was the hardest to ask: why did his father leave?

CHAPTER 23

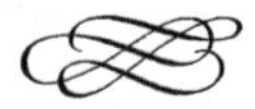

"Paul?"

Wendy's voice was stretched tight on the other end of the phone.

"What's wrong?"

"Ben was sent to the principal's office this afternoon."

He'd been worried about Ben for months, but he'd never gotten around to talking to Wendy about it. Not with everything else going on.

"Well, say something," Wendy snapped.

She was normally a placid woman, but whatever this was about, it had rattled her.

"What's happened?"

"He and a bunch of others were found smoking behind the gym. I don't know what's gotten into him. He's been different lately."

Paul had assumed Ben had only been different with him. If he was treating his mother differently, then things must be worse than he thought.

"In what way has he been different?" Paul asked, propping himself on the edge of the kitchen barstool. Wendy had called just as he walked in the door. She wouldn't ring any later because Ben and Lauren would be around to overhear the phone call.

"Sullen—reluctant to help around the place. Not his usual cheerful self." She sniffed. "I thought it was a temporary stage like Lauren went through, but she was never like this. The principal's given him a warning this time and I assured him I'd get on to it, but they won't be so lenient next time."

The last thing they wanted was a suspension. Once a student was suspended, the situation often escalated as trust was lost on both sides.

"I noticed the same sort of attitudes on our Easter holiday—"

"—and you didn't say anything to me?"

Paul stifled a sigh. It wouldn't help the situation. "I thought it was just me. Like you, I hoped I was seeing things that weren't there or that he'd settle down."

"So do you have any clues what is going on? The smoking and sullenness are the symptoms, but what is the disease?"

Paul didn't laugh, though he wanted to. She used doctor-speak when she was determined to get his attention. She'd once said it was the only language he understood.

"I did wonder if he was jealous of Lauren."

"He loves Lauren."

"I didn't say he didn't love her, but Lauren is getting a lot of attention this year. Driving, extra support for her study, her eighteenth, all sorts of extra gifts."

And Lauren was maturing into a lovely human being who was easy to talk to. Talking to Ben was like talking to a brick wall.

"That makes sense. I've been too busy being the head of a department to think straight."

A little prick of hurt lanced him. He hadn't known about her promotion. There were a lot of things he no longer knew about her, and that was mostly his own fault.

"I had thought of cancelling our week's holiday during the next school break, since Lauren will need to be studying the whole time. Maybe Ben and I should still do it."

"Do you think he'd want a whole week with you given his current attitude?"

"What if we did a long weekend or two? More often, but shorter."

He wasn't going to get many solitary weekends in the months ahead if he spent more time with Ben. Two nights ago, he'd finally rung Russ and arranged for him to come next weekend.

"Let me think about it," Paul said. "Are we agreed that I will work at giving Ben more individual attention?"

"I'd appreciate it if you did, and I'll be thinking about what I can do too."

She was going to hang up, and he didn't have the guts to say things that he should. *Come on, Paul.*

"Wendy—"

"Yes?"

He took a deep breath. "Please don't beat yourself up over this. You've done a terrific job with the kids."

He took another breath. Admitting fault was always hard. "I think the issue is on my end. I haven't made the effort with him that I should have, because Lauren is so much easier." Wendy wasn't jumping in to reassure him it was alright. "I'm only beginning to realise how deeply not having a father impacted me."

And the next weeks were only going to dig up more things from his past.

"I needed my dad and he wasn't there. Maybe Ben needs me more than I realised." He heard a murmur from the other end of the line.

"I'm not saying he doesn't need you, but there is something about boys and their father, something I'm only beginning to understand."

He had a long way to go to understand how the loss of his father had impacted him. Perhaps spending next weekend with his father would help. Or perhaps not. There were no guarantees either way.

A door slammed at Wendy's end of the line, footsteps, and Lauren's voice. "We're home."

"What's for dinner?" Ben asked.

"Got to go," Wendy said, and broke the connection.

Paul sat down and put his head in his hands. *Jesus, Esther seemed to pray all the time about everything. Is this the sort of thing I should be praying about? What do I pray, and how do I know if something would interest you?*

He was so ignorant about this being a Christian thing. How big an issue did it have to be to bother God? In the scheme of world affairs, Ben smoking behind the gym must be on the minor end of things, but it was big for Ben and potentially big for Paul and Wendy. The one good thing about this situation was that it gave him and Wendy a chance to talk. He missed having someone to talk with about daily life. He rattled around in the apartment he'd bought so he would have extra space for weekends when Ben and Lauren came to stay. Most of the time, the emptiness reminded him of all he'd lost.

He'd get dinner and relax a bit. Maybe read a chapter or two of John before bed. He was finding it harder going than expected. He'd always looked down on Christians as rather anti-intellectual, but if this book was written by the disciple John, as the notes he'd found suggested, then he didn't sound anything like the fisherman he was supposed to be.

CHAPTER 24

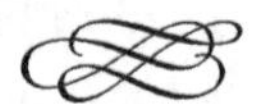

A plane zoomed overhead on its way to landing at the airport. It might even be his father's plane. Paul had timed his arrival to minimise waiting around and paying for overpriced parking.

He parked and walked into the domestic terminal, checking the arrivals board on the way. Yes, the flight had landed ten minutes earlier and the bags would come through at carousel number five. He found a seat nearby and pulled out his Saturday morning paper. He was reading the sports page when he heard the carousel start up.

He stood up and spotted his father almost immediately. A quiver went through him. That's what he'd look like in his late seventies.

His father looked up and saw Paul. He beamed, then switched off the joy as though remembering he wasn't sure of his welcome. Paul gave a quick wave and walked over, striving for calm. He took the heaviest-looking bag and nearly dropped it. It seemed a lot of luggage for a weekend.

"Welcome to Sydney. The car is this way." Paul hefted the bag and led the way. “I thought we might have lunch at the Royal Yacht Squadron. It has parking and good views and is big enough that we can talk without anybody hearing our conversation.”

His father was silent as they drove out of the airport. His eyes darted around.

“Has it been a long time since you were in Sydney?” Paul said as they drove through the city.

Russ nodded. “Decades. I never was much of a city boy.”

“Where I live is much quieter, and your bed and breakfast is only a few streets away. Very pleasant.” He hadn’t dared to have Russ stay with him in case things were uncomfortable.

“I appreciate you letting me come.”

Paul changed lanes. “There is still so much I want to know.”

His father was silent. Perhaps there were things he dreaded talking about. Well, Paul intended to dig, but he wouldn’t be cruel. If finding out more wasn’t possible this weekend, he’d wait for another chance.

“The heavier bag contains as many years of letters as I could carry, and some copies of photos I made for you.”

“Thanks,” Paul said with a crack in his voice. He’d be doing a lot of reading next week.

They were both silent for most of the trip to the Yacht Squadron. Paul parked, and they found a quiet corner outside with a view of the harbour. Paul used to come down here regularly, borrow a friend’s yacht, and sail for the day, but lately he’d barely used his membership.

Paul handed his father the menu, but he pushed it back at Paul. “Why don’t you make some recommendations?”

“Do you like barramundi?”

His father nodded.

Paul raised his hand and the waiter came over and took their order for the fish of the day. While they waited for the meal, Paul asked his father to tell him more about his life nowadays.

"I live on the Bellarine Peninsula, near the sea and near where you learned to sail. I have a little boat, and I still do a lot of gardening. Mostly my own, but some for a few people from church."

"And the nursing home you mentioned."

"Yes, there too." Russ ducked his head and avoided Paul's eye. "Some of my church friends are there."

Paul pricked up his ears. "Do you go to church?"

"Uh-huh," Russ said.

Paul leaned forward. "How long have you been going to church?"

"Since soon after I returned to Victoria." Russ shrugged. "I was struggling, and someone suggested I talk to the local Baptist pastor. I hummed and hawed for ages, but when I went to see the man, he was really helpful. Within a year, I was going to church too."

Maybe Paul would tell Russ about his own spiritual searchings sometime soon, but right now there were other subjects that were the priority.

The waiter delivered their meals, but Russ only picked at his food. His knuckles gleamed white on the fork.

"I'm sorry, Russ. I didn't stop to think that you might be uncomfortable here."

"It's not that," Russ said. "It's what you want me to talk about. I've only ever talked about it once before." He leaned forward to whisper. "I couldn't talk about it in here. We'd both be embarrassed if I bawled."

Paul's gut clenched. He hadn't been thinking about the cost of his curiosity. "If this is all too difficult, I have no right to demand it of you."

Russ looked up, gaze fierce. "You have every right." He glanced around. "You are the one who was most hurt by my choice. I never thought I'd ever abandon my own son." He looked at his plate. "But I'm not sure I had a choice."

He indicated his plate. "I don't think I'm going to be able to finish this. I'm sure it's delicious, but I don't have much of an appetite."

"Your room has a microwave. Would you like me to get it put in a container so you can take it home?"

Russ nodded. "Sorry."

"There's nothing to be sorry about. I should have been more considerate."

"I might go for a short walk while you finish your meal," Russ said.

Paul watched him go. He'd have to come up with a private spot where it wouldn't matter if either of them got emotional. He considered one place after another. Each one he discarded as either not private enough or too uncomfortable for such revelations. Then he grinned. He had the perfect place, and it was right here. He'd never seen anyone in the tiny park.

* * *

PAUL LEANED over the carpark wall and pointed. "What do you think of us going down there?"

Russ leaned over. A tiny sliver of park went steeply down to the water, and there was a bench in just the right spot. Their faces would be towards the water and their backs to the road with only fences around them. It was a place for quiet conversation, not a place for children and their carers.

Russ nodded. "That will do." He grunted. "If my knees can take the slope."

"Don't you kneel a lot with gardening?"

"That's why my knees are wearing out," Russ said, setting off.

Once on the bench, Russ crossed his arms. "This won't be easy for you to hear. I know you loved your mother."

Paul wasn't sure. His mother hadn't been the kind of woman to invite love. Too independent, too prickly, too suspicious of anyone wanting to join their family circle. He'd heard children and dogs are good judges of character. Neither had liked his mother.

"Your mother and I should never have married. Miranda had a picture of me in her mind as a knight in shining armour who was going to rescue her from her old life and give her security. And I—" He paused. "I was traumatised by the war and needed a quiet life in the country to recover. I don't know why I thought getting married and living in Sydney would be a good idea." He shook his head. "Stupid, really."

Russ stared out at a boat chugging past. "I did try an engineering job, but the smell of oil and the sound of engines revving gave me tremors and flashbacks."

"Nowadays we call it post-traumatic stress disorder."

"Whether we call it that or shell shock, I had it." Russ' hands shook. "Badly. I lasted less than two months in that job. I didn't dare to tell your mother until I had another job. Just kept leaving the house in the morning and wandering around all day, looking for work. There wasn't much to be had for someone like me."

"How did you decide on gardening?"

"I didn't, but I spent more and more time in various parks staring into space. One day I noticed some weeds in the flower bed next to me. I was bending down to pull them out when the head gardener saw me and came over and asked if I'd like a job. I was so relieved, I accepted on the spot."

"What did Mother think?"

"I didn't tell her." He shrugged. "Too scared of disappointing her. She was constantly boasting about my war service and job to her friends at the shops."

"But she must have found out eventually."

Russ nodded. "Yeah. She rang my old boss to ask me something and discovered I hadn't worked there for months. His evasive answers to her questions made her even more determined to find out why." Russ grimaced. "I tried to hide the real reason, but she could see I was getting more and more nervous as she probed closer to the truth."

Russ squeezed his eyes shut.

Paul waited. He had all afternoon. He'd let his father tell his story at his own pace.

"When she found out about the shell shock and the new job, she lost it." He shuddered. "Pounded me on the chest and demanded I leave my job and get another engineering job. I refused, and that was the start of things."

Paul wasn't yet sure what it was the start of. He waited.

"It started with little digs. Snide sorts of comments and demeaning jabs." Russ focused on the water lapping the edge of the shore in front of them. "She was clever, and most people wouldn't have noticed how she cut me down." He sighed. "After six months, I felt about six inches tall. Totally useless."

Lauren had once said something catty about Paul, and Wendy had leapt on her. It had never happened again.

"The only thing that kept me going was the gardening. My boss had fought in the first war and he understood people like me. He kept teaching me about plants, using the plants as life parables. Miranda tore me down and he built me up. As I spent more time at work, I was just about able to keep my head above water."

Russ tightened his jaw. "I didn't want to go home because Miranda was like a constantly stabbing toothache. 'You're useless'. 'You can't do anything'. 'What use is it being an engineer if you can't fix anything'?" He worried the cuticle at the edge of his thumb. "Each time she cut me down, I became more useless." He flushed. "And that affected other things."

Paul stared across the water. How would he have handled it if Wendy had belittled him? Men liked to think they were tough, but he'd treated plenty of men in the past, and seen others in the waiting room. Men who were terrified but didn't know how to deal with it. Men who wished for death rather than having surgery. Men who feared they wouldn't be able to support their families. Nowadays, a mental health assessment was standard practice and many of his patients had counselling alongside their chemo.

"I did try to ask for help, but the doctor sneered when he heard what was happening. I never went back to him again."

That was hardly surprising.

"I was close to breaking point when Miranda announced her pregnancy." Russ looked at his feet. "She questioned how the baby could be mine but said at least I'd done something right."

The silence hung between them. Finally Paul spoke. "I'm so sorry for what you had to go through."

"I don't know if it was the hormones, but things got even worse between us. Twice she attacked me with her nails. I told my boss a cat had scratched me." Russ sighed. "He seemed to accept my lie the first time, but the second time he took me aside and asked me what had really happened. I felt so ashamed, I lied again." He shook his head. "Don't think he believed me, but there was nothing he could do while I insisted I was fine."

Russ got up and paced up and down by the water, head down. Then he walked slowly back towards Paul and sat down. "I'm sorry I have to tell you all this."

Paul laid his hand on Russ' shoulder. Through the telling of the story, Russ had shrunk visibly, defeat in every line of his body. "Don't be sorry. I need to hear the truth." All these years, he'd imagined other scenarios but never this. He'd never heard any man admit to being the victim of domestic abuse and violence, which was what Russ was describing. Maybe Miranda hadn't been as physically violent as many men were to women, but the emotional toll was similar. To have survived implied there was a core of steel in Russ somewhere.

"Things were marginally better after you were born, especially when Miranda discovered I was totally besotted, and she had more freedom to get out of the house." Russ leaned forward gripping the edge of the park bench. "But soon my desire to be with you gave her more ammunition. Wanting to be a stay-at-home father was further evidence that I wasn't a man. The more I withdrew from her, the more her belittling escalated. Perhaps she would have preferred me to attack her back." He shook his head. "But my father had drummed into me never to hit a woman, any woman, for any reason, and I didn't ever want to make my father ashamed of me."

"I wish I could have met your father."

Russ turned his head towards Paul with a gentle smile. "You did once. I have a photo of you shaking his hand when you won the hurdles in second form. His company was one of the local sponsors, and he made sure he was the one to award the prizes."

Paul wrapped his arms across his stomach. He'd always felt so isolated with his mother far away and no siblings, yet there had been relatives right next to him, and he hadn't known. Paul shook his head to clear it. "Why did you eventually leave?"

Russ was silent for a long time, gently rocking back and forth. His lips moved. Was he praying or doing some sort of self-talk?

"The belittling increased from intermittent bursts to a constant barrage. Several times I considered suicide." Russ took several shuddering breaths. "But the decisive moment for me was when I imagined throttling her."

Paul drew in a sharp breath. This gentle man didn't look like the murdering kind. Russ had glossed over many of the details, but the picture was clear enough.

"I thought you'd cope better with me abandoning you than with me being hanged for murder."

Paul blinked. Put like that, he agreed. He reached over and squeezed Russ' forearm. "Thank you for telling me all this. It took guts."

CHAPTER 25

While Paul settled his father at the bed and breakfast, Russ asked if there was a church nearby. The only church Paul knew was the one he'd attended for Esther's funeral. He agreed to find out the time of the service and pick up Russ in the morning. They'd have time for church before getting Russ back to the airport.

Once home, Paul dragged out the heavy bag his father had brought and took it over to the seldom-used dining table. Inside the bag were piles of letters in bundles tied with string. He took the bundles out one at a time, checked for a date, and laid each bundle in order. The letters started in 1950 and went through to 1960. His father said there were plenty more.

There was also a large envelope. He opened this first. Inside was a selection of photos, mostly of himself as a baby: on a baby rug, in a pram, grinning to display a first tooth. There was also a handful of photos of him with his father, probably taken by a helpful stranger in the park. The best was one of him aged about two, seated on his father's lap on a swing. The chains of the swing framed the shot and his hands firmly grasped the chain for himself. He had an amazingly similar photo of Ben at the same age.

A lump clogged his throat. His father's story had torn at his heart. All his life he'd condemned his father for abandoning him. There was a lot to ponder; perhaps the letters would help him work through that process.

He picked up two piles of letters and settled in his recliner. This could be a long night.

The first letter was dated September 2nd, 1951.

Dearest Paul,

It has been three months since I had to leave. Every time I think of you I cry. You will be bewildered wondering why I suddenly disappeared. There are things a child cannot understand. Maybe one day I will have the courage to tell you.

It had taken nearly fifty years, but Russ had found the courage.

I hope your lucky bear has been able to comfort you.

That bear had been on Paul's bed until his mother had told him he was too old for such things and thrown it out. He'd rescued it and hidden it at the back of his cupboard.

It took me two days to get home. You would have loved the trip on the train, but I was too tired to enjoy it. I slept most of the way. It was easier that way.

Mum and Dad took one look at me and didn't ask any questions. Just fed me and let me sleep. I hope that one day you have friends like that, who instinctively know what to do.

Paul had always substituted work for friends. It wasn't much of an exchange.

Paul kept reading. Most of the early letters were along similar lines—Russ sharing small happenings and little things he thought a four-year-old and then a five and six-year-old would like. Paul mostly skimmed. As he finished each letter, he laid it down, careful to keep the order within each pile.

The letters were intensely personal, a father pouring out his love and longing for his son. The hurting child still hiding in the dark corners of Paul's heart craved the words. He might never read the letters again, but he'd keep them because of what they represented, proof his father had cared all along.

Today you started kindergarten. Do you even remember me? It breaks my heart to think of you forgetting the times we had together, yet it might be better if you did. There have been many times I've wanted to jump on a train and visit, but I'm afraid of what your mother would do if she saw me.

This week I finally found a job. Back at my old school. They took a gamble on me because of their respect for my dad, and references from my pastor and my former boss in Sydney. Shell-shocked survivors of the war aren't too uncommon. I have another friend there, from my war days. He teaches mathematics, and it is good to have someone who understands.

The style of the letters was intriguing. Sometimes they were written directly to him as a little boy and sometimes they were more like a diary, as though his father knew they would only be read by an adult son.

For the past two years my parents have been a solid rock when everything else in my life has cracked and crashed to the

GROUND. IT TOOK ME MORE THAN A YEAR TO AGREE TO TALK TO PASTOR LEN. HE'S A WISE MAN IN HIS FIFTIES, AND HAS PASTORED THE CHURCH FOR TWENTY YEARS. I PRAY YOU WILL NEVER HAVE TO EXPERIENCE WHAT I'VE BEEN THROUGH. THAT YOU WILL NEVER QUESTION WHETHER YOU DESERVE TO LIVE. THIS WEEK, YOUR MOTHER SHOULD RECEIVE THE FIRST OF WHAT I HOPE WILL BE MANY YEARS OF SUPPORT FOR YOUR DAILY COSTS AND SCHOOLING. I WILL SEND IT VIA THE BANK ON THE FIRST OF EACH MONTH. I CANNOT BEAR TO THINK OF YOU IN ANY NEED.

It hadn't been until he'd been in university that Paul had wondered why his mother had more money than could be expected from a secretarial job. He'd asked her once, but she'd been coy. He'd suspected a boyfriend, perhaps a married one, who supported her. Since she wouldn't talk, he hadn't pressed for answers.

The letters continued, year after year, usually about once a month. Often the actual letters were written weekly and compiled for the entire month, then put in an envelope with his name on the outside.

TODAY YOU'RE TEN. I WISH I COULD BE THERE TO HELP YOU CELEBRATE. I SENT SOME EXTRA MONEY TO YOUR MOTHER'S BANK SO YOU CAN HAVE A PARTY.

It was the first party he could remember. His mother had allowed him to invite five boys, and they'd played games in a park and eaten too much ice cream.

NOW YOU'RE IN YEAR 6 AND READY FOR HIGH SCHOOL. SOMETIMES I CAN'T SLEEP BECAUSE I'M THINKING ABOUT YOU. HAVE YOU INHERITED A MATHS AND SCIENCE BRAIN FROM OUR SIDE OF THE FAMILY? I WORRY THAT YOUR MOTHER WILL GROW TIRED OF YOU OR BE TOO POSSESSIVE AND STIFLE YOU. MOST KIDS HAVE SOME DIFFICULT YEARS BETWEEN

> THIRTEEN AND EIGHTEEN. WHAT IF YOU DO? I'M NOT SURE YOUR MOTHER WOULD COPE. I'D PREFER YOU COULD BE SOMEWHERE I CAN KEEP AN EYE ON YOU. I WISH YOU COULD COME TO THIS SCHOOL. IT'S A SPECIAL PLACE. A PLACE WHICH WOULD OPEN ALL THE OPPORTUNITIES IN THE WORLD TO YOU. I'M PRAYING HARD. SOMETIMES THAT IS ALL I CAN DO.

Paul's skin prickled with goosebumps. Both Esther and Joy prayed for him, and now here was someone else. How many recent events had come about because of all these prayers?

Five letters later, his father shared the answer Paul already knew.

> IT'S A MIRACLE. JACK HELPED ME APPROACH THE PRINCIPAL. HE HAS AGREED, SOMEWHAT RELUCTANTLY, TO OFFER A TWENTY-FIVE PERCENT SCHOLARSHIP FOR A YEAR. I'LL PAY THE REST. DAD SAYS HE'LL CHIP IN SOMETHING TO HELP. JACK AND I DRAFTED A LETTER, AND WE'VE SENT IT. I IMAGINE YOUR SURPRISE. THE LETTER IS WORDED CAREFULLY ENOUGH THAT YOUR MOTHER SHOULD ACCEPT IT. AFTER ALL, WHO WOULD TURN DOWN A FREE PRIVATE-SCHOOL EDUCATION IN ONE OF THE MOST HIGHLY REGARDED SCHOOLS IN AUSTRALIA? I KNOW YOUR MOTHER WELL ENOUGH TO EXPECT SHE'LL WANT TO ACCEPT EVERYTHING AT FACE VALUE.

The letter had arrived one Friday. Since he'd turned ten, he had been trusted to be home on his own. He'd seen the letter in the letterbox in all its official-looking formality, but he'd had to wait until his mother got home from work. The letter had looked intriguing and he'd desperately wanted to open it, but he didn't want to provoke his mother. Most of the time she was fine, but occasionally she'd explode and he never knew why. Could it have been simply because he looked like his father?

Two letters later his father wrote:

Your mother has accepted the school's offer. I will see you in four months. I can't wait. I never dared to believe the idea might work. The principal has given me strict guidelines. I can only continue to work here if I don't reveal who I am. You'd think that would be difficult, but I'm known by everyone at school as "Mr W", so it will be fine. No one should link our surnames. Even if they do, who would guess we're related?

Paul skimmed the next few letters. There was no escaping his father's eager anticipation as the time for Paul to start boarding school approached. Paul's mother had moved to Canberra for a new job and new start at the same time, and she'd accompanied him to school for his first day. He'd been more excited about being on an overnight train than changing state and school.

His mother had stayed long enough to buy his uniform and get a tour of the school before being politely told to go home. She'd complained later at how miffed she was to be pushed out the door with all the other new parents.

Paul got up out of his chair and went back to the dining table to pick up the next pile of letters written during his first year at boarding school. He hadn't found the adjustment too difficult, having been forced to be an independent child by his father's leaving and his mother's seldom being home. School had been far more exciting than home.

Today I saw you arrive for your first day. You looked bewildered, and I longed to hug you and point you in the right direction. I couldn't, because I knew the principal would be keeping a sharp eye out to see whether I was keeping my side of the bargain.

When you took off your cap, you still had the tuft of unruly hair at the front. It was like looking at photos of myself at the same age. I don't know how I'm going to keep my

DISTANCE AND NOT TALK TO YOU, BUT THIS IS MUCH BETTER THAN THE SEPARATION OF THE LAST NINE YEARS.

We nearly had a disaster yesterday. I'd forgotten your mother might come with you. Fortunately, I recognised the way she tossed her hair and was able to duck behind a convenient pillar and move my work elsewhere. A big hat helps. This hat will be glued to my head the whole time you're here, as it makes us look less similar and shades my eyes so it is harder to see me watching. Is watching all I'm ever going to be able to do? Will I ever get to hug you, my beloved son? Or will I only ever be able to pretend you mean nothing more to me than the other boys with their knobbly knees, shirts hanging out, and bright cheekiness?

Tears gathered in the corners of Paul's eyes. In these yellowed pages was the proof of a man who'd loved him. Who poured out his aching heart in pages of black ink, week after week, month after month, year after year. Never knowing whether the letters could ever be delivered. Never knowing if he'd ever be able to acknowledge his love and care. Never knowing if he'd ever speak to his son in person.

CHAPTER 26

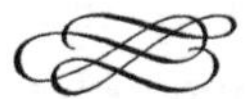

On Monday morning, Paul looked at his appointment diary for the week. Such a relief to have a normal week ahead of him after the last month with his mother's heart attack, the funeral, and dealing with her estate. Then the snowshoeing trip, Ben being hauled up in front of the principal, and now his father coming back from the dead. He'd barely had a moment to catch his breath. A five-day week of ordinary appointments would be just the thing. There wasn't even a new patient listed. Almost unheard of, but it would be great to not have to deal with anyone's tears or breakdowns. He'd had enough of those to last quite a while.

He hadn't cried at his mother's funeral. He'd never been emotional, so he wasn't overly surprised, but he'd cracked up at the airport yesterday. Talk about embarrassing. Thankfully, he and his father had been sitting in a quiet corner.

The dam had been threatening to burst from the moment he started reading all those letters. Overnight, his father had changed from being someone to be wary of to someone he could never turn away.

Going to church hadn't made things any easier. His father

moved around in the building like the people were family. Esther's grandmother and sister had been welcoming, but he hadn't dared to talk about Esther in case he upset them. Or himself.

His father had nudged him into a pew from which he couldn't escape. He hadn't known the songs, but the words had continually struck some chord inside his heart, and he'd been fighting tears the whole way. And the sermon on the Prodigal Son hadn't helped. He'd thought he'd have to content himself with a heavenly Father. He'd never thought his earthly one would appear out of nowhere around the same time.

There was a knock, and Sister O'Reilly poked her head around the door. "Are you ready to see your first patient?"

Paul gave a start. He had let time slip away and it was five minutes past the hour. "Sorry. Yes, ready to go."

At lunchtime, he went looking for Joy Wong but didn't find her out in the park next door. She wasn't there the next day either. He dashed off a note and left it with Michelle at reception asking if Joy could meet him. He had no one else whom he could question, and questions were queueing up and demanding attention.

Joy was waiting for him on Wednesday. She indicated her half-empty container. "Sorry. I started, as I thought it might not be so easy to eat once you arrived."

Paul grinned. "Fair enough. I do have a lot of questions."

"I'm sorry to hear your mother died. I've been praying for you and your family."

He'd known she'd prayed for him before, but it was moving to hear she'd kept going. He didn't really understand how prayer worked, but maybe her prayers accounted for some of the strange things that had happened in his life.

"I need to talk to someone about what happened last month." He bit into his focaccia and sifted through his thoughts. What was most important to ask in the limited time they had? "May I start by telling you what happened to me in the Snowy Mountains? I think

..." He paused. "I think ... well, I think I may have become a Christian." The words tripped over themselves. "I don't know if I did it properly, and I haven't had much time to process things because of everything else that's been happening."

"Why don't you tell me the story?"

As quickly as he could, he told her about his solitary walk, all the things that had gone wrong, the series of mini-miracles, and what he'd finally done in the hotel room. "So I read the verses and prayed the prayer in the back of the hotel Bible."

Joy smiled. "It sounds like you did the right thing. Your exact words don't matter; God focuses on your heart attitude. Did you admit you were a rebel against God, apologise, ask for forgiveness, and for him to give you a new start?"

Paul nodded.

"And was it a full surrender, or were you still trying to bargain with God and give him only parts of your life?"

Paul thought back to that night and the certainty that if he'd died in the snow, he wasn't ready to face Jesus. "I meant it, but I'm not sure it worked."

Joy laughed. "What were you expecting?"

"Something more spectacular, I guess."

"Like fireworks or angels singing?"

Paul laughed loudly. "It does sound silly when you say it like that, but I was expecting something. The whole thing was significant for me, but—"

"It didn't feel like it was significant to anyone else?"

He nodded.

"This brings up something really important in the Christian life. We need to learn to trust what God has told us through his word instead of trusting our feelings. Feelings aren't always a reliable guide."

"That might be what the section meant that was labelled 'assurance'. There were some verses there I copied out." He put his hand in his pocket and pulled out a slightly crumpled piece of paper. "I like this second one because I've been reading John. It's John 5:24. 'Very truly I tell you, whoever hears my word and believes him who sent me has eternal life and will not be judged but has crossed over from death to life.'"

Joy reached into her bag and pulled out a small Bible written in Chinese. She flipped to a place he presumed was John. She ran her finger next to the characters. "There's a similar and I think slightly clearer verse at the end of chapter three. Loosely it says, 'He who has the Son has life; he who does not have the Son does not have life because he is still under God's judgement.'"

"By 'having the Son', does it mean we've accepted what Jesus says about our sin and who he is?"

"That's right. You've accepted Jesus as saviour, but also as the king and ruler of your life."

"And if I don't do that, then I miss out on eternal life?"

"Everyone will be judged by God, but Jesus has already taken the judgement for those who choose him."

"You mean when he died on the cross?" Paul squinted at Joy.

Joy nodded. "So when Judgement Day comes, we will be found innocent because our sin is already dealt with."

"That's a relief. I used to think I wasn't really a sinner, but I've come to realise I was comparing myself with others—mostly with convicted criminals, so of course I always came out looking good in comparison. In recent weeks I've come to see we're not supposed to compare ourselves to one other, but rather to Jesus."

"Exactly." Joy clipped her chopsticks into the lid of her metal lunch box.

Paul pulled out a pen. "I want to jot down that reference."

"And look up 2 Corinthians 5:21 at home too. See if you can work out what it's saying."

Paul wrote down the two references. "One of the reasons I finally decided to follow Jesus was that my mother's heart attack was unexpected, and she never woke up from her coma. I realised I wasn't ready to die and face Jesus." Paul paused. "But I'm worried about her. She wasn't a Christian, and it's too late now, isn't it?"

Joy was silent for a long moment. Was she praying? She seemed to do that a lot.

"You say the heart attack was sudden, but maybe it wasn't sudden for her."

"Her doctor did say she'd had a previous heart episode."

"What I'm trying to say is that we don't know what your mother was thinking. If she knew about her heart, perhaps she was thinking similar things to you. Facing death forces people to think about whether they're ready to die. God is just and fair, and he died to save your mother. He would have given her every opportunity to know and trust him."

"I wish I'd already made my decision, because then I would have tried to tell her about it."

"Your mother might have known other Christians. Perhaps one of the nurses at the hospital talked about Jesus with her. Even in a coma, God is big enough to help her understand."

"Oh," Paul said. "I read the last chapters of Luke and some other chapters too."

"You see. We have no idea what she could hear or what God did through those words."

The tightness in Paul's shoulders relaxed. He couldn't know for sure, but maybe he'd see his mother again one day.

Joy glanced at her watch and finished packing away her things. He'd have to go back to work too.

"Look, Joy, I can see I need someone to help me learn more about what it means to be a Christian. I don't want to make too many mistakes."

"You'll make plenty of mistakes."

"Well, I'd prefer to minimise them. You've been very helpful, but —" His neck warmed. "I don't mean that you've not been great."

"But you'd prefer to meet with another man."

Paul nodded. "But I don't know any Christian men."

"That is something I could pray about for you."

"On Sunday, I went to Esther's church. The same guy who led her funeral gave a speech."

"Are you wondering about asking him to meet with you?"

"Well, he's the only person I can think of. He seems nice but—"

"But what?"

"Would someone like that meet with someone like me, you know, someone who doesn't attend his church?"

Joy laughed. "I'm sure it would be the highlight of his week if you got in touch." She looked across at Paul. "I got to know him a little because of the funeral. Would you like me to contact him tonight and let him know about you? Then when you ring, he'll know who you are."

"Would you? That would make it so much easier."

He'd written to Rob out of the blue, but it wasn't an easy thing to do. He'd been impressed by Stuart on Sunday and Russ had found him easy to talk to at the door after the service. He'd call on Saturday, before Ben's volleyball game. He didn't know what he was nervous about. After all, the worst the man could say was "no".

When he'd met with Rob, he'd been reading chunks of Luke, but these last few weeks it had been a struggle to read his Bible. He had so many questions, and some were questions he'd only feel comfortable asking another man.

CHAPTER 27

Paul usually went away with Ben and Lauren in the October holidays, but by then Lauren would be completely focused on her exams. She wouldn't emerge until the second week of November. Then he'd have to think of some way to celebrate with her.

Ben had decided to do a week-long camp with friends during the holidays. Was it because he was growing up or because he wanted to avoid his father?

Paul picked up the phone to call Wendy. After they'd asked each other how work was going, Paul got down to the purpose of his call.

"I haven't had much time to spend with Ben lately, and he's already made plans for the next holidays. Could I take him out of school for a day and do a three-day trip to Cairns? What do you think?"

"I don't see why not. He has more time this year than he'll have in the next two."

"Have things with him been any easier recently?"

"Being sent to the principal's office seemed to shake him up a little. His attitude towards me has been much better, although I worry more about what was behind the whole thing."

"I'm glad to hear things have improved. You haven't done anything to deserve his anger." Paul was still certain he was the main issue. Wendy had merely been in the firing line because Ben lived with her.

"But you think you have?"

"Not intentionally, but as I mentioned last time, I've been thinking a lot about being a father and father/son relationships."

Wendy was silent for a few moments. "You've been a lot more reflective lately."

He almost blurted out about his father, but it was still too new to share. He'd found the recent weeks emotional, and he wasn't ready to cope with the responses of others as well. But he needed to tell them about Russ soon, or they might be annoyed at being left out.

"Must be that time of life when we look back and think about things. Probably Mother's death has something to do with it. Talking of which, her house has sold. I'd like to talk to you about how to put some of the money aside for Ben and Lauren for the future."

"I don't like the thought of giving kids their age a heap of money."

Wendy had always worked hard to ensure the kids learned to be independent and liked to have them work for things, rather than just being given them. If they wanted a camera, they had to save towards buying one themselves. She didn't mind Paul taking them places, but she wanted them to build memories and not just go to resorts and be served by others.

"I agree, it's much better that the money be put aside for the future. There's no pressure to make up our minds immediately."

Wendy was silent for a moment. "About your idea, why don't

you check with Ben about whether there's a Monday or Friday he can take off in the next few weeks."

"I'll ask tonight."

After Wendy hung up, he sat staring at the phone. *Jesus, you know what I want. I want us to be together again, and I'd love you to do a miracle so that it happens.* He shook himself out of his reverie and muttered, "But I suspect you won't make things easy. Making things easy doesn't seem to be your style."

* * *

THE PLANE CENTRED on the runway ahead, and Paul craned his head to look past Ben's head and out the window. Paul hadn't been too surprised when Ben said yes, but after all, who would say no to three days of rainforest and reef? Ben's yes didn't necessarily mean he wanted to be with his father.

The plane landed with several small bounces before coming to a gradual stop. Ben hadn't wanted to miss his volleyball match, so here they were on Saturday evening landing in Cairns, population 150,000 according to the tourist map Paul had brought with them. They had an hour of light left to collect the rental vehicle and settle at their hotel.

Ben had selected the activities from a list Paul had researched. Tomorrow they'd do a day trip to visit the Great Barrier Reef, then on Monday they'd drive up to the Daintree Rainforest and back via the Atherton Tablelands. Before their flight on Tuesday morning, they'd work on a photography assignment for the eight-week class he'd given Ben as an early birthday present. It had taken ages to come up with something they could do together that fitted in with their timetables. The photography class meant giving up one of his squash nights, but it looked like being worth it, and besides, it was only for two months.

* * *

THE ALARM WENT off at five-thirty. It was amazing how fast a teenager could get out of bed when there was something he wanted to do.

"We need to be out the door by quarter past six," Paul said as Ben went into the bathroom.

The boat tour included snorkelling, but Paul had paid an extra fee to go diving since Ben had gained his certification last year. There was no point having the certification if he didn't keep up the practise.

Being a Sunday, the boat was packed. They chose a seat on the upper deck with the best views. The captain gave the usual introductory announcements, and they headed towards the open ocean and the reefs hidden under the surface.

Light danced off the surface of the water, and tiny waves splashed against the sides of the boat. This was the life.

"Look, Dad, dolphins." Ben pointed towards the port bow.

The pod surfed in the bow wave for a while, then moved to the stern.

"As you can see, we have specially arranged the dolphins for our customers today," the captain said over the loudspeaker, voice deadpan.

Ben leaned towards Paul. "Bet some of the tourists believe it."

Paul chuckled. "Probably."

Out here, Ben was a different kid.

When they reached the first of the two reefs where they'd spend their time, Paul led the way towards the stern of the boat. "After we've tested the equipment, you lead and I'll follow."

The boat drifted on a patch of darker blue. On three sides were lighter green patches indicating where the reef came closer to the surface.

The water was refreshingly cool after the heat of the shadeless upper deck. Paul gave a joyful kick and followed Ben, who was already zeroing in on something. He waved his arm to gain Paul's attention. He'd found a moray eel tucked into a cavity, pointy teeth bared and looking ready to dart out and devour them at the slightest provocation.

Underneath them stretched layer upon layer of texture and colour. Spiky plates and smooth bulbs of different corals, seaweeds, and seashells containing wondrous creatures. Paul preferred to hang suspended in the water and let things come to him, but Ben darted here and there like the fish around him.

Paul swam over to Ben and gestured for him to follow. Grazing along the edge of the reef was a herd of hump-headed parrot fish. Some were well over a metre long. Ben and Paul stopped and watched them until Ben moved forward, searching for something new in the kaleidoscopic world which enveloped them.

* * *

THE DRIVE to the Daintree had been long, but they'd seen crocodiles and a cassowary by lunchtime.

Now they were headed back to Cairns via the long route, up onto the Atherton Tablelands. So many times Paul had opened his mouth to ask about what had happened with the smoking incident, then shut it again. Why wreck a good day? Ben seemed to have put the incident behind him, but what if it was like a boil swelling below the surface, ready to poison other parts of Ben's life?

God, help. I don't want any more barriers to go up between us, but I must do the right thing. And the right thing was that he, as Ben's father, should check that Ben was okay. Only last month he'd had a colleague who'd lost his son to suicide because they hadn't known what he was dealing with.

Nerves danced a jitterbug in the pit of his stomach. *Jesus, help.* Jesus always did what needed to be done for others.

Paul changed down a gear to take a sharper than normal corner. He only really prayed hard when he was in trouble. *Sorry.* But he needed divine help now.

Ben reached into the side pocket of the car to put in his earphones.

"Ben, before you put on your music, I've been wanting to talk to you."

Ben stiffened.

"About why you were smoking and hanging out with those guys."

"It's okay, Dad. I don't hang out with them any more."

It was tempting to let this slide, but he was going to push on now he'd started.

"Smoking and mucking up are usually only symptoms of the real problem."

Ben snorted. "Don't start on that medical baloney. I'm not one of your patients."

Paul gripped the steering wheel. "No, you're my son and I love you."

"Funny way you have of showing it."

"What do you mean?"

"You know." Ben turned to look out the window.

"Spell it out for me."

Ben blew out a gusty breath. "Leaving us."

Anger rushed through him. Couldn't the kid see he was doing his best? *Calm down, Paul.* Look at the meaning behind the words.

"That was about your mother and me. It had nothing to do with you."

"Well, it affects us too."

"Yes, it does, and I'm sorry about that." He'd always vowed he wouldn't be like his father. Outwardly he'd succeeded, but Ben saw past the thick hedge of his excuses. Paul loved his family, but not enough. Not enough to keep loving them when his pride was hurt.

He'd wanted Wendy to beg him to come back, but she never had. And she'd never returned. That stung.

"And you love Lauren more." Ben stared out the window, presenting his rigid back and shoulder towards Paul.

Lauren was a good deal easier to love, but saying that wouldn't help Ben. "Why do you think I love Lauren more?"

"You talk and laugh with her and spend heaps more time with her."

"Once you get your learner's permit, you'll be spending hours with me too."

"Lucky me," Ben muttered.

Paul took a steadying breath. "You can't have it both ways. I may be making lots of mistakes, but believe it or not, I really am trying." It was a waste of breath saying so. No teenager believed an adult who said such a thing. Their expectation gauge was off the scale of human possibilities.

The hire car flew past the farms and patches of forest. If Wendy had been here, they would have stopped and sampled the cheese and produce on offer but Ben was still at the quantity rather than quality stage.

A sign came up advertising a farm shop ahead. "What do you say to some ice cream?"

Ben grunted assent, still too grumpy to admit he was interested.

"One of the reasons I talk with Lauren is that she talks back. I remember what it is like to be fifteen." Paul caught Ben's look. "And don't look at me like that. I was fifteen once, and my mother was a good deal harder to talk to than yours. We'd much prefer you made the effort to tell us what you think than keeping it bottled up inside." Inside, where it fizzed and fermented until it exploded. "Even angry words can be better than no words. We're not the enemy, no matter what you think."

Ben grunted again.

Paul sighed. "And grunts are not the best way to communicate."

"Okay, Dad, enough for now. I get it." Ben enunciated as if Paul was hard of hearing. "I'm not going to hang out with those kids again, and I'll do my best to talk, even if I don't feel like it."

Paul put on the car's indicator to turn into the farm gate. At least they'd talked. Now he'd wait to see if it had done any good.

CHAPTER 28

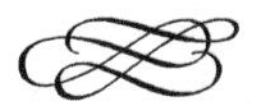

It was early Friday when Paul drove into the church carpark. He'd barely stopped the engine when Stuart exited the neighbouring house and walked towards him. Paul got out of the car.

"Good morning. I wasn't sure if you'd show up," Stuart said.

"Do people often stand you up?"

Stuart grinned. "People have all sorts of preconceptions about pastors. I hope you soon work out we're not aliens."

There was a muffled pounding on a door over in the house next to the carpark, and a shout. "Hurry up in there."

Stuart pointed his thumb towards the house. "See what I mean." He led the way towards the back corner of the house. "We'll be able to avoid the getting-ready-for-school chaos as my office has a separate entrance."

They passed through a gate into the back garden and entered the office. The walls were mostly bookshelves, and there was a big desk and two armchairs next to a small table.

Paul presumed Stuart had already eaten, although his own

stomach had been too unsettled for more than a quick slice of toast. "Sorry my work hours mean you had to get up early."

Stuart grinned. "This keeps me out of the breakfast-time squabbles. My son is not a morning person."

He sounded like Ben.

Upstairs, footsteps pounded down the stairs. Stuart pointed at the ceiling. "Sorry."

"Don't be sorry. It's a friendly sound." A sound he hadn't known he liked until it was gone. "I didn't expect you to have a family." Paul's neck warmed.

"You expected me to be unmarried." Stuart laughed. "It's only Roman Catholics who can't marry. Most Protestants are encouraged to marry and have families." He winked. "One wife, and three or four children. We've exceeded the quota with five, hence the pressure on our two bathrooms."

That explained the amount of noise.

"Why don't you tell me about yourself." Stuart leant back into his seat. "Just whatever you feel comfortable talking about."

"Life was pretty normal until a year ago." Paul told him a little about his work and his family. "Meeting Esther really made an impact."

"I didn't know her well, but her grandmother has been a member of this church since before I joined," Stuart said.

"I saw Esther's sister here the day I visited with my father."

"Yes, she comes with Naomi each week," Stuart said. "Why did Esther make such an impact on you?"

Paul described what Esther had been like and how she'd challenged him to examine some of his prejudices. Of course, he hadn't thought they were prejudices at the time. "Up until Esther, once a patient is in palliative care, we pass them on to other specialists."

Stuart shifted in his chair and indicated Paul should continue.

"It's one way of coping with the fact that we lose a good proportion of our patients." Paul rubbed his eyebrow. "Esther was the first person I'd visited in palliative care for many years. I'd only intended to make a quick visit but got trapped in one corner of the room when all her family arrived." He'd been too embarrassed to push past them, then too intrigued to leave.

"I remember you saying at the funeral that you were there the night before Esther died," Stuart said.

Paul nodded. "I'd never heard anything like it. She scolded us and said we ought to know going to be with Jesus was far better." He shook his head. "It raised a lot of questions in my mind. Esther had been challenging me to read the Bible since the end of her first round of chemo, but I didn't do much more than glance at it." Paul shrugged. "After the funeral I decided I needed to investigate properly, so I contacted one of the other men at the funeral to ask if he'd read and discuss Luke with me."

"Was he a Christian?"

Paul shook his head. "That was the point. I wanted another sceptic, not someone who was already a Christian."

"And how did it go?"

"Surprisingly well. We discussed a few chapters every week. I nearly gave up at one point, but Esther's letter arrived just in time to keep me going."

Stuart sat forward in his seat.

"Yes, the letter got lost. I wanted to think the timing of its arrival was a coincidence, but there have been too many coincidences recently."

"Hmm," Stuart said.

"Halfway through Luke, my mother died, which unleashed more questions. Then my father got in touch. I hadn't seen him since I was four, and I'd been told he was dead."

Stuart raised his eyebrows. "You have had an interesting few months."

"I want to tell you how I finally became a Christian."

Stuart listened and occasionally asked clarifying questions as Paul shared his epiphany in the snow and in the weeks following.

Paul had dreaded talking to someone like Stuart, but it seemed like he'd been wrong, yet again. Almost none of his assumptions about Christianity had proved to be true.

"Thank you for trusting me with your testimony," Stuart said. "I'm always asking people how they came to know Jesus, because every single journey is different."

Testimony. Paul blinked at Stuart's use of the word. A formal statement? A record of evidence or proof? The word fitted Paul's account of finding faith. He must ask Joy about her testimony someday soon.

"Now have you read any books of the Bible apart from Luke?" Stuart asked, pulling out an index card. "Would you be okay with me jotting down some of your answers on this card? I meet up with a lot of people, and my memory isn't great. I don't put your name, just your initials."

What an unusual job, talking about the Bible all day with people. "I've previously read all of Genesis and half of Exodus. Now I'm reading John, but I'm finding it harder than Luke."

"So would you like us to discuss John together?"

Paul sat back and digested this offer. Rob had been a fellow sceptic, safe and familiar terrain. Stuart claimed not to be an alien but he felt alien to Paul.

"Would you be happy to read, say, a chapter each day and bring your questions?" Stuart said. "I prefer people to do some reading at home." He pointed to the houseplant near the window. "Like most of us, that plant thrives best with regular, small waterings rather than a dousing once a week."

Paul nodded. Wasn't this why he'd come? To understand more?

"Does this time suit you?" Stuart asked.

Paul wrinkled his forehead. "Wouldn't I be taking too much of your time from your family?

"My wife and I have a deal. I meet working men several mornings a week, then I look after our youngest while she visits stay-at-home mums and older folk during school hours."

Stuart wrote down a quick heading and John on his card. "Normally, we'll start with a quick prayer asking God to help us to understand him better, then study John or talk about an issue that has come up, then finish with prayer. I'm guessing you're not used to praying out loud with someone."

Paul shook his head. "Never done it."

"Why don't I pray for you this week? You can pray another time, once you're used to the idea."

Paul sucked in a breath. He wasn't used to exposing his feelings and doubts to someone he'd just met.

"As Christians, we often bow our heads and close our eyes when we pray, it's a sort of respect thing and to keep us from being distracted. Feel free to do whatever makes you comfortable."

Stuart bowed his head and Paul followed. The whole thing was strange, but this was an opportunity to get used to what other Christians did.

"Dear heavenly Father. Thank you so much for bringing Paul here today. Thank you for how you've been working in his life and for the impact Esther's life has had on his. You've promised that when we are adopted as your children, you give us your Spirit to help and guide us. Please help Paul as he reads John this week, to increasingly understand it, and see its relevance to his life. Please help him to remember every day that you love and care for him and will never leave or forsake him. Help him grow to trust you more each day, and give him wisdom in the decisions he has to make at work and home. In the name of your son, Jesus. Amen."

A lump formed in Paul's throat as Stuart prayed. Esther and Joy had said they were praying for him, but actually hearing the prayer was different. God had a universe to run, and he'd never thought God cared about his daily decisions.

Stuart escorted him out to the carpark. "See you next week." He gave Paul's hand a firm yet friendly shake. "Feel free to call any time."

Any time? Did he mean it, or was he just being polite?

The session hadn't been nearly as uncomfortable as Paul had expected. Stuart made him feel at ease and hadn't even pressured him to turn up to church—a pressure Paul would have resisted, as Sunday was his one sleep-in morning each week.

Paul took a deep breath before turning the ignition on in his car, feeling strangely like he'd just had his first solo drive after gaining his licence, as if he'd achieved a solid step towards the new direction he wanted in his life.

CHAPTER 29

Paul picked up the phone and dialled his father's number. It rang eight times before his father picked up.

"Hello, Russ speaking." He sounded breathless.

"Did I call at a bad time?"

"It's never a bad time for you to call, but I was talking to a neighbour at the front gate."

Paul would have to go down and visit his dad sometime soon. Before he did that, he was going to tell the family about their grandfather. There were now two major pieces of news he hadn't told them, and he wasn't sure whether they'd greet either with joy.

"Thanks for sending that huge pile of letters. I've been reading them whenever I get a chance."

"Hope it's not too overwhelming."

"Yes and no." Sadness did sweep over him at the thought of all the years he'd missed with his father, and that he'd never know his grandparents. They'd seen him a few times, but he had no memory of it. He'd have given almost anything to have talked to them, even for an hour. "I wish I could have known your parents."

"They would have loved to have known you."

Paul bit his lip. Grandad had died at seventy-five, but Grandma had lived into her late eighties.

"Tell me a little about them."

His father's chair squeaked as he settled into it. Russ' voice vibrated with pride and affection as he related how the family had migrated from Sussex and settled into life in Geelong.

Conversation flowed more freely every time he and his father talked, but getting to know each other more fully would be a long process. The letters were an immense help as they revealed his father's heart. Paul had cried more tears over the letters than anything in his life. For his father's loneliness, for his desire for Paul's best, for how he had to go about his work and pretend Paul was just another schoolboy.

"That's more than enough of me talking for one evening," Russ said.

"There is still so much I want to know," Paul said. "Could you write some of this down for me?"

His father laughed. "I already have. I haven't thought of much else than you in the last few weeks."

"And I've spent most evenings reading your letters." Paul took a deep breath. "Look, Dad—"

There was silence on the other end of the phone. "Yes, son?" Russ' voice was as shaky as Paul's emotions.

Paul swallowed the emu-egg sized lump in his throat. "Father's Day is coming up. Would you be happy for me to tell the rest of the family about you?"

His father blew his nose, the sound trumpeting down the phone. "It would mean a lot to me. Do you think Ben and Lauren might be willing to meet me one day?"

"Hopefully, but we'll have to take things at their pace. Lauren is in the home stretch towards her final exams, and Ben ... well, I can't predict Ben at the moment. I'd appreciate your prayers for both of them. Wendy and I need wisdom to help Ben work through some issues."

"I've been praying morning and evening for you all."

Nerves danced in Paul's gut. Joy and Stuart knew he'd become a Christian, but no one else knew so far. Rob might not be surprised, however they hadn't been in touch since finishing their Friday meetings. While reading Luke, there'd been a voice in his head that had said, "How could you?" to Peter when he'd denied Jesus. Yet here he was, afraid to tell people. It wasn't as if he faced any threat of death, but it was embarrassing how much he feared being ridiculed. *Grow up, Paul.*

"I'm only just beginning to understand the power of prayer." Paul's heart began to do a foxtrot. "I think prayer must have played a part in me becoming—becoming a Christian recently."

His father swallowed loudly. "Oh, son, I've been praying for you for years. Knowing Jesus probably saved my life."

The rigidity in Paul's spine relaxed. That hadn't been too bad. There were always going to be people delighted about his decision and others who would be indifferent or antagonistic. He'd better get used to it.

"Can you tell me what happened? Why you became a Christian?" his father said.

Paul gave the ten-minute version. "I want to hear how you became a Christian too."

"Mine isn't that exciting, and you already know some of it."

"I still want to hear it. Stuart, the pastor helping me read the Bible, asks Christians he meets for their testimony, and you're the first person I've asked."

"I'll get a glass of water first, if that's okay? My mouth gets parched with all this talking."

The phone knocked against something and his father's footsteps retreated across wooden floorboards to turn on the tap. Dad's letters indicated he lived alone and had never remarried. His mother had never said they were divorced. He'd ask sometime.

The footsteps returned, energetic and firm.

Russ cleared his throat. "I was raised at the church but drifted away when I went to study engineering. The start of the war made everything else seem urgent, and any free time was used for sleeping, drinking, or dancing."

Not too different from any man of that age during any era.

"The war hardened me against God. It seemed unlikely that a God who allowed a Hitler or a Changi prison camp truly cared about the world."

This line of thinking made a certain kind of sense. He'd have to ask Stuart.

"I fooled myself into thinking my salvation was a gorgeous blonde who tantalised me with her occasional letters." He sighed. "War without Jesus is similar to the deserts we were fighting in. Dry and bleak. I wish I could redo the past. One of my friends tried to get me along to meetings, but I always refused. He died in Italy."

"Didn't his death make an impact?"

"Not at the time, because I'd blocked my ears, but he did tell me if you have Jesus you have everything you need and he wasn't afraid to die because he knew where he was going."

His father gulped some water. "I've told you about how low I got after I left you and your mother. My parents gave me plenty of space, but Dad also dragged me along on all sorts of hikes. He'd had some struggles of his own and believed in a mix of prayer, fresh air, and exercise. I left the praying to him, but the rest was helpful."

"Why did you eventually agree to go to see the pastor?"

"I reached a point where I realised I needed help to process the past. There wasn't much understanding about situations like mine in those days, and I'd already had a bad experience with a doctor. My parents had been patient, but I needed a job and I couldn't even apply for any when I still heard the voice in my head calling me a useless failure. I agreed to four sessions with Dad's pastor."

"But ended up doing more?" Paul asked.

"Yes. Len was a huge help. First he listened without judging me, then he helped me discern the difference between what was true and false. He pushed me to talk about the war and process all the gunk I wanted to avoid, and he encouraged me to get all my doubts about God out in the open." Russ chuckled. "There were a lot of them, but Len never got angry or defensive. He said God was more than capable of defending himself."

"And how did you become a Christian?" Paul asked.

"It wasn't anything dramatic. Just step by step, beginning to believe in truth instead of lies. After about six months of meeting up with Len, I turned up at church one day. He knew introducing me would make me run a mile, but some folk invited me to meals and treated me as one of the family."

And for a man separated from his son, this was something that had been missing for a long time.

"I don't really know when I actually became a Christian. One day I looked back and realised I now believed what God said in his word and had trusted my life to him. At that point, I got baptised."

Paul frowned. "Isn't that something that only happens to babies?"

"It depends on the church. Baptist churches prefer to baptise people who are old enough to make up their own minds. You'll see lots about baptism when you read the book of Acts."

"I think Stuart is planning to study Acts once we finish John."

"Is it really quarter past ten?" his father said. "I'm supposed to start at the nursing home at eight tomorrow morning. I'd better hit the sack."

"Dad, before you go, could you remember to pray for me as I speak to the family?"

"Son, you don't have to ask. I've been praying already and will keep on praying." His feet thumped on the floor. "Look, why don't I pray right now."

"On the phone?"

"Why not? It doesn't matter to God where we pray."

"Okay." Paul bowed his head even though no one could see him.

"Great and mighty Creator. Thank you for the grace and mercy you've poured down on us lately. To have Paul back in my life is such a wonderful gift. Thank you he was willing to let me back into his life even though I hurt him so much in the past."

The past—all those years Paul had believed terrible things about his father when in truth he'd been deeply loved as a son. All those lies had disappeared like debris swept away by rushing flood waters.

"You know we long to see the relationships in the whole family restored. Please prepare Ben and Lauren to discover they have another grandfather. I pray we can get to know each other in time. Please help Wendy as she helps them process their emotions, and give Paul your courage to talk with everyone. In Jesus' name, Amen."

Jesus, thank you for giving me back a father. Thank you that he knows and loves you and that he is a prayerful man.

"Are you okay, Paul?"

"Yes, Dad. I'm a little overwhelmed. That's all."

"Son, I understand. Life has been overwhelming recently, but it's the best kind of overwhelming, isn't it?"

It was.

CHAPTER 30

The following Friday, Paul woke more excited than nervous. Last week had been far less scary than he'd expected. Stuart had a way of making him feel comfortable and that his ignorance on various matters was normal.

Over the past week, Paul had even managed to pray each morning. It was only a few minutes before he ran out of things to say or got spooked by the discomfort of not hearing anyone talk back, but it was a start.

Paul had focused on thanking God for things this week as he'd noticed that both Stuart and his father always thanked God at the start of their prayers. As a result, he'd noticed how many things he'd taken for granted, even at work. Sister O'Reilly had nearly fallen over when he'd bought her flowers and thanked her for all her hard work. The woman was a saint to have put up with him for the past fifteen years.

Once seated in the study, Stuart said, "Let's start by praying. I always pray before I read the Bible, that God will help me understand it and notice what he wants me to notice."

"Even after all these years?"

Stuart nodded. "It would be nice to think we could graduate from asking for help each time, but I still get distracted by daily life and can treat God's word too casually. Praying helps me slow down."

Paul decided to add this to his morning routine.

Stuart prayed. "Now, has anyone given you a quick introduction to the Bible as a whole?"

"No."

Stuart went over to the desk and picked up a piece of paper and a pen. He did a quick sketch of book spines along a shelf.

"I'm not an artist, but you get the idea. Think of the Bible as more like a library than a single book. Sixty-six books, with thirty-nine in the Old Testament and twenty-seven in the New." He wrote the numbers and the abbreviations OT and NT above the book spines. "The Old Testament covers the stories of the Israelites before the time of Jesus, and the New starts just before Jesus is born. Like any library, there are different genres of literature. Which ones have you noticed?"

"Well, history, of course. Biography, and whatever you'd call all those rules and regulations at the end of Exodus."

"The first five books are often called the 'Pentateuch' or the 'Law'." Stuart wrote the genres on his paper. "And there are poetry and wisdom books, and prophetic books too. Have you looked past John's gospel?"

"I have flipped ahead. Some of the books looked like letters."

"Yes, that's exactly what they are. Letters to individuals or churches or groups of churches. Have you worked out what the numbers are?"

"Chapters and verses?"

"The numbers weren't in the original scrolls. They were added later to make it easier for us to find things."

"Like an address?"

"Yes, that's a good way of thinking about it."

Tonight Paul would check the table of contents to see if he could spot the different genres.

"How did you go with John?"

"It was easier the second time through. It's so different to Luke that it takes a while to adjust."

"As a doctor, it might be easier for you to resonate with Luke's style. John is more philosophical. It is also likely that Matthew, Mark, and Luke were written first, so John didn't have to repeat what they'd written. He'd had years to process his experiences, so John tended to group things in themes rather than telling the story in chronological order." Stuart reached to the side and picked up his Bible and flipped it open to John 1. Paul did the same.

"The hardest part of John is the prologue in the first eighteen verses. John is introducing the themes he'll flesh out later in the book. Why don't you read aloud the first five verses?"

Paul cleared his throat.

"In the beginning was the Word, and the Word was with God; and the Word was God. He was with God in the beginning. Through him all things were made; without him nothing was made that has been made. In him was life, and that life was the light of all mankind. The light shines in the darkness, and the darkness has not overcome it."

The words had a pleasing rhythm.

Stuart looked at Paul over his reading glasses. "These verses scare people off, but does the first line remind you of something in the Bible?"

Paul looked out into the garden. "In the beginning was the Word." The words were familiar. "In the beginning …" Ah, he had it. "It's the beginning of Genesis."

"Yes. The original readers would have immediately recognised the opening words, but John puts a new spin on them. Instead of God, he talks about the Word. What do these verses say about the Word?"

Paul traced his finger along the sentence. "The Word was with God, the Word was God. Wait. The next section seems to contradict the first sentence. It implies the Word is separate from God."

"It is mysterious, isn't it? The verses also say the Word is the creator. Check out verse fourteen for another clue."

Paul looked further down the page and read. "The Word became flesh and dwelt among us."

"Who is John talking about?" Stuart asked.

Paul wrinkled his brow. With the capital letter it had to be a person. "Jesus?"

"Now go back and substitute Jesus instead of Word and see if it makes sense."

Paul went back and read the verses. It did make a sort of sense, but created another problem. "I don't get why it says Jesus is God but also implies he's separate."

Stuart chuckled. "You've hit one of the big mysteries of the universe. How can there only be one God, yet somehow he's Father, Son, and Holy Spirit?"

Paul was having enough difficulty with just the Father and Son, and there was now a third! It seemed like more than one god to Paul.

"I'm going to ask you to put this question aside for the moment and let John reveal it to us. The disciples were Jewish and therefore monotheistic, yet after the resurrection they did come to accept that Jesus was God. If you flip to chapter twenty, verse thirty-one, John tells us his purpose in writing this book."

Paul wrote down the reference, flipped ahead in the Bible, and read. "'But these are written that you may believe that Jesus is the Messiah, the Son of God, and that by believing you might have life in his name.'"

"So why did John say he wrote this book?" Stuart asked.

"That we might believe Jesus is the Messiah, God's son, and that we might have life."

"John is using terminology his original readers understood. We'd say something more like, 'This book was written to prove Jesus is the Saviour who was going to come into the world and that trusting Jesus would lead to real life.'"

A question burned in Paul's mind, but it felt stupid. *Come on, Paul, surely you're not still afraid of what others think?* "I note it doesn't say eternal life. The promise of eternal life seems rather abstract. I'm more concerned about now."

"It's a common misunderstanding," Stuart said. "When the Bible talks about eternal life, it's not just length of life, but a life full of meaning and depth. When we accept Jesus' gift of himself, we start a new life, an eternal life, right at that moment."

"But we still die?"

"Yes, but death becomes more like a gateway to something better, rather than a full stop."

What had Esther said the night before she died? "Don't pity me. My life is about to start, with every day better than the one before." He'd thought her out of touch with reality.

"Now, why don't you reread the first eighteen verses and see if things make more sense. John adds lots of words in there that are going to be themes he comes back to, words like 'life' and 'light' and 'testimony'. This whole book is a big testimony, full of smaller testimonies about who Jesus is and how through him we can come out of the darkness into the light and into real life."

Paul reread the verses. They were easier to understand now he had the key that 'Word' equals Jesus.

"I've noticed you're a notebook man," Stuart said. "What questions do you have?"

Most of Paul's questions were from chapter three but he had a quick one from chapter one before that. Paul peered at his jotted reference. "In chapter one, verse fifteen, John wrote, 'This is what I meant when I said, "He who comes after me has surpassed me because he was before me."' It sounds like some sort of riddle."

"And it is not helped by the number of people called John," Stuart said. "This John isn't the writer of the book, the same John who is one of Jesus' twelve disciples, but the John who is Jesus' cousin. You would have read about his miraculous birth to Zechariah and Elizabeth."

Paul raised an eyebrow. "The old couple who were visited by an angel and told they'd have a son?"

Stuart nodded. "In that culture, the older cousin should be superior. But John is saying that in this special case, Jesus is superior not just because of who he is but because he's older—older in the sense of existing since before creation."

"Mmm, I see," Paul said. He sat and thought for a few moments before he turned the page to chapter three of John. He tapped the verses in front of him. "I think I understood the part where Jesus talks about a new birth. Not a physical birth but a spiritual one."

"John's gospel has a lot of ordinary things from daily life that Jesus gives an extra spiritual meaning. You'd have read another in chapter four, where Jesus says he gives living water, and if the Samaritan woman drinks, she'll never be thirsty again. Can you see what Jesus is getting at there?"

"That he quenches any thirst we have, whether it is for love or significance or anything else, I guess."

"Right."

Paul found it a powerful image. His chest tightened. Ben needed this Jesus as he struggled for his identity. Lauren didn't look thirsty at the moment, but the Bible said everyone was thirsty, whether they knew it or not. Sometime soon he was going to have to tell his family about his decision. His gut ached at the thought. Would his decision drive more distance between them? He might well have distanced himself from them if the roles had been reversed. He'd have equated someone becoming a Christian with losing their mind or joining some sort of cult.

"My main question is in verse fourteen," Paul said.

Stuart grinned. "Yes, that verse causes a lot of confusion. What's your question?"

"John is obviously making a quick reference to a story his readers were familiar with, but I don't get the reference."

"It's not surprising you're unfamiliar with the story as it's in the book of Numbers."

Paul had seen the book of Numbers when he checked the Old Testament table of contents the night before. It was somewhere at the front of the Bible.

Stuart leaned back in his armchair. "After the Israelites were rescued out of Egypt, they wandered in the desert for forty years. God provided food for them every day, but the Israelites began to grumble and complain about eating the same food day in and day out. So God sent poisonous snakes to bite them."

Paul blinked. "That sounds a bit extreme."

"It wasn't the first time they'd complained," Stuart said, his tone wry. "As more people died, the people came to Moses and asked him to pray to God on their behalf. God told Moses to make a snake out of bronze and put it up on a pole. Anyone who looked at it would be healed." Stuart sketched a drawing on a piece of paper. "Like that."

He'd drawn the pole like a cross, with the snake hung over the crossbeam. Now the verses made more sense. Like the bronze snake, Jesus would be lifted up on a cross and when people looked up to him in trust, they could be saved.

They discussed a few more verses from the chapter.

"We've just about run out of time, but I think we need to talk a bit more about prayer," Stuart said. "Prayer is both a great privilege and one of the hardest things in the world to do. It is so easy to get distracted and to forget how important it is."

"I don't really understand why people pray. Doesn't God already know everything we're going to ask?"

Stuart paused. "When your children were little, didn't you usually know what they wanted before they asked?"

Paul snorted. "It was usually related to playing with them, ice cream, or a puppy."

"But didn't you like to see their faces as they asked?"

"I guess. They were pretty cute, especially as they worked themselves up to ask."

"Prayer is more about building a relationship than the actual words. God loves to hear us pouring out our hearts."

"It would be much easier if I could see him."

"Almost everyone thinks that, but over the years you'll learn to trust and perhaps even appreciate the way God has arranged things."

Paul hoped so. Talking to himself before bed felt strange, but if he didn't talk out loud, he fell asleep mid-prayer.

"I often give new believers this sheet about prayer." Stuart reached for a paper on the desk next to him. "It gives some ideas and guidelines to get you started."

Stuart passed it over and Paul scanned it. "Could I take this home and ask questions next time? I need to head off in a few minutes."

"Have we got time to pray?"

Paul nodded. He'd known Stuart would want to pray.

"Do you want to try? Just a few lines of thank yous based on something we've talked about or something that has happened this week."

Paul gripped the edge of the chair. He'd feel less nervous standing in front of a room full of doctors than he did at this moment. "I'll have a go."

Stuart prayed first, then Paul bowed his head and took a deep breath.

"Dear heavenly Father, I'm not very good at this yet, but with your help I'll get there. Thank you for giving me a new start. I didn't think I needed it, but each day it becomes clearer that I did. Thank you for the conversation I had with Dad during the week, and that we're more and more comfortable each time we talk. Please help me to be able to tell my family I'm following you now." He couldn't think of anything else to say. "Amen."

Stuart gave him a thumbs up. "See, it wasn't so bad."

"You didn't see my knees shaking."

"It gets easier. One of the reasons I like meeting with new Christians is that it reminds me how difficult it is embarking on a whole new life."

Difficult was an understatement. It was how Paul imagined it would be to walk on the moon. All the rules he'd lived with had changed. Instead of walking firmly on the ground, the lack of gravity meant he might float off into a new direction he'd never intended.

What would Ben, Lauren, and Wendy think?

CHAPTER 31

Paul was seated on a picnic mat in the park in front of their old home, where Wendy and the children now lived. Lauren handed him a bread roll. "Happy Father's Day, Dad."

"Thanks, honey." He looked at the roll. "Have you been baking?"

Lauren flushed. "Baking is a nice break from studying."

"Bet your brother doesn't mind," Paul gave Ben a wink.

"Nope, and she makes enough for me to share. Now my friends all want me to introduce her to them."

"They're too young for me," Lauren said, passing round the butter. "Help yourself to whatever you like."

"Lauren's got a boyfriend," Ben chanted.

"Have not," she said, swatting his shoulder. "Just someone to go to the formal with."

Paul raised his eyebrow at Lauren.

"I met him at some of my hockey games. His twin sister is on my team." She shrugged. "He was easy to talk to, and his sister vouches for him. She sort of set us up, and we'll both go to each other's formal."

He had a heap more questions he'd have to ask Wendy. No use

being the overprotective father, although he wasn't sure he could help it. Lauren was special, but maybe every father thought that about their daughter.

They ate their way through salmon and fresh salad rolls, followed by mini-meringues with kiwifruit and strawberries for dessert.

A strong blast of wind lifted the far edge of the picnic blanket. The sky had suddenly turned dark. "Looks like we're in for a drenching."

"I thought it wouldn't rain until tonight." She knelt on the rug. "Quick, Ben. Hand me the lids and I'll get everything covered."

A spot of rain splattered into an empty dish.

"Hurry—we're going to have to make a dash for it," Paul said.

Ben grabbed the empty plates, while Lauren and Paul gathered up the leftover food.

More heavy drops of rain fell, releasing the smell of damp earth.

"Head home, Lauren, and take this with you." He handed her an opaque plastic folder. "Ben and I will bring the rug and everything else."

Lauren grabbed her belongings, scampering across the park and up their steep drive. Paul picked up the rug and shook it.

"Check the ground and bring the picnic basket. I'll bring the chairs." Paul turned to fold them up, gathered them under his arm, and the two of them ran for shelter. The heavens opened as they got to the front gate. They were partially wet by the time they reached the house and stood panting and laughing at the entry porch.

"Sorry, Dad. I thought we had more time," Lauren said, "I should have picked a different spot for our picnic."

"It's fine. A little rain never hurt anyone." He put down the chairs. "Can you ask your mother if I can come inside? I have something I wanted to talk to you all about."

Ben and Lauren trooped inside, leaving him staring at the metal security door.

He hadn't been in the house since he'd moved out, but he was fairly confident Wendy would allow him in. If not, he'd have to gather them in the garage or the pavilion in the park.

Lauren put her head out the door. "Mum says come in."

He bent down and took off his wet shoes, leaving them outside the door. He checked his socks. There was a little hole on the right-hand toe but at least they were clean.

He and Lauren walked through the hall and living room. He glanced around. Many of the familiar paintings were still there, but there was a new enlarged photo on the wall—one Ben had taken on their Snowy Mountains trip. He'd have to remember to compliment him on how well it had turned out.

The glassed-in front porch looked out over the park.

Wendy shivered. "That was a quick change of temperature. Sorry it ruined your picnic."

Paul chuckled. "It didn't ruin it. It just meant we didn't hang around. I left the chairs on the side porch." He spotted his folder and picked it up. "Glad this didn't get wet, as I have some things I want to show you."

"Well, I'll go and clear away the lunch things." Wendy stood.

Paul looked up at her. "Please stay. What I have to say concerns you, too."

She squinted at him, uncertainty and maybe a flicker of fear on her face. What was she afraid of?

"Nothing to be concerned about. I'm hoping you'll think it's good news, but it was a total surprise to me. Something appropriate to talk about on Father's Day."

Wendy perched on the edge of Lauren's armchair. Ben and Lauren looked at him expectantly.

He'd prayed about how to share this with them and he knew his father was praying too, as was Stuart.

"First, I'd like to thank Lauren and Ben for the picnic."

"I didn't do much," Ben muttered.

Lauren winked. "I did the baking and you did the carrying. Perfect, as far as I'm concerned."

"I appreciate you making an effort on Father's Day and making this one special. This was always my worst day of the year when I was a kid. The only good thing was that it was on a Sunday, so once I was away at boarding school I didn't have to see everyone playing happy families."

But he'd had to hear boys at school talking about what they'd done with their father. He'd tried not to mind, but every year a painful arrow or two pierced his defences.

Ben tapped his finger on the arm of the chair.

"Don't worry, Ben. I'm not going to give a speech, but I can't tell you my news without a little background. You might remember I never had any contact with my father after he left, and I was told he died years ago. I was almost relieved, because I didn't want to meet the kind of man who would abandon his family without a word."

"Yeah, a real drop-kick," Ben muttered.

"Well, I certainly thought so," Paul said. "But his death also left a hole, and Mother refused to talk about him."

"And there were never any photos in her house," Lauren said. "I looked."

"When your grandmother had her heart attack, I realised I might have missed my only chance to find out."

"Have you found out now?" Lauren asked, clasping her knees to her chest.

"Do you remember the extra key Ben found behind the mantel clock?"

They all nodded.

"Well, it opened a bank safety deposit box."

"And what was in it, something valuable?" Ben said, eyes wide.

Paul chuckled. "Not valuable in the way you mean."

"What did you find, Paul?" Wendy asked, moving to a more comfortable spot.

"Lots of legal papers, including my parents' marriage certificate and some photos."

"Is that what you've got in that bag?" Lauren asked.

"I'll show them to you in a minute. Most importantly, I learned that my father's name was Russell James Webster. When I looked at the photos, I remembered him." Paul's voice cracked and he swallowed. "I remembered the games we used to play and how he'd throw me in the air. I can't describe it except it was like he'd come back from the dead."

"Show us the photos, Dad," Lauren said.

Paul picked up the plastic bag and took out the folder. "I've put each one in a separate clear plastic sleeve to protect it." He'd brought six of his favourites and handed them around. Even Ben seemed interested.

"Goodness, he looks like you. I mean, you look like him," Wendy said.

"And look, Mum, Ben has his nose." Lauren held up the photo.

"Pity these are all black and white. We don't know his eye colour," Wendy said.

His secret wanted to explode out of him, but he stuffed it down as they looked at all the photos. This slow story was more fun.

"Once I knew my father's name, I went looking for his death certificate. But I couldn't find it."

"Maybe he wasn't from Australia. Do I look Spanish, Mum?" Lauren cocked her head to one side.

"Not Spanish." Wendy laughed.

He let them babble on before saying, "A few weeks after Mother's funeral, I received a letter from a man claiming he was my father."

Lauren stared at him, Wendy slumped back into her chair, and Ben said, "Whoa!"

Lauren was first to recover. "And was he?"

"That was my immediate question. The letter included a photo of him with me, and plenty of proof. It took me a few days to absorb the news and decide what to do. I was scared that meeting him would be a disappointment."

"There's an adopted girl in my class who wants to meet her birth mother. Her parents are suggesting she waits until after the exams."

"Smart parents. I was certainly distracted at work." Fortunately, Paul had Sister O'Reilly to keep him on track.

"So have you met him?" Ben asked.

"You remember that weekend I was so pleased your volleyball game was early and close to the city? Afterwards, I went to collect him from the airport."

"And was it awkward?" Lauren asked.

"At first. It's incredibly difficult to bridge forty-plus years of absence. We both had so many questions. And of course, I couldn't ask the most important questions at first."

"Like why he'd abandoned the family and had never been in contact," Ben said.

Paul looked at the photos he'd laid on the carpet, each a smiling snapshot showing only part of the truth. Behind the smiles were uglier things. He'd spent last night debating how much to tell the family now and how much to leave for the future.

"Over the last weeks I've moved from calling him 'Russ' to calling him 'Dad'. That's mainly happened because he's totally different from what I expected." He sighed. "I started from a position of wary antagonism, but he has patiently answered all my questions." And he'd been vulnerable and humble. "One amazing thing is that he's given me hundreds of letters he wrote to me during the intervening years but never sent."

Another box had arrived on Friday.

"Yes, but why did he leave?" Ben thumped the arm of his chair.

"Patience. I'm getting there," Paul said. He summarised his father's war experience. "You've studied World War One and Two in school. Can you remember some of the emotional impacts of war?"

"You mean shell shock?" Lauren asked.

"Exactly. Not much was known about it, but Dad definitely continued to suffer when he returned. Jumping when car doors slammed, nightmares, and in his case, an inability to go back to his old job. He switched to gardening instead."

"I bet Miranda loved that: being married to a gardener," Ben said.

"Your grandmother had her own issues. I'm not going to go into all the details, but their marriage was a mess. For your grandfather, it was a choice between leave or find himself doing something that couldn't be undone."

"You mean kill himself?" Lauren was always the sensitive one.

"Something like that. It took him years to recover after he returned home to his parents."

"But it doesn't explain why he never got in contact." Ben was a bulldog when he caught onto a train of thought.

"No, and I only asked about that last night."

"Took you long enough," Ben muttered.

Wendy flashed Ben a warning look.

Things had been better between him and Ben since their talk had cleared the air, but his old habits sometimes still came to the surface.

"I needed to build trust between us before I asked that question. Dad doesn't like talking about my mother's failures with me." Sadly, he hadn't found anything his father said too surprising. Everything fitted with what he'd seen of his mother.

Ben was sitting with his arms folded, waiting for an answer.

"Dad did have one contact with my mother after he recovered. He arranged to deposit money into her bank account every month.

She accepted that, but said she'd change our names and disappear if he ever tried to contact me."

"But that was when you were a kid. Why not contact you when you were an adult?" Ben asked.

"By then, he'd gotten used to things as they were. He was afraid to make things worse, and didn't want to drive a wedge between her and me."

"Do you really think she would have been that vindictive, Paul?" Wendy asked.

"It's possible. He was definitely afraid of her."

"How did he find out she'd died?" Ben asked.

"The bank contacted him about stopping payments."

"What?" Wendy's voice rose. "He sent her money all those years, even after you no longer needed it?"

He nodded. "Incredible, isn't it? He must have felt some sense of obligation to her too." Or pity. "They were never divorced."

"What do you want us to do now?" Lauren said.

"Mostly I wanted you to know what's been happening, but I'd also like him to have a chance to meet you all."

Ben frowned.

"I know it sounds awkward, but I thought I might bring him to watch you play sport to start with. That way you don't have to talk to him much, but he gets to see you and the things that are important to you. We'll go slowly. Your Mum might have some good ideas." He glanced over at Wendy. "She usually does."

Wendy was quiet for a long moment. "Thanks for letting us know what's going on. I'll get back to you soon." She got to her feet. "Lauren can see you out now that the rain has stopped."

* * *

PAUL AND LAUREN walked across the park towards where he'd parked his car. Water dripped off the trees and pale sunshine made everything glisten.

Lauren linked her arm through his. "Thanks for coming and telling us about our grandfather. I want to meet him, even if Ben isn't keen."

He squeezed her arm. "I was sure you'd be the first. Your grandfather is going to love you."

She turned to look at him. "One thing I don't understand when I see you and Mum together. Why are you still separated?"

He'd seen that question in her eyes the last few months. He kept walking, running through a few ways he could answer the question.

"It seems to me that you like each other a lot and neither of you has remarried."

"I don't know," he mumbled, his face warming. As he said the words, he knew she wouldn't let him get away with such a pathetic response.

"Don't know what? Don't know whether Mum would say yes?" She shook her head at him. "You'll never know unless you ask."

"I'm not sure it's that simple."

"Why not?" She narrowed her eyes at him. "What are you afraid of?"

Was it only yesterday he was marvelling that Lauren had grown up? Now she was proving it.

"Lots of things," he muttered sheepishly. He was terrified the door would be slammed in his face forever. Terrified he'd lose what they had at the moment.

"Really, Dad. When Ben and I have a fight, you expect us to work through things. Why can't you do the same?" She peered at him. "You've changed this last year. You're more—much more—approachable. And considerate. You're really making an effort. Why can't you be the same to Mum?"

"Has she ever said anything to you that makes you think I might have a chance?"

"Nope." Lauren shook her head, and her fringe swished over her eyes. She swept the hair aside. "But she wouldn't. It's more that she's never criticised you." The side of her mouth twitched. "And she pretends not to, but she listens closely, very closely, when Ben and I talk about you."

A warmth filled Paul's chest. He'd caught himself daydreaming about Wendy several times recently, but he hadn't dared hope. Maybe he should think seriously about it.

Lauren kept walking. "You will think about it, won't you Dad?"

"I promise I will." He'd think, but would he dare act? That was the question. Lauren saw things in black and white, and maybe she was right. But then she wouldn't be the one taking the risk.

CHAPTER 32

Paul hadn't been able to get Lauren's words out of his head. He'd been planning a strategy all week. A huge bunch of daffodils—Wendy's favourite—were on the car seat next to him, and he was parked within sight but well out of the way of his former home.

Ben and Lauren came out the front gate in their sports uniforms and headed across the park to the train station. He waited ten minutes before picking up the flowers, getting out of the car, locking it, and heading to the house. *Please, Lord help her not to be on her way out the door.*

He wiped his hands on his trousers and rang the doorbell.

A vacuum cleaner whined inside. Good. That meant she was unlikely to be going out any time soon.

The vacuum cleaner cut off and he heard Wendy's footsteps come towards the door. There was a pause as she checked through the spy hole. He smiled with what he hoped was a friendly and disarming smile.

She opened the door and looked at the flowers. "Wasn't exactly expecting you today," she said in a neutral tone.

"Can I come in?" Paul asked, heart racing.

"I guess you'd better."

As she unlocked the security door, he wiped the sweat off his hand again. He didn't blame her for her wariness, but he'd hoped for more warmth.

She didn't take him into the sunroom, but into the formal lounge that they used for guests. The sofa showed no more wear than when he'd left. She sat across from him in an armchair.

"These are obviously for you." He handed her the flowers and laughed nervously. *Paul, relax.* She wasn't likely to eat him, but she might toss him out on his ear if he didn't get to the point.

Wendy took the flowers and laid them gently on the coffee table. Was it a good sign that she hadn't thrown them at him?

"I didn't want to talk while Ben and Lauren were here." Sweat prickled along his hairline. He'd gone for a haircut last night and dithered about what to wear today. He'd chosen a shirt in her favourite colour, the one she'd always said brought out the blue of his eyes. Probably too obvious, but at the moment he needed all the confidence boosters he could get.

Wendy sat quietly waiting for him to speak. *Help, God. I don't want to do this, but Lauren is right. I must take the risk if things are ever to change.*

"I don't know where to start." He swallowed, the sound loud in the quiet room. "When you left, it was a shock. I was happy with things the way they were and assumed you were too."

"A common male failing," she said, voice still neutral.

He nodded. "Yes. We men are pretty blind."

She folded her arms and leaned back in the armchair. Uh-oh.

"I was one of the blind ones. Once you left, I was too shocked to do anything and … well, too afraid to make things worse. I did what you'd expect—buried myself in work and hoped things would sort themselves out."

"They seldom do unless you make an effort."

His face warmed. "And I didn't make any effort, so it wouldn't be any wonder if you thought I didn't care."

"And do you?"

He leaned forward. "I do. More than I know how to express."

She just looked at him.

And his mind was blank. The people at work would laugh to see him so tongue-tied, but he'd fooled himself into thinking that Wendy would welcome him back. He'd expected her to at least meet him halfway, but that obviously wasn't going to happen. *Help, help, help.* Say something. He said the first thing that came into his head. "Lauren—"

She jerked forward and slapped her hand on the table, her face a harsh mask. "Don't you dare bring the children into it. This is about you and me."

"I d-didn't think—"

"And that's the problem. You haven't thought this out. You think your good looks and charm and the security you offer make you irresistible. Well, they don't!"

A bright spot of pink glowed in each cheek, making *her* look rather irresistible, but he wasn't going to add to his mistakes by saying anything about her looks. While Wendy was generally a placid person, she got riled up every now and then, and she wasn't going to let him explain that she'd misinterpreted his intent.

"I didn't come here today with any confidence, because I've wronged you all along. I should never have let our marriage drift along. I should have cared for you as you deserve, and I should never have let things slide all these years. There's no other woman in the world for me, and if the answer is no, then I'll have to live with it."

She was shaking and gesticulating for him to leave. If he did what he wanted and gathered her into his arms, she'd probably scream for the police. He stood and headed for the front door, pent-up emotion choking him as he went. Total and utter disaster.

The only satisfaction was that he'd been able to say some of what was on his heart.

He closed the two doors behind him and stopped. Behind him, he could hear the faint sound of Wendy crying as though her heart would break. At least he hoped that's what it was and that she wasn't crying because she was angry. His gut twisted.

Jesus, help her, because I can't.

CHAPTER 33

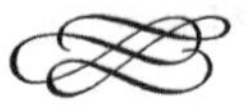

Paul didn't sleep much that night or the next. He got through work because he'd always been skilled at shutting down his emotions.

When his father rang, excited to announce he'd booked flights to come up and meet Ben and Lauren, Paul hadn't had the heart to ask him to delay his visit. How upset was Wendy? Ben might not notice if Wendy wasn't herself, but Lauren would certainly pick up the general vibe.

She had. On Thursday, there was an unstamped envelope in his mailbox. Lauren must have walked over after school.

> Dad,
>
> I'm assuming you said something to Mum. She's really upset but pretending it's nothing. I knew you'd been because of the flowers (unless some other man has popped up out of nowhere???!!!)

He would have liked to deceive himself that there was hope if

Wendy hadn't thrown out the flowers, but he'd bet they were in some obscure, dark corner.

> Let me know when Grandad is coming, and I'll make sure to come for dinner. I won't be able to come over for the weekend until after the exams as it's too disruptive. I need to keep my head down. As you'd say, these exams are important. Only two months to go and they'll be over and I'll be FREE!!!!

He laughed. At least someone was still themselves. No need to worry about Lauren. She'd been working consistently and would do well.

> Do call and let me know what's happening and when Grandad is coming. It will be good to have something apart from study in my diary.
>
> All my love,
>
> Lauren

He brushed his eye. *God, keep her like that. No. He shook his head. No, I want her to have a chance to know you.* There were still more conversations ahead of him, and none of the outcomes were predictable.

* * *

Paul had barely read the Bible the whole week. He'd thought he was beginning to understand how to pray, but he hadn't managed anything more than whimpers. Every time he thought about Wendy, his stomach cramped. He'd been scared of losing what they'd had over recent months, and now he'd thrown it away. Why did things between men and women have to be so complicated? Although, come to think of it, his relationship with his father had also faced many hurdles, and each hurdle had the potential to derail their reconciliation.

Paul got out of his car and headed into Stuart's study.

"Good to see you, Paul. Just let me get the coffee pot." He disappeared back into the main house.

Paul put his Bible, pen, and notebook in a stack on a small table and walked around, looking at some of the photos scattered around the room. Photos were funny things, almost always posed shots or records of celebrations. What would it be like if photos were taken of the actual events with all the fights and misunderstandings? It might be more real, but no one would put those pictures on display.

Having no memories of his parents together, Paul had no role models, good or bad, to compare with his situation. In boarding school, adult supervision had been distant and he'd never had a married couple to observe. Not that they'd have shown him any of the gritty stuff of life. That went on behind closed doors, which was of no help to someone like him. The only public model offered was soap operas, and they were hardly real life. Even books created conflict to make the story interesting. In real life, conflict didn't happen according to predefined templates.

Stuart came back in and closed the study door. "Not so noisy this morning. Two of them are away on a school camp."

Paul hadn't noticed things were any quieter.

Stuart poured the coffee.

"You're not very chatty this morning," Stuart said. "Got things on your mind?" He handed Paul a full mug. "Anything you'd like to share?"

Good question. Stuart had grown up in a church cocoon. What would he understand about marriage difficulties?

"I messed up big time with my wife." Paul cleared his throat. "My estranged wife, this week."

Stuart merely raised an eyebrow.

"I told you we've been separated for five years but never divorced. It was entirely my fault, as I was taking her too much for granted."

"Been there, done that," Stuart said.

Paul blinked. "Really?"

"Yeah, there were a few years when we had four children under six and coming home was like entering a barnyard. I invented tasks away from the house and left Anne to handle it on her own."

"Bet she loved that," Paul said.

"Mr Understanding I certainly was not. Just when my wife most needed me, I opted out and pretended I was doing God's work. God had to grab me by the shoulders and shake me to make me pay attention."

"How did he do that?" Paul asked.

"Made me feel a failure." Stuart stretched out his legs in front of him. "I found Anne crying her heart out in the bathroom, saying she'd had enough. Soon after that, my father came over and gave me a much-needed lecture."

"Doesn't sound like much fun."

"It wasn't, and it took about six months of hard work for me to see there were some major things that needed to change. Amazingly, Anne stuck around, trusting that God could change me."

Paul had misjudged Stuart, just like he'd misjudged his wife and his father. They had more in common than he'd realised. "I'm not sure whether God can change my situation. My wife doesn't even know I'm a Christian, and I can't tell her now or she'll think it's just a ploy to convince her I've changed and she has to give me another chance."

Yet another thing he'd blown.

"You'd better tell me what happened."

Paul certainly wasn't going to give a line-by-line description. He'd been humiliated once. He didn't plan on another round.

"Up until the middle of this year, we've only talked occasionally on the phone. Conversations have been strictly business. Finances and schooling and the children. But things have been different this year, and she surprised me by coming to my mother's funeral. Considering how my mother treated her, I thought that was a fine gesture."

Sometimes in his dreams, he could feel the ghost of her kiss on his cheek and her whispered condolences.

"There's been so much happening this year that we've had far more time together, and I find myself missing her more and more."

He'd been lonely their first year apart, but mostly he'd been angry and sulky that she'd dared to leave him. Then he'd stuffed his anger in an emotional deep-freeze and concentrated on work. Lots of academic papers, lots of conferences, lots of sport and activities.

"And then Lauren said some things that made me think it was worth the effort to see if we could start over, so I went to see Wendy on Saturday and got thrown out."

"Did she listen to you?"

"She heard the words." Paul's neck warmed and he didn't look at Stuart. "I got more and more nervous and incoherent and that made things worse. She kept misunderstanding me and then asked me to leave."

He'd been swept out the door like discarded rubbish.

"And how much did you pray before going to see your wife?"

Paul looked up sharply. "What do you mean?"

"It was an important life decision to go and see her." Stuart spoke quietly. "So how much did you pray beforehand?"

Paul flushed. "I prayed lots of help-me prayers during the conversation, but I don't think I prayed beforehand. In fact, I've been struggling to pray and read the Bible this past week."

"You're going to struggle to read the Bible and pray all your life."

All his life? He'd presumed this was going to get easier.

Stuart picked up his Bible. "The Bible keeps us centred on foundational truths. It reminds us who God is and how he works. Reading the Bible is like reading God's letters to us."

Letters? Like the ones stacked all over his dining room table.

"And praying keeps us humble, keeps us listening to God. It allows us to process what we're feeling. Prayer became my lifeline when I messed up my marriage. Maybe now is a good time for it to become your lifeline too."

Paul couldn't imagine it. Sure, he prayed, but he prayed because he felt he ought to, and because it was something Christians did. It wasn't natural except when he was in need.

"Rather than study the Bible today, let's spend the time we've got left in prayer."

Paul glanced at his watch. Thirty minutes. How could anyone spend thirty minutes in prayer?

"One secret to spending more meaningful time with God is breaking it up into sections." Stuart rummaged into a drawer and pulled out a slightly crumpled piece of paper with one printed side and a clean back. He wrote A-C-T-S down the side. "First, A for adoration."

Paul flushed. Adoration sounded like something he felt for his wife, not something he ought to feel for God.

"It does seem an unusual term, but you might remember a Christmas carol with the line, 'O come let us adore him, Christ the Lord.'" Stuart sang the lines, including the three repeats of the first phrase.

Paul had heard the carol often in his school days and at the annual *Carols by Candlelight* Wendy dragged him to when Ben and Lauren were small.

"To adore means to strongly love and respect but also to praise and worship. I'll quickly tell you the other three letters of the acronym, then we'll come back to adoration because it's the hardest for people to understand."

Stuart wrote down the page.

C - Confession

T - Thanksgiving

S - Supplication

"Supplication is an old-fashioned word, but it just means making requests to God. It's what most people think of when they think of prayer. We're great at asking for God's help and blessing in our lives, but I like to teach adoration, confession, and thanksgiving first because they're less natural to us. Of course, this is just a useful memory tool. It's by no means the only one, nor is it a kind of magic spell that must be followed to produce results. Prayer is a relationship, not a magical formula." Stuart looked across at Paul. "Ready to have a go?"

Paul nodded because it seemed to be expected of him.

Stuart flipped through his Bible and reached the centre. He skimmed some verses, then turned another page. "Yes, let's look at Psalm 46 and try to turn the words into praise and adoration to God."

Paul found the place by aiming for the centre and landing close by the chapter he wanted.

"The Psalms were the Israelites' prayer book. I often work my way through the Psalms from chapter one. I read a verse or two then turn it into prayer. I'll do the first verse and I think you'll catch on quickly. Psalm 46, verse 1. 'God is our refuge and strength, an ever-present help in trouble.'"

Stuart closed his eyes. "Dear heavenly Father, you are a great and mighty God, a refuge to all who come to you. We praise you that you care enough to offer refuge and you're always ready to give us strength. We praise you that your strength is greater than the greatest power on earth." Stuart opened his eyes. "Okay, why don't you do verses two and three?"

Paul looked down at the text and read. "'Therefore we will not fear, though the earth give way and the mountains fall into the heart of the sea, though its waters roar and foam and the mountains quake with their surging.'"

The words seemed to describe his current emotional state, but he still didn't see how they were going to turn into prayer. *Help, Lord. Teach me how to do this.* He opened his mouth. "God, when I read these verses, they describe some of the things I've felt this week and over the last months with Mother's death and Dad's appearance in my life. Like a series of earthquakes or huge waves. It's all been a bit chaotic, and I'm not used to all this emotion. It's disconcerting. But these verses tell me there is no need to fear because you're in charge." He leaned his head in his hand. "I didn't behave like you're in charge on Saturday, and went and wrecked everything by relying on myself. Sorry."

He'd stomped over everything with steel-capped boots. Wendy's crying had gotten to him. He'd caused her enough pain already. The last thing he wanted to do was be the cause of more.

"You've naturally shifted to confession," Stuart said. "Why don't we pray silently saying sorry for any recent words, thoughts, or deeds that wouldn't have honoured Jesus."

There were lots of those. He'd silently cursed an annoying patient this week. He'd wished Ben was more like Lauren, instead of accepting that he was his own individual, and he'd failed to appreciate Sister O'Reilly, yet again.

The next few minutes seemed long, but Paul still hadn't finished when Stuart interrupted. "Now what about things we can be thankful for. We'll do this ping-pong style, with short sentence prayers back and forth."

Paul chuckled at the vivid analogy.

Stuart started. "Thank you that we can meet together."

Paul said the first thing that came into his head. "Thank you that things with Dad are going well, and he's coming to visit soon."

"Thank you that you love Wendy and Ben and Lauren, and you'll give them chances to know you," Stuart said.

Paul straightened in his armchair. Stuart's prayers showed him where his prayers fell short. He should have been praying for his family to come to know Jesus.

They prayed back and forth and included some requests scattered through the prayers.

"Amen," Stuart said. "Before you go, let me show you my prayer notebook. If I don't write things down, I end up drifting off to sleep or thinking about everything but God." He stood, went to the bookshelf next to his desk and pulled out a book with a lurid picture of cats on the cover. "My ten- year-old made the cover and gave it to me for my birthday."

Paul couldn't help grinning at the colourful squiggles and splotches all over the cats. "She's obviously the creative type."

Stuart gave a proud father grin, opened the first double page, and held it up for Paul to see. "I write down my requests and the day I start praying for them." He pointed to the column. "The next column is the date of the answer, and the final column is whether God said 'yes' or 'no'."

Paul raised an eyebrow. "Why would God say 'no'?"

"For many of the same reasons any father would. If we requested something that would hurt us or lead us away from him."

"I don't think Wendy comes into that category."

"No, but there is also the mystery of human freedom. Wendy can still choose her own way, no matter how much you pray."

But Paul was going to pray that God changed her heart as God had changed his. After all, God hadn't won him over easily, and it wasn't proving easy to learn how to rely on God. Maybe Saturday would have gone differently if he had left God in control.

CHAPTER 34

Paul had bought a new notebook on his way back from work. The next morning, before getting ready to take Ben to sport, he ruled up some pages and wrote in the first request alongside the date.

** Wendy will change her mind.*

He tapped his pen on the page. No, the request was too broad. He needed a list of mini-steps towards the overall goal. What made sense?

He jotted down:

** W. will still talk to me*

** W. will agree to both of us being at Ben's sixteenth birthday party*

** For courage not to give up*

** Pray twice a day for this situation*

That would do for now.

In the front of his notebook he wrote the A-C-T-S acronym, then turned to Psalm 1. He would follow Stuart's suggestion and read through the Psalms. That way he wouldn't have to make another decision about what to read and pray, for a hundred and fifty days. That sounded good at the moment.

He read the Psalm through twice. Short and poetic, but he couldn't see how to turn it into this thing Stuart called 'adoration'. Instead he prayed the Psalm for Ben. That he would choose to walk with the righteous and not people who'd lead him astray. That he'd be a tree that was fruitful, and would choose to follow Jesus one day.

Paul prayed each of the requests twice a day for four days. It made him feel good to be doing something positive.

He was driving home on the fifth day when a question flashed into his mind. Did he feel good because he expected God to be impressed by his prayers? Did he subconsciously expect God to reward him for being a good boy? He thumped the steering wheel. Every time he thought he was making progress, God would expose his motives. His motives stank, certainly not something he should be congratulating himself about.

And his requests? They were completely selfish. He was telling God what to do and expecting that fervent prayer would convince God to listen and grant his request. If Paul's children had treated him like this, he'd have been disappointed.

When he got home, he picked up his notebook from the bedside table and took it back to the kitchen where he'd eat dinner. As he ate, he examined each request. Then he got out his pen and wrote:

* *Wendy will be comforted from any hurt*

Judging from her crying, he'd inflicted some even if it hadn't been intentional.

* *Wendy will somehow think about Jesus*

How was that going to happen? He added some sub-points.

* *Help her to have a Christian friend who supports her*

She'd had a close Christian friend years back. Now, what was her name? Cathy? No, Cecilia? Close, but not quite right. He gnawed the end of the pen. Cecily, that was it. He'd discouraged the friendship because he'd feared Cecily had too much influence in Wendy's life. *Forgive me, Jesus.* How arrogant to think he could dictate Wendy's friends. Apart from Cecily being a Christian, there hadn't been anything else objectionable about her. The friendship had died because Cecily had moved away from the area.

His dinner grew cold while he prayed for Wendy. Prayed for God's comfort, encouragement, and that Wendy would have a chance to know Jesus.

When he finished praying, he warmed his dinner up again in the microwave, finished eating, and then did the few dishes. He had homework tonight. Ben loved the photography class, and Paul loved seeing Ben come alive. Every week they learned about different sorts of photography. Tonight, he had to photograph common objects from unusual angles. Since it was usually dark when he got home, he was going to look through the apartment and the public parts of the apartment block and see if he could find anything.

For the next two hours, he lay on the floor staring at objects on the ceiling or the shadows cast by the downstairs ornamental railing. Three neighbours saw him, but only one spoke to him, the woman from apartment six.

"What are you doing?"

"It's for my photography class homework, so my son isn't embarrassed by my lack of effort."

The woman, whose name he'd never bothered to find out, said, "Good on you. I like to see a father spend time with his son."

Paul's heart warmed. Here was someone who could see he was making an effort. Even better, it seemed to be bridging the gap between him and Ben. Probably because Ben continually took excellent photos and Paul praised him so often.

He'd told Stuart about the difficulties in his relationship with Ben, and Stuart had mentioned a helpful book about how people give and receive love. Paul thought Lauren seemed to appreciate quality time and gifts, but Ben drank encouragement like it was the half litre of milk he consumed every day. Once Paul started really encouraging Ben, things improved beyond what he had thought possible. It also helped that Paul's mother was no longer around to cut Ben down. She used to do the same to Lauren, but Lauren could laugh it off. Ben was much more sensitive.

As for himself, he did lots of acts of service, yet that hadn't really communicated much to Wendy. He'd always made sure things around the house were fixed and in good repair. Not that he'd usually done them himself, but he'd paid others to do them and Wendy hadn't needed to tell him more than once. Stuart had also explained about the language of touch. As Paul had listened, he'd wondered if that part of him might have become stunted because his mother hadn't been a touchy-feely woman.

He didn't regret summoning the courage to ask Stuart to meet up. He was learning just as much from hearing Stuart pray, the books he was reading, and even how Stuart set boundaries such as not accepting calls during their meetings, as he was from studying the Bible together.

* * *

ON FRIDAY, after discussing another chapter from John, Stuart asked, "And how are your prayer times going?"

Paul stopped and thought for a few moments. "It's pretty hard going. I stick at it for two or three days, then get distracted or forget to pray for something important. The notebook is a huge help."

"Another thing I do is change things up a bit. Such as, praying for different people each day."

"So not everybody, every day?"

"No. For example, you might pray for Ben on Monday, Wednesday, Friday and Lauren on the other days." Stuart looked across at Paul. "And you can pray for different things for them."

"Like studies and emotional maturity on different days?" Paul asked.

Stuart nodded. "And praying for their salvation."

"Yeah, I've started doing that. I worked out that my prayers for Wendy were incredibly selfish. I was reading some of Jesus' teaching about prayer, but I'm not sure I really understand what it means to pray according to God's will."

"Yet we're all fairly clear on what our will is. We all want happily-ever-afters and plenty of smooth sailing."

"It's certainly what I want," Paul said.

"And it's good for us to acknowledge our desires, because it's only when we see them out in the open, exposed by the light of day, that we can appreciate our true motivations aren't necessarily ideal."

"Mine certainly aren't, but I'm not sure what to do about it."

Stuart leaned back in his chair, hands clasped behind his head. "What do you think God's will might be for you and your family?"

"Reconciliation and forgiveness would be part of it, wouldn't they?" Paul sure hoped so.

"Definitely, although we also need to ask another question—what needs to happen for there to be forgiveness?"

Paul stared out the window at the tree blowing back and forth in the breeze. "An apology, I guess, and asking for forgiveness."

"That's what I had to do with my wife. I wanted to skip that part because it made me feel uncomfortable. However, with God, joy comes second."

Paul raised an eyebrow.

"I mean we want God to give us the joy up-front so that it's easier to obey, but God wants us to obey whether we feel like it or not. Joy doesn't come before obedience, it follows our obedience."

Paul grimaced. "That doesn't sound like much fun."

"It isn't, but you'll find that if you shortcut the process, then you've only papered over the cracks. The original problems will break through again later and cause even more pain." Stuart sat up straight. "What else is in God's plan for the world?"

Paul rubbed his eyebrow. "The world is too much for me to get my head around. For my family? I assume God cares about their spiritual well-being and wants them to know him."

"That's something God is working towards for the whole world. He wants your family and your squash partner and your neighbours and every one of your patients to know him."

Paul hadn't even considered them. Maybe he should start by writing to Rob and telling him he'd become a Christian.

"Wouldn't it be more efficient for God just to write in the sky?"

Stuart laughed. "God values maturity more than efficiency. He chooses to work through human beings to accomplish his purposes."

"Like he's used you and Esther and Joy in my life."

"And probably a lot of others you don't know about."

Like his father. He hadn't known his father had been praying for all those years. It made him feel small and humble. Now it was his turn to pray for his own family. He hoped he'd be as faithful.

CHAPTER 35

Lauren had come over early to help Paul cook. Russ should be arriving at the local train station within the next ninety minutes or so, as his plane had arrived on time. Paul had planned to collect his father from the airport, but Russ insisted he would catch the bus and train.

"Mum sent over a cheesecake," Lauren said. "I put it in the fridge."

So Wendy didn't totally hate him. Surely she wouldn't make a cheesecake for a father-in-law she'd never met if she hated them both. Or maybe she was just trying to lighten Lauren's load. He sighed as he followed Lauren's instructions to chop the mint for the sauce to accompany the roast lamb. There was no use second-guessing what was in Wendy's heart. He'd been wrong before.

"I think that's chopped up enough, Dad," Lauren said as she went over to the oven, opened the door, and checked the meat. "Time for the potatoes and pumpkin to go in. Then I can go and do a little more study."

She'd driven herself over, something that still made him

nervous for no reason at all except that he wasn't used to her independence.

"When Dad calls, I'll walk down to the station and meet him."

"Oh, I'll come with you." She looked at him. "If that's alright. It will be good to get out."

"You sure? Your presence might make him cry."

"I don't mind, but will he?"

"Why don't I ask him when he calls? Leave the decision to him."

She leaned across and kissed his cheek, then went back to the dining table where she'd laid out one of her revision notebooks. Maths, he guessed. That was her weakest subject.

Forty minutes later, the phone rang. Paul picked it up and talked briefly to his father. He put down the phone.

"Dad said he'd love you to come to the station."

Lauren turned the meat and vegetables, and they set off. She clasped his arm. "Do you think he'll like me?"

"Are you kidding me? He'll adore you. What grandfather wouldn't be proud of a granddaughter like you?"

"I wish Ben was here, but I think he's scared."

"Scared of what?"

"I'm not sure. Maybe scared of being disappointed."

"Or perhaps he feels a bit disloyal, since he loves your Pop and Nana."

"Maybe."

Things with Ben had continued to improve. He was making an effort to talk with Paul, and had a new friend who not only seemed to be having a positive influence but went to a local church. A Christian friend for each of his family members was something Paul had been praying for. One tick and answer 'yes' for his prayer book.

The train was right on time. Paul called his father's name, and a big grin creased his father's face. Lauren didn't wait but rushed ahead and gave him a hug. Paul blinked back tears. Lauren had the courage to risk her heart. A lesson he needed to learn and keep on learning.

Russ returned the hug, then held her out at arm's length. "And how come this gorgeous creature is hugging an old man like me?"

Lauren laughed. "It's not every day I meet my grandfather for the first time."

"No," Russ said, voice cracking. "No, it isn't."

"I'll take your bag, Grandpa."

"I think that's your father's job. You and I get to walk together."

Paul laughed and picked up the bag.

Lauren took her grandfather's arm as if she'd been doing it all their lives. She pointed out various places as they walked along.

Lord, help the visit to go well, and may Ben be willing to let Dad attend his volleyball game next week.

He'd suggested his father stay until the following Sunday in the hope that Ben might relent and agree to at least the volleyball. Dad also wanted to go to church with him and have a good long talk with Stuart.

* * *

"DID you really make all this on your own?" Russ asked.

"Well, Dad made the mint sauce." Lauren winked at Paul.

"With full instructions from Lauren, as I'm not much of a cook. Wendy sent along one of her famous passionfruit cheesecakes."

"You peeked, didn't you Dad?"

He nodded. "Couldn't resist."

During the meal, Lauren asked lots of questions about where Russ lived and what he did with his time. In turn, Russ asked questions back.

"After dinner, I'll show you my yearbook. It only came out a week ago."

His father looked pleased. "And I brought some more photos of your great-grandparents, and your dad as a little boy."

"Ooh," Lauren said. "That should be fun."

Lauren had brought a game with her in case the conversation lagged, but it wasn't needed.

Lauren stood up at nine. "Got to get my beauty sleep."

"Any more beautiful, and your father will have a full-time job beating off the boys," Russ said.

Lauren kissed them both and breezed out the door. Paul accompanied her to the car.

"Thanks, Lauren. The meal was great, but most of all, thanks for making Dad feel so welcome."

"He's a dear. I'm glad you found each other."

He waved her off and headed inside. Time to get Dad settled for the week. Thanks to Lauren, it was off to a good start. Dad would be alone during the day, but he assured Paul he wouldn't mind. He intended to catch the train and visit the garden where he used to work, and the botanical gardens.

"I may as well enjoy the things the city has to offer."

PAUL AND BEN spent two hours taking portrait photos of the other students in the class. Paul had been worried the class would be too much for Ben and that he might neglect his homework, but the reverse was true. Doing something he loved motivated him for everything else.

"This week," the photography teacher said, "I want you to take a series of portrait shots using the techniques we've practised. And extra points if your various subjects are of different ages."

Paul grinned. Ben had reluctantly agreed to let Russ attend his volleyball game on Saturday. What would he say to some family photos? Taking photos might just break the ice between Ben and his grandfather and it was much easier than trying to make polite conversation. Paul would ask and Ben could always say no if he didn't want to do it.

* * *

"DAD, if you drive me home, we could take some photos in the park. The pillars of the rotunda would make a good frame," Ben said, his hair still wet from his post-game shower.

Paul didn't glance across at his father. This offer seemed too good to endanger by any smug looks when the idea to bring Ben and his grandfather together had worked.

"Sure, we'll drive you home. I brought my camera just in case."

When they got to the car, Paul held his breath. Ben always sat in the front, and he hadn't yet acknowledged his grandfather. Would politeness win?

Ben opened the front door and turned. "You sit in the front. It'll be more comfortable." Then he held out his hand to his grandfather. "I'm Ben."

A glow of pride spread in Paul's chest. *Well done, Ben.*

"I am mighty pleased to meet you, Ben," Russ said.

"What am I to call you?"

"If you're not ready to call me Grandpa, I don't mind if you call me Mr W. That's what the kids at your Dad's school called me." Russ looked across at Paul in the driver's seat. "If that's okay with you."

"Ben, you do what you're comfortable with."

Ben jumped into the back seat and clicked his seatbelt.

"I didn't call Dad 'Dad' for the first few weeks either," Paul said, reversing out of the carpark.

"I understand my sudden appearance on the scene is hard," Russ said. "It doesn't upset me that you're wary."

Ben didn't say anything, but when Paul glanced in the rear-view mirror, it was obvious some of the tension had drained out of him.

It was only a short drive, and once they reached the park, Ben got out of the car. "I'll get my camera and the tripod."

"And let Lauren know what we're doing, in case she wants to join us," Paul said, locking the car. Wendy wouldn't show her face. *Lord, let there one day be a reason for a whole family photo.*

Ben jogged across the park, and Paul led the way towards the rotunda. The thud of tennis balls from the nearby courts accompanied them.

"Is this where you lived before?" his father asked.

"Uh-huh. Wendy and the kids can easily catch the train to both schools."

"I loved seeing the school. It's much easier to pray for people when you've seen them in their natural environment."

It had been Lauren's idea to ring her grandfather and show him around her school. They'd run into Wendy during the tour, and Russ had been touched that she'd come straight across and welcomed him into the family and then invited him for a cup of tea.

He came back, bubbling. "That's one nice woman."

It was another shared opinion in a growing list.

They took a seat near the rose garden and waited for Ben.

"God's answering our prayers," Russ said. "Ben hasn't been as unwelcoming as you warned me he might be."

"He's made a real effort."

"I never expected I'd ever have the pleasure of doing the grandfather thing and get to watch my grandson playing sport. Volleyball was new to me, but it's obvious Ben has quite the talent for it."

Ben appeared on the far side of the park and walked towards them, various bags hanging from his shoulders and, carrying the tripod. "Lauren will come out in about twenty minutes, and Mum knows what we're up to."

Paul turned away to hide his face. The desire to see Wendy was overwhelming, but he didn't think she'd come within a mile of him for a while yet. It would be interesting to see how they'd manage Ben's sixteenth birthday. He'd had a terrific idea on how to celebrate the day. Before he'd messed things up with Wendy, they'd agreed to make more of a fuss about the party than normal, since Lauren had already had lots of special things throughout the year, with two official farewells yet to come.

Ben had his camera out and was checking the light. "Mr W, why don't we take some photos of you first." He reached into a bag and came out with a set of hedge clippers. "I've heard you're a gardener. What about taking some gardening shots?"

That's why Ben was the much better photographer. Paul would have sat his father down and ended up with a posed, formal shot with Dad looking uncomfortable. Already his father had the clippers in his hand and stood near the rose bushes looking like he belonged.

Ben took a few shots, then a few more. He frowned. "Mr W, can you think of anything you could do that would make you look like a gardener?"

"Well, I'd better not start digging anything up, but a wheelbarrow might work. If you could find one."

Ben's eyes gleamed. "A wheelbarrow would be perfect." He looked around. "There's one over there."

They strolled over. The wheelbarrow contained pots of flowering plants. Someone was going to get in trouble for leaving it out.

"If these photos turn out as well as they look from here," Paul said, "you're going to win the best photo again."

Ben flushed. "Well, it helps that Mr W has an interesting face and the light is good."

"He means I've got plenty of wrinkles," Russ said.

Ben laughed, a real laugh full of the confidence of youth.

"Sounds like I've been missing out," Lauren said from behind them.

"Just in time," Paul said. "Ben has some terrific shots, and I haven't taken a single one. Can I borrow the tripod and take some shots of Lauren on the swing?"

"Only for a while. I want to take some photos of both you and your dad together."

Ben took photos of Paul and his father, and Lauren with her grandfather.

"If you set up the tripod and timer, would you be willing to join us in a three-generation photo with your grandfather and me, and then we could add Lauren to the group too?" Paul asked.

Ben paused, his hand frozen on the camera, and then nodded.

They took the photos, after which Lauren headed home. A few minutes later, she came down the drive and waved them over.

"Mum has sent some snacks."

Paul's throat narrowed. Was Wendy being polite again, or was her attitude softening? He and his father had been praying every morning before work. Could this be the new beginning they'd been praying for?

CHAPTER 36

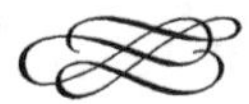

Paul was still praying, and his prayers had changed as the weeks went by. He seldom prayed for the situation between himself and Wendy to change. Instead, he concentrated his prayers on Wendy herself, that she would be surrounded by Christians who would love and support her.

Paul had thought hard about whether to wait until Wendy's birthday to send her flowers but decided a 'just because you're special' gift was better. He attached an extra envelope and he'd ask the lady in the flower shop to write

Do not throw away, contains tickets

so that no one would recognise his writing and Wendy wouldn't immediately reject the gift. Inside were two tickets for the latest musical for Wendy and Lauren, and two tickets for a photography exhibition Wendy could see with Ben. Maybe Ben's photographs would be exhibited one day. He'd won the class best-photo competition for the second time—the class had unanimously voted one of the wheelbarrow shots and one of the group shots as the winners. Not the staged shot, but the photo that revealed relationships. Paul's hand was resting on his father's shoulder with relaxed affection. Lauren looked thrilled with her new grandfather and Ben still looked like a slightly wary outsider. Ben had accepted the prize of a fifty-dollar voucher to a local camera shop with ears flushing pink.

Paul sat down to compose a letter to Wendy that he could include with the tickets. He'd be praying she'd read it.

Dear Wendy,

He'd daydreamed about writing 'Dearest Wendy', but that would guarantee the letter would be tossed in the bin.

This letter is going to contain many apologies.

Next week, he'd write a thank you letter. *Jesus, help me to apologise properly, without excuses or light-hearted jokes.*

I don't think I have ever apologised to you in more than an indirect or half-hearted way. It wasn't because I didn't feel sorry, but because I was too proud to admit my many failures. But recently I've been meeting with a guy who has really helped me. Dad has also been a good example in this respect. It must have been all the letters he wrote to me but never sent (I've spent weeks reading them) that gave me the idea to write to you.

You know speaking about emotions is difficult for me.

Sorry that this letter has taken so long. It should have been written the week you left, but I let pride get in the way of doing what I should have done. Sorry for caring more about my hurt than about yours.

Paul stared at the wall. *God, help me be genuine and help Wendy to be willing to read this.*

Sorry that during our marriage I took you for granted. I didn't think it anything special that you had a meal waiting for me when I got home or that you had given up your dreams of further study so that I could follow my dreams. It was inconsiderate not to think that you might want something more out of life than to be my wife.

Once the children came along, I didn't stop to consider your needs. I assumed you would be the carer, and I wasn't there enough for you. My friend Stuart

Paul nibbled the end of his pen. Should he say Stuart was a pastor and name his church? It would give the barest hint of what had been happening in his life. He bowed his head. *Should I add it, Lord?*

He didn't hear any voices and had learned not to expect them, but he didn't sense any warnings either.

is the pastor of the local Baptist church, and has five children. He's made me aware of how much work they are when they're small. I'm sorry I left you alone too often and didn't hide my lack of enthusiasm for bed and bath-time routines. I wish I could redo those years. Stuart describes it as one of the best times of his day and how it's made an immense difference to his relationship with each child.

Paul reread what he'd written. It wasn't eloquent, but he wasn't aiming for eloquence.

You are the most important person in my life, but I didn't make that clear. I'm sorry. I should have encouraged you to have time for yourself and encouraged you to spend time with your friends.

Another thing I did that was wrong was to pressure you to

END YOUR FRIENDSHIP WITH CECILY. I WAS AFRAID OF HER INFLUENCE ON YOU AND WAS SCARED YOU MIGHT BECOME A CHRISTIAN. I HAD A HOST OF PREJUDICES AGAINST CHRISTIANS WHICH I NOW KNOW WAS FOOLISH IGNORANCE. YOU HAD THE RIGHT TO CHOOSE YOUR OWN FRIENDS. I'M SORRY FOR HURTING YOU.

IN FACT, I'VE HURT YOU AT EVERY TURN. I'M SORRY FOR MY ARROGANCE, MY INSENSITIVITY, AND MY SELF-CENTREDNESS. IT IS ONLY BECAUSE YOU'RE SUCH AN AMAZING PERSON THAT YOU STUCK WITH ME FOR SO LONG.

THIS LETTER AND THE GIFTS COME WITH ALL MY LOVE,

PAUL

Paul's father had been gone just over a week. He'd never expected to miss him, but he did. He especially missed having someone to pray with every morning. It had been his father's idea, and the thirty minutes each morning had slipped by. They'd concentrated on praying that Wendy, Ben, and Lauren would have opportunities to meet Jesus. Prayer was beginning to make sense, although it was obviously one of those things in which no one ever dared to claim expertise. There was always another mountain to ascend behind the one the pray-er had just climbed.

God, I trust you to do work in Wendy's life. She needs you. Help her to realise this. As I discovered you were the best Father, may she discover that you are everything she needs. Even if we never end up getting back together, help me to rejoice in you and work for her best. Thank you for the wonderful woman she already is, but help her to discover the greatest blessing of them all, knowing you.

CHAPTER 37

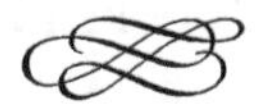

"Dad, there's some man sending Mum flowers," Ben said on their way home from volleyball.

Paul kept his voice steady. "Is that so?"

"The second bunch arrived this morning, but Mum hasn't said who they're from."

Paul worried the cuticle on his thumb. "And what's your mother's reaction?"

Ben opened the car door. "I didn't see the first lot arrive, but this morning she blushed. Haven't seen her do that for ages and thought you'd want to know."

He did indeed. Paul leaned forward to peer out the open door. "See you next week at Berowra Waters."

"My friends are all looking forward to it." Ben slammed the car door.

Paul put the car into gear and headed towards home. Wendy had chatted to him on the phone about Ben's party. She'd been dubious about mixing boys and boats, but he'd assured her he'd manage all the logistics.

Paul glanced at the dashboard clock. Would Stuart be at home? He'd always told Paul he could drop in at any time.

Stuart and his three eldest children were washing their car on the lawn. Paul parked and went to join them.

"Dad, you've got a visitor."

Stuart looked up with a grin and introduced them all. Then he gave Paul's car a once-over. "Looks like your car could do with a wash too."

"I haven't had time to go to the car wash."

"Our service is much better, isn't it?" The children nodded. "Kids, why don't you finish off our car. I'll help Paul with his."

One of the children handed Paul her bucket and cloth. "You can use mine, but it needs new water and soap." She pointed towards the corner of the house.

Stuart brought the hose over and sprayed water over the top and sides while Paul poured out the dirty water, rinsed two buckets at the second tap, and refilled them.

"Were you dropping in for a specific reason?" Stuart asked once they started washing the car.

Paul looked around. The children were packing up their buckets and heading back towards the house. "I guess I never expected to have to wait so long for my prayers to be answered."

Stuart kept his voice low. "It can take months to rebuild trust."

Paul moved over to the same side of the vehicle as Stuart. He told Stuart what Ben had said about Wendy blushing. "I'm hoping that's a good sign."

"And did you send her the list of thank yous?"

Paul nodded. "I mailed it this morning. It stretched to three pages. I did what you suggested and started with things about her character rather than things she'd done for us."

Stuart bent towards his bucket and thoroughly soaked his sponge. "I hide a little note somewhere in the house each week for Anne to find. Keeps some spice in our marriage."

"If I ever get my marriage back, I'll be changing a lot of things."

"Years ago, I asked the church to allow us a weekend to attend a marriage enrichment course."

"Didn't you run out of things to talk about?"

Stuart laughed, and his breath blew bubbles across the surface of the car. "Nope. There's always something to learn. Now we go almost every year. I think of it like changing the oil in the car." He rubbed a particularly dirty spot on the paintwork. "It made such a difference to the way we functioned that the church now insists on paying."

Looking back, Paul had invested more time in checking his stocks and shares than he'd ever invested in his marriage. The last few months had shown him the huge difference investing in his relationship with Ben had made. He was more settled at school. When Paul had bumped into the principal a few weeks back, he'd remarked on how well Ben was doing.

God, give me another chance with Wendy. Surely this growing desire for us to be together must come from you. It would be so much easier to walk away, but you've given me courage to pursue her. Thank you.

They finished the last side of the vehicle and rinsed off the car. Paul arched his back. "Haven't done this for years."

"It's a good task to do with the kids. The boys in particular find it easier to talk if they're doing something else."

Yet another simple task he could do with Ben. The photography class had been a win all round. He now understood more of what Ben was talking about, and they also had all their Christmas presents sorted.

"I haven't yet told you how thankful I am for all the time you've spent with me," Paul said.

"I love spending time with people who are hungry to learn."

Paul rubbed his eyebrow. "I've often felt totally out of my depth, trying to navigate a new language, culture, and norms, like what that missionary who talked in church last week described."

"Becoming a Christian in your fifties must be tough."

"Mostly it's been great. I didn't realise how isolated I'd become. Now I'm making new friends, and even my work relationships have improved."

Michelle and Sister O'Reilly were much more relaxed now he took the time to appreciate them. He'd added them to his growing prayer list, although he was fairly sure Michelle was a new Christian too. He'd have to ask her one day how that had happened.

"Last week, the colleague I play squash with asked me why I was different."

"And what did you tell him?"

"I was terrified, but I remembered you'd told me to send up a quick prayer. After that, it wasn't too bad. I managed to tell him I'd become a Christian and share with him a few ways my decision was impacting my life."

"Did he ask any more questions?" Stuart walked over to the low wall next to the car and sat down.

Paul shook his head. "But I told him he could if he ever wanted to, and I'm praying regularly that he will."

The eldest boy came out of the house carrying a dog lead. "Cornflakes," he called. "Cornflakes."

Stuart chuckled. "My kids thought it was funny to name the dog after breakfast cereal. I promised them we'd all go for a walk together."

"That's okay," Paul said. "I only needed some encouragement, and you've given that." He gestured towards the car. "And I got a clean car in the bargain."

"See you Friday?" Stuart said, standing and picking up their empty buckets.

"You bet."

Paul whistled as he drove the few streets home. If someone had told him six months ago that his two best friends would be a

Baptist pastor and his own father, he'd have scoffed. Yet he'd never before experienced the kind of conversation that dug below the surface. The first few times had been scary but now he always ended up feeling like he'd eaten a home-cooked meal instead of late-night takeaway from a fast-food joint.

CHAPTER 38

"Ben, is your team ready to go?" Paul asked.

The six teenagers gave a throaty roar and piled into the small motorboat. Paul checked one last time that they all had their life jackets on. Four more boys were in a boat with Wendy and Lauren. Paul had the final five of Ben's classmates in his boat.

Wendy had been worried the boys couldn't be trusted not to ram each other, but he'd assured her the boat hire included a compulsory safety lesson. Anyway, Ben was sensible enough to play within the rules and had helped him divide up the teams. The shyer, less confident boys were with Wendy and Lauren, and Paul had the only two likely to get carried away.

Paul blew his whistle and all the excited chatter died down. "This is a scavenger hunt. Every boat leader has a map of Berowra Waters and the list of everything you need to collect." Paul held up his map and list. "Remember, the water will be cold if you fall in. We'll meet in Bennets Bay for lunch."

"There are extra points for boats that see birds or fish—just record a list and the number you see. But for that, you'll need to be quiet," Wendy said in her best teacher's voice, putting her fingers to her lips.

This last idea had been Wendy's way of preventing the boys hooning around and showing off.

"You have ten minutes to organise yourselves before I blow the whistle to start. You will then have two hours to find everything."

Paul turned to the boys in his boat. "I'm here for the ride and to keep my eye on the other boats, so I suggest one of you is in charge of the map, two take turns with the steering, and two keep charge of the list and make sure we don't miss anything. Who wants which job?"

They divided the responsibilities with lots of jokes and friendly squabbles.

"Have you decided where we're going and how we're going to do this?" Paul asked.

"Do you think it's easiest to zigzag a bit?" The map-reader traced the route with his finger.

"Does that look best to the rest of you?" Paul asked.

The team had a quick discussion before agreeing. Paul checked his stopwatch, put his whistle to his lips, and blew.

Wendy's boat took off with a rush. She saluted him as they went past. He'd forgotten how competitive she was. Her boat might be the one to beat.

"Stick to the right-hand side," the map-reader said. "We have to pick up two white rocks from Camp Point, then go straight across and around Calabash Point, and into Calabash Bay."

"One thing at a time." Tom frowned as he concentrated on steering the boat. Paul looked around for the other two boats. Wendy's was already about one hundred metres in front.

A few minutes later, he watched as Wendy's boat reached the point and carefully pulled in close to shore. But they were wasting time, as they obviously hadn't thought through who was getting out of the boat.

"Okay, team, who is getting out of the boat?" he asked.

"Geoff's at the front," Tom said.

"You happy with that, Geoff?" Paul asked.

The boy nodded.

The white rocks were all in one patch, but it wouldn't be fair to tell him exactly where.

Wendy's team were still mucking about on shore when Geoff scrambled out of the boat. He turned out to be a good choice, because he took the time to scan the shore and spotted the rocks almost immediately, but he didn't go straight to them. Rather, he meandered around and pretended to pick up rocks in other spots. Ben's team were joining the hunt when Geoff strolled back to the boat and climbed on board, and they were off first. Wendy shook her fist at him. He gave her a lopsided grin, and forced his attention back to the task.

"Next stop, Calabash Bay where we're supposed to find a fake calabash floating in the water with a red ribbon around it." William rubbed his ear. "Anyone know what a calabash is?"

"Something for bashing people with?" one of the boys asked.

"No, it's not a weapon," Paul said.

"I'm fairly sure it's a gourd or container. They use them in Papua New Guinea." Dave's father worked for an oil company, and his family spent most of their holidays overseas.

They found the two-litre bottle floating in a clump of three in the inner part of the bay. Wendy's boat was only thirty seconds behind, and Ben's had obviously gone elsewhere first.

They proceeded on their zigzag way. Geoff was now the nominated gatherer, and he collected different-coloured leaves, various twigs, and tin cans. Each boat had to pick up rubbish, one point per piece, and put it in the designated bag. William spotted an eagle but forgot himself and yelled, so the other boats also gained the points.

With the marina's permission, Paul had placed three bags of

drinks on a buoy two-thirds of the distance along the route. He'd left a label on them.

These are here for a birthday party—please don't drink 😊

Their boat was last to arrive, as they'd taken their time to collect all the rubbish and spotted more birds and some fish.

Lauren waved and grinned at him as their boat left the buoy. Did Wendy give him a genuine smile as she took off? Maybe he'd misread it, but his pulse accelerated all the same.

They proceeded along to the furthest point of their travels. The trees came down to the water's edge and a bright blue sky with dazzling white clouds stretched high above them. Every now and then there was the splash of a fish jumping.

"At the next beach, all but one of us has to get out and run to the end and touch the dead tree," the boy in charge of the list said. "That will have to include you, Mr W."

In the past, Paul would have mentioned he was a doctor but now he just grinned to hear the nickname.

As they approached the shore, Tom slowed the boat down to the merest putting purr. He edged it closer. "Mr W, can you use the oar to check how deep the water is?"

Paul manoeuvred one of the emergency oars forward and placed it in the water. "It's still thigh deep. Come in closer."

Tom carefully steered the boat in.

Paul checked again. "Okay, that's knee depth. I'll go first and hold the boat for the rest of you."

They all got out safely and made a run for the end of the beach, scattering sand and whooping as they went, yet still getting back to the boat in double-quick time.

"Off we go," Tom yelled, turning the boat in a wide semi-circle. Ben's boat came into view and the boys around him erupted into waves and whistles.

"I think he's already gone around the furthest buoy and is coming back," Paul said above the din.

The sound of their engine grew in volume as Tom pushed it towards the top speed they were allowed.

"Remember, there is only one bonus point for arriving at the lunch spot first. We can still gain points spotting fish and birds," Paul said.

"There's a group of cockatoos," Geoff said, careful not to yell or point. "Four of them. Have you got that written down?"

The scorer added them to his paper, and they proceeded towards the lunch spot.

"Everyone else is already there," Dave said, disappointment in his voice. The beach area was awash with scampering boys, while Wendy and Lauren were unpacking some of the baskets and boxes.

"The race isn't lost yet," Paul said. "We might have picked up more rubbish or seen more birds."

William had spent much of the trip with a stick in hand, plucking plastic bags and other pieces of rubbish from the water.

"And look at the bottom line on the list."

"It just says that there's an extra ten points for a task that isn't listed." William rubbed his ear. "Doesn't say what it is."

Paul looked around the boat. "Can anyone guess?"

"Can't be for wearing life jackets, because everyone has done that," Dave said, steering towards the beach.

Paul kept his mouth shut.

"Give us one clue, Mr W," Geoff said, eyes pleading.

"Look at the beach and see what's happening and what isn't," Paul said.

All the boys looked ahead.

"I see everyone running around," Tom said.

"But no one is helping Mrs W," Geoff said.

Bingo. The kid was smart.

"Is that it?" Geoff said. "We get bonus points for helping with the picnic?"

"I'm not saying," Paul said holding up his hands. "I'd prefer you helped because it's the right thing to do."

There was a little jetty, and it didn't take long to tie up alongside the others, unload the boat, and carry their portion of the picnic stuff over to where Wendy and Lauren were working.

Wendy had her back to him. When she straightened and turned, a smile like a ray of sunshine shone out. He beamed back, and she flushed and turned away. Oops. Maybe she hadn't intended to greet him so warmly.

"What do you want us to do, Mrs W?" Geoff asked eagerly.

Wendy looked around at the line of helpers and narrowed her eyes at Paul. "Did you cheat and tell them?"

"I only gave them the tiniest clue."

She shook her fist at him. "We'll have to talk about that later. Not sure that's allowed, but I won't turn down the help." She pointed to a big flat rock and handed a tarpaulin to the nearest boy. "If you can drape that over the rock, then all the food can go on there." She indicated the bags they were carrying. "And all the containers can go on the rock. Please leave the container lids on until we're ready to eat."

The boys scurried to do her bidding.

"And what do you want me to do?" Paul asked.

"You'd better add up all the scores, although I'm not sure you can be trusted."

"I'll be good, I promise. I'll only give one point to our team for helping, instead of ten."

"That's mighty generous of you."

He hadn't heard the gentle bantering tone in her voice for years. Was it just the boating and fresh air? Or a determined effort for Ben's party? Or—his heart rate pulsed in his ears. Or, was she warming up to him?

"Well, jump to it, Mr W. We're about to eat, and everyone will want to know who has won."

He snapped his heels together and saluted her.

* * *

THE PICNIC WAS A GRAND SUCCESS, with rolls, ham, cheese, and salad. There was also fried chicken and fruit and plenty of drinks. Wendy had catered for an army. Like an army, they ate every crumb, and had a burping competition to finish off.

Wendy stretched out her shapely legs and laughed. "I knew there were advantages to working in a girls' school. Paul, are you ready to tell us the results?"

He gave a toot on his whistle.

"I've tallied up the points. Each boat team had a specialty. Wendy's crew—" He bowed towards her. "Saw the most birds and fish." He winked at Ben. "Ben's crew was the fastest and won on organisation." The team whistled and stomped. "And our team picked up the most rubbish."

"But who won?" a lanky boy called out.

"Actually it was almost a three-way tie."

"Almost? But who won?" The kid wouldn't give up.

"The team with the most beautiful members." He turned to smile at Wendy and Lauren.

"Well done, Mum, well done," Ben called.

Paul had hoped Ben's team would win, but they'd concentrated on speed rather than picking up all the possible extra points. It didn't seem to bother him.

"The prize is back at the marina, as are the cake and ice cream," Paul said.

There was another burst of stomping. "First, we have to clear up here. When we get back, we'll put all the rubbish in the back of my car."

The boys scrambled up from where they'd spread out.

* * *

As THE PARENTS arrived to pick up their sons, Dave called out, "Three cheers for Mr and Mrs W for this terrific party."

Paul couldn't look at Wendy, but it sounded good to have his name linked to hers.

As he turned to go, Wendy handed him a small bag. "The left-over cake, and something extra."

Something extra? He licked his dry lips. What would Wendy give him? If he didn't have to play the host and see everyone off, he'd be delving into the bottom of that bag right away.

CHAPTER 39

The extra thing in the bag with the leftover cake had been a note. A note asking him to go over to Wendy's place at three the following afternoon. Apparently both Ben and Lauren would be out.

Paul had read the note twice, hands shaking and a sick feeling in his stomach. *God, is this your answer?* Then he'd spent a restless night over-analysing everything. In the end, he'd concluded he had nothing to worry about. If his presents were annoying Wendy, she'd have said so in a letter and she wouldn't have been so friendly yesterday. Or would she?

Lord, keep me calm.

At two minutes to three he was on Wendy's doorstep. He'd asked Stuart and his father for special prayer, although he hadn't told them why. It was reassuring to know both were praying, but his hand still wobbled as he reached out to press the doorbell. He'd had to take a second shower and change his shirt before he came.

Wendy avoided Paul's eyes as she opened the front door. Once he was inside, she locked the screen door and led the way into the sunroom.

She sat down and crossed her hands in her lap. "Thanks for coming." She swallowed loudly. "Especially after how I treated you last time."

"I don't blame you for that. I upset you."

She unfolded her hands and gripped the arms of the sofa. "Yes, but I don't think you meant to. Once I calmed down, I realised it took a lot of guts to come and say what you said."

Paul kept quiet.

"Never thought you'd do such a thing."

The corner of his mouth twitched. "Me neither."

"But you've changed a lot recently." She leaned back in the chair. "You're more considerate and kind." Her voice trailed off. "More humble." She gestured at the flowers, sitting in the middle of the dining room table. "The kids think I've got a boyfriend."

"And do you?" He kept his voice light, but he could feel the strain in it.

The room went silent apart from the ticking of the clock in the hallway.

"I'm not sure. Not yet."

He bit his lip. *Please Lord, keep her talking.*

"When I sent you away last time, I cried for an hour. I was so confused and conflicted, and I didn't have anywhere to turn."

He forced himself to lean back into the seat. All he wanted to do was gather her into his arms.

"I couldn't talk to the children, and I didn't want to talk to Mum and Dad. They'd want to protect me, and I needed someone with more objectivity." She hugged her arms round her body. "I've been so busy looking after the children that I haven't had much time for friendships."

And he'd disapproved of one of the closest friends she'd had.

"And then a miracle happened."

He pricked up his ears.

"Lauren asked me to pick up an eighteenth birthday present for one of her friends in that specialty music shop in Turramurra. You know the one."

He nodded.

"Who do you think was walking out as I walked in?"

He raised his eyebrows.

"Cecily," Wendy said.

"I thought she moved to the Blue Mountains?"

"She's still there, but it just so happened that her daughter wanted a particular piece of music for a recital, and the only place it was available was in Turramurra."

Awe filled him.

"I thoroughly embarrassed myself by throwing my arms around her and bursting into tears." Wendy laughed. "She handled it well, and within a few minutes, we were catching up."

Wendy blew her nose. "We talked for two hours, and I had to ring Lauren and tell her it would be pizza for dinner. We've been talking several times a week ever since."

"Wow."

"Want a cup of coffee?" Wendy asked, standing up.

"Yes, please." He wanted to hear the rest of the story but if she needed time, he'd have to accept it. She headed towards the kitchen and he heard the gush of water, then the click of the kettle being turned on.

Give me patience, Lord.

He stood and looked at Ben's photos displayed on the walls of the formal lounge room. He spotted the new one immediately. Wendy stared into the lens with pensive sadness. Her pain was etched onto her face, and yet she was so beautiful that his mouth went dry as chalk.

Wendy bustled in with the coffee cups on a tray, along with a plate of something he was too nervous to notice. He couldn't face eating, but he sipped the drink. Wendy perched on the edge of a chair and watched him from under her eyelashes. What was she looking for?

"Lauren mentioned that you've been praying for her, and I think she said something about you going to church."

Paul swallowed his coffee down the wrong way. He'd been praying for an opportunity to tell Wendy about his new faith, but now the opportunity was here, he didn't know how she'd take it. Things were at such a delicate stage. What if his decision put her off? He'd like to think he'd choose Jesus first, but the choice between Wendy and anything else wasn't so clear-cut. He adored this woman, and he'd been a fool to think he could stop doing so just because they were separated.

God, help. Don't let me deny you. His stomach ached but he answered her unspoken question. "Yes, that's right. I became a Christian a few months back. I haven't regretted it."

She stared at him. "That's unexpected. You were always so disparaging about Cecily's beliefs."

His face warmed. "I was an idiot." He swallowed. "Didn't know what I was talking about." *Lord, help.*

Wendy was quiet for a long moment. "I don't know what to think about the whole thing. Cecily only talks about Jesus if I ask a direct question, and I appreciate that. Her beliefs are the opposite of so much I've taken for granted."

Disappointment oozed through him. He wanted Wendy to know Jesus as soon as possible. Like yesterday. Why didn't God make himself clearer?

Wendy took a gulp of her tea and set the cup down. "That's what I wanted to talk about."

He looked blankly at her. He'd missed something.

"The presents and letters are nice, but I want you to stop."

Stop. What was she saying?

"I don't want to feel pressured. We need to go slowly."

He struggled to breathe. Slowly. It already felt like snail's pace to him.

"You've communicated what you want, but I'm not sure." She wrapped her arms around her waist. "We've already messed up once, and I couldn't handle messing up again."

No, no, no, God. I didn't want this.

"Please don't look like that," Wendy said.

Like what? Was the devastation gripping his heart mirrored in his expression?

"I'm not saying a definite no, but I can't say yes at the moment. I need more time and it might be quite a while. Cecily has recommended a counsellor I can talk to."

He walked over to the window and stared out.

"You're not angry at me, are you?" Wendy's voice was quiet.

He turned. "No, but of course I'm disappointed."

"I knew you would be, but I couldn't let you go on imagining that everything was suddenly okay. Things take time."

Outside, a group of children ran across the grass playing chase. Stuart had said trust took time and Paul knew it to be true. It had taken time for him to trust his father. And it had taken time for him to trust Jesus. Looking back, he'd believed Jesus existed and was God weeks before he was willing to entrust his life and future to him. *God, help me to rely on you to work in Wendy's heart as you've worked in mine.*

"Paul, say something."

Wendy's voice was tinged with worry.

He turned back to look at her. His heart ached at the fear in her eyes.

"You're right." His words were hesitant. *Help me, Jesus.* "Trust takes time." He smiled wearily at her. "You take whatever time you need. I'll wait." He sent up another prayer. "If in the end you still decide no, then somehow God will help me deal with that."

As he said the words, a certainty filled his heart. Much as he loved Wendy, he wanted whatever was best for her even more. Of course, he'd prefer to avoid any pain ahead, but Jesus had promised he could satisfy any heart. Paul didn't know how that was possible, but he was going to choose to take God at his word, no matter how impossible that seemed right now.

He squared his shoulders. At least he was no longer alone. God had already given him the friendship of his father and Stuart and was restoring his relationship with Ben. And God was a better father than he or any earthly father could ever be. God wouldn't withhold any good gift.

Being a Christian was still new and strange, but it was far better than what he'd had before. God was a father who promised to never leave or forsake his children.

And Paul was going to take him at his word.

ENJOYED GRACE BENEATH THE FROST?

The best way you can help others find out about this book is by telling them about it. Writing an online review is one way of doing this. Every review is a gift to an author.

How to write a review – easy as 1-2-3

1. A few sentences about why you liked the book or what kind of readers might enjoy this book. Even one word turns a mere star rating into a review.
2. Upload your review - the same review can be copied and pasted to each sales site.
3. If you loved the book please also share your review on your personal social media. Anywhere you can spread the word is appreciated.

A book can never have too many reviews.

STORYTELLER FRIENDS

Becoming a **storyteller friend** (http://subscribe.storytellerchristine.com/) will ensure you don't miss out on new books, deals and behind the scenes book news. Once you're signed up, check your junk mail or the 'promotions' folder (gmail addresses) for the confirmation email. This two-stage process ensures only true storyteller friends can join.

Facebook: As well as a public author page, I also have a VIP group which you need to ask permission to join.

BookBub - allows you to see my top book recommendations and be alerted to any new releases and special deals. It is free to join.

NON-FICTION BY CHRISTINE DILLON

1-2-1 Discipleship: Helping One Another Grow Spiritually
(Christian Focus, Ross-shire, Scotland, 2009).

Telling the Gospel Through Story: Evangelism That Keeps Hearers Wanting More (IVP, Downer's Grove, Illinois, 2012).

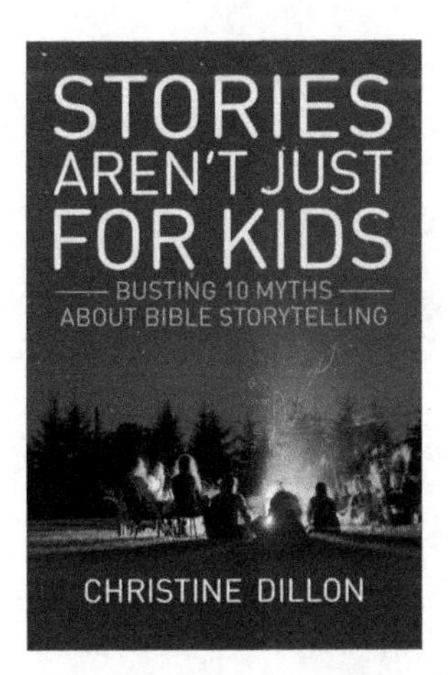

Stories Aren't Just For Kids: Busting 10 Myths About Bible Storytelling (2017).

This book is free for subscribers. It's a 'taster' book and includes many testimonies to get you excited about the potential of Bible storying. All these books have also been translated into Chinese.

NON-FICTION BY CHRISTINE DILLON

Sword Fighting: Applying God's word to win the battle for our mind (July, 2020).

FICTION - GRACE SERIES

Book 1 - Grace in Strange Disguise (October, 2017).

Book 2 - Grace in the Shadows (July, 2018).

Book 3 - Grace in Deep Waters (July, 2019).

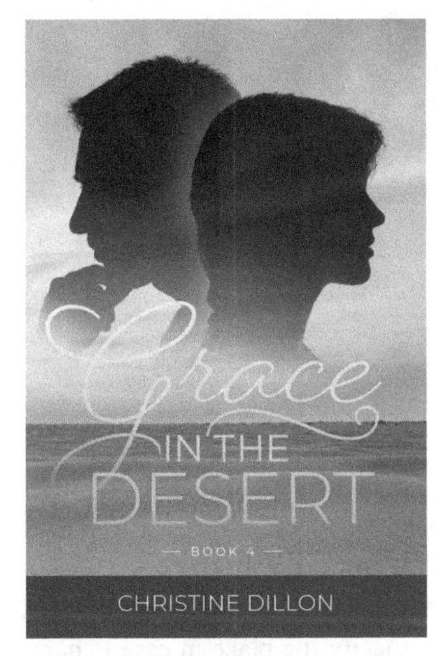

Book 4 - Grace in the Desert (June, 2020).

The digital novels + audio for books 1-2 can be bought directly from the author (https://payhip.com/ChristineDillon). You need a PayPal account to make your payment. PayPal is also free to join.

AUTHOR'S NOTES

With regards to setting: The first book mentions places I knew and loved but I didn't specify the place in case I changed details to suit the story. In the second book, I started to name the places and for book three, I consciously showcased different areas of my beautiful country. This fifth book highlights Canberra, the Snowy Mountains, and Cairns/Great Barrier Reef in Queensland.

Using real places also allows me to use these settings as the visuals for the book trailers, which you can find on Youtube.

ACKNOWLEDGMENTS

I am so thankful that God is in charge of my timetable. Since my first standalone book turned into a series, I have planned to release one book a year which means research and preparation is done in August and September and then I write from October to December. For this book, God surprised me once again and the book planning came together early and the first draft was already written by mid-September. Being ahead of schedule turned out to be a blessing as things became a little chaotic with a sudden house move, needing to live with various friends, and then leaving Taiwan earlier than expected. As God has proved over and over, he knew exactly what he was doing.

Thank you to all of those who are waiting for this book and faithfully write reviews and tell others about the previous books. Every review is appreciated.

Continued thanks to my editors, Cecily Paterson and Iola Goulton (we've done this five times now) and cover designer, Joy Lankshear (five novels and three non-fiction books).

I am so grateful to those who read the early manuscript (the beta reading team) and then those who do the proofreading. Every year we're improving as we all learn how to do this and as we master the various technologies. Thank you to David U., Kim W., Lizzie R., Anne M., Sarah L., Kate B., Jane C., Suzanne R., and Laura T. I've come to rely heavily on your input.

Thank you to Lizzie and Cecily who told me to change the ending. You were right! Many of the places in this novel are places I've visited. Writing the scenes brought back many good memories.

Discussion Guide

There are discussion guides for each of the novels on my website.

www.storytellerchristine.com

ABOUT THE AUTHOR

Christine has worked in Taiwan, with OMF International, since 1999.

It's best not to ask Christine, "Where are you from?" She's a missionary kid who isn't sure if she should say her passport country (Australia) or her Dad's country (New Zealand) or where she's spent most of her life (Asia - Taiwan, Malaysia and the Philippines).

Christine used to be a physiotherapist, but now writes 'story-teller' on airport forms. She spends most of her time either telling Bible stories or training others to do so.

In her spare time, Christine loves all things active – hiking, cycling, swimming, snorkelling. But she also likes reading and genealogical research.

Connect with Christine

www.storytellerchristine.com/

facebook.com/storytellerchristine

instagram.com/christinedillonstoryteller

pinterest.com/storytellerchristine

CPSIA information can be obtained
at www.ICGtesting.com
Printed in the USA
LVHW010445211221
706819LV00010B/808